SAVAGE
LOVE
ASHLEE ROSE

Dedication

For all the fairy tale lovers, if you like it dark and hot.. this one is for you

Other Books by
Ashlee Rose

Entwined In You Series:

Something New
Something To Lose
Something Everlasting
Before Her
Without Her

Standalones:

Unwanted
Promise Me

All available on Amazon Kindle Unlimited
Only suitable for 18+ due to nature of the books.

Prologue

Xavier Archibald III

I still remember the first time I laid eyes on her. Her flowing red hair sat in waves down her back, her piercing blue eyes shined and twinkled like the stars above us. Her ivory skin was so pale, yet so beautiful.

I wanted her in that moment.

To claim her and make her mine.

But I had to bide my time. Play the part. I couldn't rush this. I had been planning this moment for the last five years, and I wasn't about to fuck it all up now because of testosterone.

She wouldn't want me; she would come kicking and screaming. Because who in their right mind would want to be with me?

People said I was cold-hearted, callous and spiteful. Hate ran through my blood like poison. My mouth was vicious, my heart black. And they were right… I am all those things, but I'm also incredibly selfish and want her for myself.

Perfectly imperfect is what I recall her saying to me on our first meeting.

My face scarred, my eyes so different. One brown and one icy-blue.

But it didn't stop me from seeing how fucking beautiful she was.

I just had to bide my time.

I could hear them whispering and sniggering. They were right.

How could a monster like me love?

Who could love a monster like me?

I was wealthy, strong and a force to be reckoned with.

My name might be Xavier Archibald the third, but to everyone else, I was known as *The Beast*.

Chapter

One

Royal

Tonight, my parents were throwing me a ball for my twenty-first birthday. I mean, of course they were. Their only born child, heir to the throne with a ring-less finger, they wanted to marry me off. I knew it had to happen, but I wanted a choice. I didn't want to be suited off with whomever they chose. The truth was, I was already in love. My heart belonged to my one and only Christopher. But my parents would never allow the future queen to marry a servant. He was a peasant in their eyes. But not in mine.

He was my only friend. Don't get me wrong, I had the other pompous princesses and princes around me, but none of them were really my friends, more like acquaintances. We had to get along because of who we were.

Royals.

The last big ball thrown for me was my sweet sixteen, and everyone from our kingdom, Auradell, was there, plus the most cold-hearted man to walk the earth.

Xavier Archibald.

Even saying his name sends shivers down my spine. His eyes on me made me feel uneasy. He watched my every move. He was my first dance, waltzing me around our large ballroom, sweeping me off my feet. I couldn't lie, he was a fantastic dancer. We got lost in small conversation, and he asked me what I would like to have been if I wasn't heir to the throne. He piqued my interest in that moment. I had always wanted to be a doctor, I'm not sure why. Maybe it was the hours and hours I used to spend playing doctors and nurses with my teddies? I had a very lonely childhood, but you get used to being on your own. My mind drifted back to our dance, a hint of a smile crossing my pink, bow lips.

"Tell me, Royal, if you weren't next in line to be queen, what would you be?" he asked in a low, gruff voice as he glided me across the high-gloss floor.

"No one has ever asked me that before." I smiled at him; my head held high as we continued our show for the spectators. I looked into his eyes; they were mesmerizing. I had never seen eyes like it. His left eye was the darkest of browns, almost black, yet his right eye

was an icy-blue, pulling me in and hypnotizing me in that moment.

"You going to answer me?" he said with a small laugh as he spun me round, my pink gown twirling round my feet.

"A doctor," I said shyly, a small blush creeping over my face.

"I wasn't expecting that," he said, slightly shocked. "But that's wonderful."

"Thank you." I nodded as the song started to slow down.

"No, thank you, Royal. Thank you for accepting my dance. Not many people would." His lips pressed into a tight line as we started to slow, my hand still firmly in his, his other hand gripping onto my hip.

"Why's that, Xavier?" I asked, his name slipping off my tongue like silk.

"Because of what I am... Who I am." He bowed his head for a moment, showing a vulnerability. I took my hand out of his, placing my gloved index finger under his chin and tipped his head to look me in the eyes.

"You are perfectly imperfect. Don't let anyone else tell you any different." I smiled at him. His mouth dropped open for a moment, before he bowed down in front of me. He took my hand, kissing the back of the glove as I curtseyed.

That was the moment he walked into my life.

I sighed at my thoughts.

I never saw that side to him again. He had changed, he was callous and cold. He wasn't the man I met five years ago. I looked over my shoulder as I saw my bedroom door open, my beautiful mother waltzing in.

"Royal, darling," she said as she leant down to kiss me on the cheek. "Are you excited for tonight?"

"Not really." I shrugged as I looked back into the dressing table mirror.

"Why not?" She looked confused as she stood up, Betty walking up behind her as she started styling my long, red hair.

"Because it's going to be filled with loads of stuffy, no-good, pompous arseholes. I would have been happy with just you and Daddy," I admitted, looking at her in the reflection of the mirror.

"I know you would have, honey, but we also need to find you a suiter. Me and your father were married by your age."

"Well, it was different then." I rolled my eyes.

"Hardly." She shook her head at me. "These are the rules, some we can bend, some we can't break. This one is a can't break. Now, finish getting ready. Our guests will be arriving in an hour." She smiled at me before closing the bedroom door.

"Betty, do you think I could escape if I jumped out of

the window?" I asked, spinning round in my chair to look at my maid.

"If by escape, you mean die, Royal, then yes, jump out the window, my dear." She let out a small laugh as she gripped my shoulders and turned me back round to face forward.

"I can get ready by myself," I said a little sarcastically.

"I am quite aware of that, but unfortunately, this is my job. So, sit tight, button it and let me finish your hair," she snapped before giving me a pat on the back.

An hour later, I was finished. My long, red hair loosely plaited, then tied halfway down as the loose curls hung down my back, which had small white roses entwined through it. I had an ice-blue off-the-shoulder fairy-tale gown on with a multi-layered tulle skirt. My ivory skin popped somehow against the blue in the dress. I took a deep breath, I really didn't want to do this, but I had to. This wasn't just my twenty-first, this was also to find me a suiter. I hated the fact that we were in the modern day, yet we still had to follow the rules from hundreds of years ago.

Betty stood on the footstool as she placed a delicate, silver diamond tiara into my hair.

"Beautiful," she muttered as she stepped down. "You ready?" she asked.

"As ready as I'll ever be." I sighed.

"It'll be a wonderful evening." She winked at me.

"I'm going to be stuck with an uptight arsehole, aren't I?"

"Of course not, your father wouldn't do that to you," she said confidently.

"Ha, we will see." I shook my head from side to side as I made my way out of my bedroom.

Here we go, time to seal my fate.

I walked slowly down the sweeping staircase, my hand running along the solid gold bannister, my heart skipping a beat when I saw the crowds of people gathering in the extravagant ballroom. Creams and golds wrapped around the room, with gold chandeliers and hanging candelabras. The chattering and chanting silenced as I floated to the bottom of the stairs. I stood for a moment, watching the sea of people bending down and bowing as I walked towards my father's throne, my mum smiling, my dad's face stern, but his lips turning into a small grin as I stepped closer to him. I bowed my head occasionally to the curtseying and bowing guests as I reached for my father's hand. I stepped up next to him and his lips pressed to my cheek before he spun me out to face the never-ending crowd.

"Thank you for all being with us tonight to celebrate my beautiful daughter's twenty-first birthday," he cheered out. "I promise the night will be filled with good drink, good food and a beautiful princess." He laughed as he held my hand high and the crowd started clapping. I hated things like this. I hated being the centre of attention, believe it or not.

Once he dropped my hand, he pulled me close and craned his head as he spoke quietly. "I already have your suitor lined up, but I will announce it a bit later this evening." He pulled back, then grinned at me like a proud father.

I swallowed the large apple-like lump in my throat down as far as I could. I knew it was happening, but it still didn't make it any easier. I looked over at my mum, and her facial expression concerned me. It made me feel uneasy as the panic crawled up my throat, my heart pounding in my chest. I bowed my head as I walked down the steps that led me onto the grand ballroom floor, holding my gown as I did. I looked around the room for a familiar face; my *fake* friends. I felt a pull, and my skin tingled when I saw Christopher standing with a solid silver tray holding glasses of champagne. I rushed over there as quick as I could when I felt a hand grasp my skinny wrist, pulling me back before spinning me round as my body bumped into a steel-hard chest. My hands landed on a crisp white shirt, my breath catching as my eyes steadied on my fingers before I darted my eyes up to meet his gaze. His eyes burned so deeply into mine.

"Princess Royal." His voice was raspy, his tongue darting out and licking his bottom lip. His voice vibrated through to my core, setting my insides alight. His eyes were hypnotizing, and I lost myself in them. I felt my eyes moving from one to the other, and the difference in his eyes was mesmerizing. The warmth of the dark chocolate-brown was warm, comforting, inviting, but the icy-blue was cold, heartless, callous. A shiver ran down my spine, making me shudder in front of him.

"Xavier," I whispered, my shoulders relaxing as his hands moved to his chest, curling his long fingers around my delicate wrists as he pulled them from his shirt, dropping them into my large gown-skirt.

"Happy Birthday." He smiled at me, his lips twitching as he kept his eyes on mine.

"Thank you." I bowed my head down, a blush creeping onto my pale skin.

"You're most welcome." He winked at me. "May I have this dance?" he asked as he held his hand out for me.

"You can." I nodded as I placed my gloved hand in his and he pulled me close, his other hand snaking round my back as he started waltzing with me. "This brings back memories," he growled lowly, so only I could hear before the smile faded slightly. "Five years ago, I got to dance with you, you were so young, innocent..." His voice trailed off. "And now, here we are again, but now you're twenty-one, and you're mine." His voice was now harsh, gruff. I felt the colour drain from my face; my palms instantly sweaty. "Keep smiling, princess," he ordered, and I felt my blood run cold at his tone.

I did as he said, and I kept smiling as my eyes darted round the room, looking for my father. Our eyes met, interlocking. I could tell by the look on his face that Xavier was telling the truth.

"Now, I can't indulge in too much information, but you are mine from this moment, do you understand? Me and your father have an *agreement* so-to-speak. But it's not for me to tell you what exactly that agreement is. You'll have to speak to Daddy dearest. We will be leaving tonight; your housekeeper has already packed your belongings," he snarled.

I tried to pull my hand from his grip, but it only got tighter. "Not so fast, princess." He shook his head, his grin spreading across his face which creased the scar that ran from the side of his face and down to his cheek, sitting just under his eye. My chest tightened; my restricting corset felt like it was crushing my ribs. I couldn't breathe. I needed to get away, my eyes were wide with panic.

"Finish the dance, you don't want to cause a scene now, do you?" he said sarcastically as he sensed my panic, viciousness lacing his thick voice. He made me quiver, and not in a good way.

The music quietened down, and he craned his neck to my ear. "I am going to ruin you," he whispered before kissing me on the cheek. The devil himself had claimed me, and my dad had made a deal with him. I couldn't do this. I had to go and speak to my dad.

No, surely he wouldn't have agreed to hand me over to him? Surely I meant more to him than that?

I ran towards my dad as quickly as I could in this heavy gown.

"Royal, what's wrong, darling?" my mum asked, standing from her cream and gold throne.

"Ask Dad." My eyes narrowed on my father. My chest was heaving up and down quickly, the panic searing through me.

"Patrick?" she asked, raising her perfectly shaped brow.

"Mya," he said, agitation in his voice as he reflected his glare towards his queen.

"Can we move this out of the ballroom?" he asked, coughing to clear his throat. I didn't give anyone a moment to talk, I turned on my heel and rushed towards the double doors leading out to our hallway, my father and mother following me.

"Can someone explain what's going on?" my mother asked, throwing her hands up in frustration as we stood in the main lobby of the house.

"Daddy?" I jeered at him.

"I have already paired Royal off. I did it five years ago..." His voice trailed off, his pale face blushing a crimson red.

"Patrick, what have you done?" my mother said in a

ghost of a whisper.

"I have suited her off with Xavier Archibald——"

"No, no, Patrick, no!" My mother shook her head, her glowing skin instantly paling, her hands covering her mouth, her ice-blue eyes wide as she looked at me. "Why have you done that? What possessed you to agree to him? Out of all the princes out there looking for our daughters' hand in marriage, you have agreed to give her to that beast?" her voice raised, anger consuming her.

"I had no choice." His head dropped; his voice was small.

"You are the fucking king, Patrick. Of course you had a choice." She stepped towards him, slapping him hard around the face. I felt the sting, and the noise echoed around the room. My dad's head turned from the contact, and he slowly turned back to my mother, his eyes wide with shock.

"Royal, sweetie, you won't be going with Xavier." She shook her head.

"Actually," I heard Xavier's voice. My skin was crawling, and I was frozen to the spot. My eyes ripped from my mother's as I watched him take a step forward, hands in his suit trouser pockets as he rocked towards me, cockiness swamping his persona.

"Royal will be coming with me, it was the agreement, wasn't it, your highness?" he fired at my father, who was looking at his feet like a coward.

"What agreement?" my mother snapped, stepping in front of me.

"Am I going to tell them or are you going to grow a spine, Patrick?" I saw Xavier raise his eyebrows, his finger and thumb rubbing over his blonde beard. My eyes darted to my father. He was staring at me, his hand taking his crown off before running his shaky hand through his red hair. My father's eyes glassed over before he bowed his head back down.

"Tick, tock, tick, tock." Xavier laughed softly, cocking his head to the side.

"I'm paying a debt," my father spluttered out quickly.

"A debt?" my mother squealed, aggressively.

"Not just a debt, Patrick, come on." Xavier's eyes narrowed on me as he licked his lips.

"Patrick, speak now. Or I swear it, I will walk out into that ballroom and cause such a scene," my mum threatened.

"Mya," my dad snapped at my mum, his voice raised and aggressive. I could see his blood boiling, his face red like a beetroot.

"Don't you shout at me." She stepped towards my dad, puffing her chest out, her head held high. I tore my eyes from my parents before I looked at the monster beside me, his eyes on me.

"You're killing me, Patrick. I want to get my wife-to-be home," Xavier snarled before throwing his arms in the air, rolling his eyes. "Let me just tell you, I haven't got time hearing the back-and-forth of a lover's tiff. Me and your king, Mya, sat down five years ago, for a little gambling game. I have never seen a man so passionate and hungry to win." He laughed as he stepped closer to me. "After a few games of losing, he threw his last penny into the pot. And again, he lost." He shook his head. "He begged me, and I mean begged me to reconsider, to bail him out. So, I made him get on his hands and fucking knees and plead with me to let him go..." He trailed off as he ran his finger over his full bottom lip. "I did think about it, but after a while he got desperate, pleading with me, saying that he would do anything, give *anything* to not have to pay out. So, obviously, I asked. My ask was marriage to his daughter, to take her and do as I please. She was mine from the moment she turned twenty-one. He made the choice that you would abdicate the throne, passing it on to his brother who will reign as king." He took his bottom lip between his teeth as he stood in front of my father. "So, now I am ready to take your daughter away from her title, away from you and away from her perfect little life. She belongs to me; she will always belong to me." He towered over my dad, glaring his eyes into my dad's as he cowered down in front of him. My mother couldn't even speak, she was shocked. As was I.

A debt? A fucking gambling debt?

"Now, Royal, go get changed, grab your bags and we

will be on our way." He smiled as he turned back to me.

"Never. I won't leave with you. You can't make me." I shook my head, the fear apparent in my voice.

"Oh, baby girl, I can make you do anything. If you don't go and get your bags, I will get them for you, put them in my car then throw you over my fucking shoulder and drag you the fuck out of here." He stood in front of me, growling. "Do not fucking test me, *princess*."

My throat went dry, my eyes wide as I just nodded in agreement. I didn't even look at my parents, I couldn't. I felt betrayed by my father, the one man who was meant to protect me and look after me to the end of time.

But he had given me away, because he didn't want to lose his kingdom.

His money and the kingdom were more important than me.

I turned on my heel, making my way to the staircase before looking over my shoulder at Xavier, giving him a filthy look. I looked him up and down, taking in his appearance. "It's true what they say about you, you're a monster. Nothing more than a beast with no heart," I spat at him. "I will not take orders from you. I will leave with you, I will live with you, but don't you dare, for one minute, think I will bow down to your every request. You are very much mistaken, *Beast*. I am a princess, born to be a queen. I will not drop to my knees for you. No, you will be on your knees in front of me. Begging for forgiveness. And I will be smiling down at you, watching you plead and I will love every single minute of it," I snarled before turning my head to keep walking, when I felt his hand wrap round my arm, pulling me round to face him.

"Oh, Red, baby, I would love to be on my knees in front of you, but I won't be begging. You'll be begging me to stop, to stop my tongue caressing the most intimate and sensitive part of your body. I know you're already wet for me; your body language has changed. Now, go and get your stuff. It's time to go home," he whispered, dropping his hand from my arm as he looked me up and down, licking his lips.

He was right, my breathing had changed, I had a burning ache deep inside my body that was so overwhelming I couldn't even explain it if I wanted to, and my knickers were damp.

Fuck.

Chapter Two

I scurried upstairs as fast as I could, my dress constricting my chest. Fuck, I couldn't breathe. My eyes were stinging, my lungs burning as I gasped for air. I felt like I was going to have a heart attack.

"Betty!" I screamed; my voice hoarse as my burning tears streamed down my face. I was pacing up and down the halls of my floor of the palace. What the fuck was going on? This had to be a nightmare. I stopped outside my bedroom, pinching my pale skin with my fingers, trying to wake myself up. Fuck, fuck, fuck!

"Royal?" she said panicked as she ran out of her dorm.

"I'm being taken tonight, by the beast," I cried as I collapsed to the floor, bending over small, wishing I could disappear.

"No," she called out as she ran towards me, grabbing

my arm and pulling me up. "Royal, look at me, darling, look at me," she said. My red, raw eyes looked at her sad expression. "It'll be fine, I am coming with you. Let's just get your bags and get you changed. Let me get dressed. It won't be forever, okay? I promise." She pulled my shaking body into a motherly embrace before rushing into her room.

"Royal..." I heard my mother's timid voice.

"Mum," I wailed as I threw myself into her arms.

"I am so sorry." She wrapped her arms around my body as she pressed her lips to the top of my head. I felt the anger rattling in my stomach and I pulled myself away as I looked at her through my teary eyes. "Are you? But not that sorry to put a stop to this?" I said spitefully.

"You know I have no control over this..." She looked at me with sad eyes, her mouth drooping slightly, her voice quivering. "Royal, please." She reached out to take my hand, but I snatched it away.

"How could you?" I sniped at her as I turned on my heel towards my room. "Don't follow me," I screamed out as I slammed my bedroom door to see Betty standing there, her eyes looking me up and down.

"Don't be mad at your mother, dear," she said quietly.

"I am mad. So fucking mad." I balled my fists.

"You're allowed to be mad, but not at her. This isn't her doing. Now, let's get you changed."

I felt like I could breathe a little better as I stepped out of my gown, leaving it on the floor and slipping into my fitted tracksuit, wearing a tight white tank-top underneath. I pulled my hair out, brushing through the curls and tucking my now-wavy hair over my shoulders. I took my gold bangle off, placing it into my full jewellery box. I wasn't taking any of my expensive stuff with me. It can stay here where money obviously means more than your own flesh and blood.

I looked at myself in the mirror. I could do this. I was strong, I wouldn't bow down to him. I am a daughter of a king, albeit a cowardly king but nevertheless, I was still a princess who was born to be a queen. And nothing less. I may have been a gambling debt, a win, but that was it. I wouldn't let him get away with it this easily. I was going to fight until my last dying breath if I needed to. I grabbed my bags, Betty behind me with the rest before we made our way downstairs, my head held so fucking high. I didn't want it to drop for a second. If I did, he would see my crown slip. And that wasn't about to happen.

"Finally," I heard him mutter as he rolled his odd-coloured eyes. He stepped towards me as I stood at the bottom of the stairs, not even looking in my mum or dad's direction. I was so mad, and if I looked at them, I would rage out and I wasn't about to put on a show, not in front of dear old Xavier. I was holding my rage ready for him. Behind closed doors. A small grin spread across my lips at the thought. I couldn't wait. I revelled in bringing him down in front of me. He thought I was going to bend over when he asked, but he was so fooled. He was a damn fool if he thought I was going to jump as soon as he clicked his fingers. I may be his prize, but I wasn't going to act the trophy-wife. No. Not for one minute.

"What you smiling at, princess?" he asked as he took my bag from me.

"Nothing." I flicked my fiery-red hair over my shoulder as I walked towards the entrance of the palace, Betty scuttling behind me as he struggled with the bags that she had. He needed to know from day one that he was my bitch. Not the other way around.

"Erm, Red... What the fuck is the wench doing?" he bellowed. I felt my blood boil. I snapped my head round at him, my face screwed as if I had the taste of poison in my mouth. Betty was more like a mother to me than my mum was at times.

"Excuse me?" I sniped at him, my eyes narrowing on his.

"I said, what the fuck is the wench doing?" he repeated slowly as if I was thick.

"Were you not brought up with manners, you vile human?" I spat.

"No, darling, I don't do manners. I don't ask, I don't beg. I tell. I order, and people obey." He dropped my bags to the floor. "Do I need to ask again?"

His eyes were hooded, dark and stormy. He rubbed his hand against his blonde, neatly trimmed beard.

"Go on, ask me one more time," I goaded him, licking my lips as I stepped towards him.

"What. The. Fuck. Is. The. *Wench*. Doing?"

"Betty. That's her name. Maybe practice it a few times, you bully. Betty," I said again, nodding at him. "Betty comes with me. We are a pair, and I won't be leaving without her. So, my darling husband-to-be, what's your choice?" I folded my arms across my chest, Betty standing next to me.

"Hmm, let me think about it," he said as he dropped his hand from his beard, his footsteps getting closer to me. Before the next words came out of his perfectly kissable lips, he wrapped his arms round my waist and threw me over his shoulder. "Wench," he snapped. "Bring her fucking bags, put them in the boot then walk back to your maid quarters where you belong. You weren't part of the agreement. Just the princess. I suggest you do as you're told." He spun to talk to Betty like pure filth, like she was nothing more than dirt on the bottom of his shoe. It was disgusting.

I wanted to scream, to shout out, to smack him as hard as I could, but it was pointless. I wasn't going to win this battle. Bide your time, Royal, your time will come.

I looked up at my mum and dad as I was marched out onto the main steps. My mum fell to her knees, her screams would haunt me, and my dad... Yeah, he didn't do anything. Couldn't even look at me.

He was spineless.

A fucking coward.

I washed my hands of him the moment I was out of the palace. That bridge had been burned.

My heart broke as I saw Betty, her choked sobs destroyed me as I was taken by the beast. I would never forgive him.

His driver opened the door to his hummer, a single nod to his man as he threw me into the back of the car, slamming the door behind me as he snatched the bags off of Betty, putting them in the back and closing the boot as he dismissed her. He opened the passenger door in front and climbed in. His driver started the engine, the tyres spinning on the gravel as he accelerated quickly to get away. I spun myself round on the back seat, to see Betty and my mum running out onto the driveway, watching me drive away. I swallowed the lump down in my throat, watching them disappear as we pulled out the gates, the guards moving out the way as his little henchman drove through them.

After fifteen minutes, I didn't even know where we were. I had never ventured far out of the palace, so this was all new to me. I hadn't been spoken to at all from the moment I was put in the back of the car like I was invisible. I felt the tears stinging my eyes, my throat burning, but I wasn't going to give into them. I wasn't going to show him how weak he made me feel, no. I was going to fight him with everything I had.

I made that promise to myself.

Chapter Three

We had been in the car for at least an hour by the time we slowed, pulling through black iron gates, a thick mist sat over the huge, grey mansion in front of me. I sat forward in my seat in the middle as I looked through both head-rests. I didn't want to keep staring but there was something beautiful about it.

As we approached, lights either side of the door automatically turned on which showed an archway that had a steel looking door sitting flush with an iron knocker. A shiver swept over me. The windows were huge, the whole demeaner of the house was beastly looking, suiting its owner down to a tee.

"Get out." His voice was thick and gruff. His little bitch opened the door for me, not even looking me in the eyes. I tutted as I climbed out of his stupid car and stood before the steps, Xavier grabbing my many bags, and little bitch helping him as I stood watching them. Who was the boss again? I smirked, rolling my eyes at them.

Xavier looked me up and down with pure hate in his eyes as he opened the front door, dumping my bags in his hallway. I stood, in awe of his house. The walls were grey, but it didn't make the rooms dark. The staircase was in the middle of the entrance hall, breaking off in two directions. There were solid, dark oak doors that led off the main hall, and I wanted to know what was behind them all, but that would have to wait until tomorrow. I was beat. I reached in my pocket to find that I had left my phone at home.

Fuck.

I threw my head back, the tears threatening.

"What's wrong?" Xavier snapped at me; his voice was harsh.

"Nothing." I shook my head from side to side, my voice small.

"Red," his voice pierced through me, his eyes were softer, which made me feel uneasy.

"I left my fucking phone back at the palace, okay? My one little bit of normality and I left it at home." I tipped my head back, sighing and annoyed that I showed a small bit of vulnerability.

"Alan," he bellowed. "Go back to the Sorrell's and get Royal's phone."

Little bitch, who I now knew was called Alan, nodded and scurried out the door. I may know his name, but little bitch suits him so much better.

"Thank you," I mumbled, bowing my head.

"You hungry?" he asked as he kicked the floor, his eyes watching his feet before they dragged up my body.

"No." I shook my head.

"You need to eat, you are skin and bones," he growled.

"I'm not hungry. I don't need you telling me anything about my body," I sniped at him.

"Fine." He pushed his hand through his hair. "Fucking go hungry." He shook his head as he grabbed my bags and started walking up the grand staircase, turning to the right and walking down a long, narrow hallway. It seemed like I was over the other side of the house. I couldn't help looking at all the photos of these well-dressed men, I was assuming they were his ancestors, but I wasn't going to ask him. I was so engrossed that I bumped into him as we stopped outside a door, which I was assuming was my room.

He pushed the door open with his shoulder, dumping my bags just inside the door. The room was huge and painted cream. A queen-size four-poster-bed with white lace drapes that hung over the frames and were tied back with gold ribbon. A large footstool sat at the end of the bed. There was a large, ornate gold shabby-chic mirror that sat over a cream French-style dressing table with a velvet cream chair tucked neatly underneath. Next to the dressing table was an open archway, leading through to a large bathroom. There was a grand free-standing bath on gold legs that sat in front of a big window overlooking the beautiful flower gardens. My heart skipped. I loved gardening, the soil underneath my nails soothed me.

"I trust all is okay?" Xavier's voice was soft.

"Yes," I said in barely a whisper.

"Good." His voice was chilling, sending shivers down my spine as he slammed the door behind me, a lock sliding across.

No.

No.

Fear prickled over my skin. I ran for the door, grabbing the handle and tugging it with all I had. He had locked me in.

What the fuck?

I slid down the door, my chest heaving, my heart breaking as I cried out. I cried so loud, knowing full well he couldn't hear me. I was alone. Completely and totally alone.

I was a prisoner to this beast. This monster.

I felt my soul slowly dying. It wouldn't be long until he had sucked the life out of me.

But I needed to fight, and I would definitely fight.

***

I woke, cold and stiff. It took me a moment for my eyes to adjust to my surroundings. I wiped my sore eyes, my throat hoarse from screaming into complete emptiness. I crawled towards the door and noticed a note that had been slid underneath.

You won't win this battle. Don't be stubborn. You'll lose, Royal, you will always lose.
X.

I screwed up the note as I kicked the door, anger seeping out of me as I continued to kick with all I could. I was panting by the time I had finished, trying to catch my breath before standing and walking towards the bed, a cup of water, a sandwich and my phone was sitting on the bedside unit. Had he walked in whilst I was curled up on the floor asleep?

The thought made me sick to my stomach. I climbed onto the bed, grabbing my phone and holding it to my chest. I didn't want it to speak to the outside world, no, I wanted my books and my music. They were my escape. My escape from my reality. Even as a princess, I wanted out. I have always been trapped. I have never been able to walk down the street without being noticed, I can't just go for a cup of coffee or clothes shopping. No, I had to have everything bought for me, and whether I liked it or not, I had to wear it, had to have my hair in a certain style. I had no freedom. Life is too short to not have freedom. But now, I was a prisoner against my will. I turned my phone on for it to beep with messages from my mum, which I ignored. I just went straight into my reading app, and lost myself before falling asleep, dreaming of my fantasy world. It was the best place to be.

***

I woke up, stretching my hands above my head. I had fallen asleep in my clothes and I felt dirty, but I had honestly had the most amazing sleep. The bed was comfortable, I couldn't complain about that. I threw back the heavy duvet and headed towards the bathroom when I heard a knock on the door. I rolled my eyes, opening the handle when I realised it had been unlocked. I could make a run for it, but then again it would be no use, he would catch up with me.

I pulled the door open to see a youngish, black-haired maid standing outside with a covered tray and a single deep-red rose sitting next to the silver lid. I scoffed out a laugh. *Prick of a bloke.*

"May I come in, your highness?" she asked politely.

"If you must." I sighed, extending my arm out to let her into my room.

"Thank you," she mumbled as she placed the tray on the end of my messy bed.

"Are you a prisoner too?" I asked her as I closed the bedroom door behind me, walking over to the bed.

"No." She shook her head and laughed. "My family have always worked for the Archibald's, but I am really

36

mad that he has kept you up here." She shook her head. "I'm sorry." She reached out and rubbed the top of my arm.

"It's okay, it could be worse, I suppose." I shrugged.

"I suppose so." She nibbled her lip.

"You don't have to stay, making small-talk." I smiled at her softly, my eyes scoping the room.

"I'm not, I just thought you could do with a friend. I'm Mabel." She held her hand out and I stepped towards her, taking her hand before giving it a gentle shake.

"I'm Royal."

"I know, it's an honour to meet you, your highness." She went to curtsey, and I shook my head, letting out a small laugh.

"Please, no. I'm just Royal. I don't expect you to curtsey for me. Please?" I asked again.

"Of course, your highness… Shit, sorry, Royal." Her hand flew to her mouth, she looked completely mortified.

I let out a throaty laugh, flicking my red hair over my shoulder as I did. "Don't say sorry." I giggled as I walked towards the tray, lifting the silver lid off the plate and seeing eggs, French toast and strawberries. Bit of a weird combination. I scrunched my nose up before picking up a strawberry, covering the plate with the lid again and popping the strawberry into my mouth as I reached for the rose.

"Was this from the devil himself?" I asked as I

37

brought the flower to my nose, smelling the beautiful rose.

"It was," she said timidly as she walked towards the door. "He cut it from his garden especially this morning." She shrugged her shoulders up quickly as she held onto the door handle.

I just nodded my head as I dropped it to the tray, dismissing it as I walked towards the bathroom. "It was nice meeting you, Mabel, hopefully I get to see you again soon."

"I hope so, see you soon, Royal," she said softly as she closed the bedroom door. I smiled to myself as I disappeared through the archway of the bathroom, running the water for the bath. Why did he think I would accept a rose from him? He was deluded. I stripped out of my clothes and left them on the floor as I dipped my toe into the hot bath, my pale skin instantly turning a blush-red. I let out a soft moan as the water swept over my aching body. I didn't know why I was aching, maybe it was the tension crushing down on me or the fact I slept for a couple of hours on the hard, wooden floors? I leant my head back, so my neck was resting on the roll-top bath, my eyes fluttering shut when I heard a cough behind me. I sat up in the bath, throwing my arms over my bare chest as I turned to face the door to see the beast himself standing there. His eyes trailed over me, a wicked grin crossing his face, his thick scar creasing as he smiled.

"Leave," I groaned at him.

"This is my house, Red, I don't take orders from you," he said as he strolled towards me, cockiness consuming him. He was in a suit jacket, an opened collar white shirt and matching suit trousers. I would be lying if I said he didn't look handsome. He looked delicious. A fire set off deep inside me as he ran the tips of his fingers along the rolled bath top. His eyes burned into mine. His fingers moved to my delicate, innocent skin, trailing up my spine which sent tingles all over me, but I couldn't work out if it was a nice feeling or a feeling of disgust.

"So delicate, so beautiful and all mine," he growled as I moved forward, away from him.

"Yours?" I snapped my head round at him.

"Yes. Every single bit of you is mine." He groaned before he dropped to his knees next to the bath, pushing his hand into the hot water and gliding his hand between my legs. "Especially this. This is mine only. It's all mine." I froze as his fingers stilled. My eyes wandered up to his, an evil smirk graced his face. "Oh, Royal, you're untouched?" He licked his lips. "Even better." His head moved toward my lips when I let out an ear-piercing scream.

I slid back in the bath, my heart thumping in my chest, my eyes wide with panic. My eyes flitted to him, his eyes looked back and forth to mine as I saw a small change on his face. I wasn't sure if it was the realisation that I was a virgin, or if he was more shocked at my reaction.

"Don't touch me," I screamed.

"Royal," he growled low.

"Get out," I shouted as I turned my face from him, the hot tears falling from my eyes and down my face. I heard his footsteps walking towards the archway before he stopped, his eyes burning into my back.

"I SAID GET OUT!" I screamed, then I froze, waiting until I felt his presence leave.

"I'll go, but just know this, Royal, when I'm finished with you, there won't be a single inch of you that hasn't been broken by my touch."

The room stayed silent, my heart was beating in my chest, but I held my breath. When I heard his footsteps fade and my bedroom door slam shut, I burst into tears.

I got out of the bath on shaky legs, I was trembling. I wrapped the white, fluffy towel round my petite frame as I walked numbly over to my bed before falling onto it, his threat spinning round and round in my head. The thought of him touching me again petrified me. He really was a monster. I walked towards the huge wardrobe and pulled out a navy-blue summer dress with white polka dots covering it and white sandals. I pulled my long, red hair into a high messy bun and flicked some mascara on my lashes. I chose a coral matte lipstick which made my ice-blue eyes pop. I don't know why I got dressed up to sit in my room and stare out the window, but I needed to do something to distract my thoughts.

I slumped on my bed, grabbing my phone and seeing missed calls from my mother. I rolled my eyes. I was still too angry to speak to her. I didn't have anything to say to either of them. My eyes were pulled to the door, when I saw a shadow underneath the gap. I darted off the bed and grabbed the round door handle, twisting it and hearing it click.

Shit, it was open.

I pulled the door towards me slowly as I stuck my head out into the hallway, looking down the narrow corridor. My heart skipped a beat when I saw it was empty. I closed the door behind me and ran as quickly as I could down towards the main landing. Once I reached the opening, I stilled for a moment. I didn't know where anything was in this house. I walked slowly towards the stairs, looking over my shoulder constantly, feeling on edge. I was fearful of him; I didn't want to be, but I was. I let out a deep sigh of relief when I stepped into the main entrance hall at the bottom of the stairs. I walked towards the door, my freedom literally just beyond that threshold but something made me walk down the hallway, through the kitchen and towards the large French doors that led to a huge, green lawn. The flowers caught my eyes straight away. I walked cautiously towards the doors, pushing them open. The spring air filled my lungs, the scents from the flowers consuming my nostrils. I felt like I was in a haze as I ran my hands through the yellow tulips that were in full bloom, the petals soft against my skin. I felt a small smile grace my lips, it felt like a lifetime since I last smiled. And I mean, genuinely smiled. I was in my happy place.

I carried on walking through the flower garden, past the roses, peonies and the hydrangeas until I reached an orchard. Full bloom fruit trees climbed high into the sky, stretching their roots so deep into the ground as their branches tried to touch the sky. I knew how they felt, everything was so close, yet they were being anchored to the ground. I felt anchored. Heavy, imprisoned.

I spun my head, looking behind me to the back gate which was in touching distance. I took a deep breath before holding it and running as fast as my legs would take me. I pushed through the black iron gate. I felt a sense of freedom in that moment, even though I still had the driveway to get down. But I wasn't going to worry about that now, I was just going to keep running. I let out a sigh of relief as I reached the end of the driveway, bowing my head for a moment as I tried to catch my breath.

"Where you going, princess?" His voice crashed through me, shivers running up and down my spine. The fear was instilled in me. I turned slowly, looking him up and down in his signature suit and white shirt, my blue eyes taking every inch of him in. I hated that my body betrayed me when I hated everything about his beastly self.

He stepped towards me, his large hand coming out

of his pocket as he ran his finger across his bottom lip before he flicked his eyes up to mine. He darted his hand away from his mouth and pushed it forward, wrapping his fingers round my neck, pushing me back towards the cold iron gates as his lips hovered just above mine. "Thinking of escaping, were we?" he said in a callous voice, pressing his knee in-between my bare legs, pushing them open and thrusting his rock-hard body up against me before he wrapped his fingers a little tighter round the base of my throat, his mouth lowering towards my ear.

"What's the matter, Red, cat got your tongue?"

I pushed my hand up to his wrist, trying to pull his hand from my throat which only made him growl and tighten his grip. "Oh, baby, I don't think so." He shook his head. "You're mine, always mine." He smirked a sickening grin. I gave him the best, sweetest smile I had as I moved my face closer to his before I spat in his face then kneed him as hard as I could in his dick, which made him drop his hand from my throat and fall to the floor on his knees before I ran as fast as I could back towards the house.

I continued running, turning for the stairs and barging into my room. I slammed the door shut, my back against the wooden door as I tried to calm my breathing. My eyes scanned the room to put something against it, but it was too late, the door swung open so hard, crashing into the wall, denting it instantly. I had never seen eyes turn black as quickly as Xavier's. I was terrified, but I wasn't going to let him know that. I was going to put up the best fight I could.

I stood by the bed, both my arms across my chest. I had never seen someone so angry. He was standing in the doorway, his left hand still on the door handle that was now stuck in the wall. His shoulders were hunched over, his neck lowered slightly, but his eyes were on me, not leaving mine for a second as he marched over to me, his hand on my chest as he pushed me back onto the bed. My eyes widened as I scurried backwards, towards the headboard. I watched as he climbed in-between my legs, his hand gliding up my thigh, exposing my creamy skin and knickers. I heard his breath hitch, his eyes looking down at my bare legs before he looked back at me.

"You might be royalty, Royal, but not here. You belong to me. Do you understand?" he said in a low, calm voice that scared me even more than when he was angry.

I didn't say anything, I didn't move. I just stayed frozen. His finger hooked under my knickers, his fingertips barely touching my pure skin before he pulled them out quickly. His teeth sunk into his bottom lip, biting it as if he was trying to control himself. To stop himself.

"Fuck," I heard him growl before his hand was back round my throat, tipping my chin up with his other hand. "Don't ever fucking run from me again. Do you understand?" he said, a little more frustrated now. I stayed mute.

"Answer me," he snapped.

I didn't.

"Royal, answer me before I fuck that stubborn, pretty little mouth of yours." His hand left my throat. He ran his thumb across my bottom lip. My breathing fastened, my chest dipping and heaving. "Do you understand?"

I nodded. My eyes were brimming with tears, my throat burning.

"Good girl." He smiled as he climbed off of me, sitting on the edge of the bed before standing. He readjusted his suit, his hand pushing through his hair. I couldn't work out if it was out of frustration or habit.

"I can't wait to fuck you." His voice was raspy. "The thought of being the only man inside of you is enough to make me come over there right now and brand every part of you." His eyes hooded as he looked me up and down, my dress was still sitting round my waist. "But I have to stop myself, the mood I'm in, I will destroy you. But mark my words, Royal, it's coming. I'm not a patient man. You either give it up soon or I'll take it when I want to. You're mine, to do with as I please." His breath hitched, his eyes closing for a moment before they were burning into my soul. "And what I want is to fuck your tight pussy, claiming you as my own," he hissed before he walked out the door.

I let out my held breath, my heart racing in my chest and my knickers soaked.

This man was the devil, and as much as I was petrified of him, my body wanted to sacrifice itself to him.

Chapter Four

After crying for what felt like hours, I jumped in my skin when I heard a gentle knock on the door. I shuffled off the bed, bending down and looking in the dressing table mirror. My eyes were swollen and red, my cheeks blotchy.

"One moment," I called out as I ran into the bathroom, splashing my face with cold water to try and ease my appearance. I dabbed the towel on my face and neck. I took a deep breath then started walking towards the door, surprised that it opened when I turned the handle. My mouth dropped a little when I saw Xavier's little bitch standing there with a note.

"Royal, your highness. A note from Sir." He bowed his head slightly as I took the note with trembling hands.

"Thank you," I mumbled, my eyes flitting from the note to Alan. I took a moment just to take in his appearance. He was around the same height as me, five-foot-six, and stocky with dark brown hair. His eyes were a honey colour, they were intriguing. I pulled my eyes from him, giving him a small smile as I batted my eyes back to the note in my hand.

Dinner at six, get dressed up.
X

Brilliant. Just what I wanted.

I sighed and handed the note back to him.

"Shall I tell Sir you will be attending?" little bitch asked as he stepped back and away from my door.

"Don't tell him anything. Bye, Alan," I said with a sweet smile as I closed the door on him.

My smile soon faded when I realised that I would have to sit in his company for a couple of hours tonight, with his crude, hot mouth and his mysterious eyes. I tilted my head back, so it banged softly against the door. I just needed a moment to gather my thoughts.

I sombrely walked over to my bed, checking the time on my phone. It was already four p.m. I had two hours to prepare myself and find something to wear. I didn't bring anything dressy, I brought clothes for convenience, not for dinners with *him*. Dropping my phone onto my bed, I wandered through to the bathroom, running myself a bath. I must have spent a good hour in there, soaking in the bubbles. Occasionally, I emptied the bath, then topped it up with boiling hot water so my skin burned.

I reluctantly pulled myself out, wrapping my slender body in a towel. I padded out to the bathroom, gasping when I saw a long-sleeved, black dress hanging up on the outside of my wardrobe. A note sat on the dressing table alongside a deep-red rose.

I scrunched my nose up as I took the note.

Don't be late, I don't like waiting. Especially for something that is already mine.
X

I rolled my eyes, placing the note on the table then reached for the rose and sniffed. It smelt divine. I brushed the petals along my lips, smiling at their softness. After a moment, I placed the rose delicately back down before standing in front of the dress, running the material of it through my fingers. I dropped the towel to my feet as I strolled over to the wardrobe drawers to grab some underwear that wouldn't show under the tight material. I chose a lace thong but decided to go braless, my breasts were small enough to not need a bra but still enough for a little handful. I slipped my thong on after pulling my red hair from its messy bun, letting it fall down around my breasts before I ran my fingers through the ends, breaking up the small knots that had formed.

I stood in front of the dress again, just taking a moment. I didn't like that he had bought a dress for me. But from the small insight I have seen with his temper, when I piss him off it makes me not want to do it again, not this soon anyway.

I reached up, pulling the dress off the hanger and slipping it over my body. The boat-neckline sat just under my visible collarbone and my shoulders before my arms disappeared into the long sleeves. The dress clung to my body as if it had been made for me. My eyes trailed down my body as I looked at the two large splits up each leg of the dress, my heart fluttered knowing that I was exposed to him slightly. I took a deep breath and walked over to my dressing table, applying a small amount of bronzer and flicking my lashes with mascara. I covered my lips in a matte-red lipstick. Reaching for my perfume, I sprayed some on my neck then slipped into my black-heeled, open-toed sandals. I ran the brush through the ends of my hair, forming it in natural waves where it had been sitting in a messy bun all day. I smiled at my reflection, but my insides were a bag of nerves.

It had just gone six, and I was still sitting on my bed. I don't know why I do it, but I wanted him to stew. I wanted to rile him up. Even though it made me anxious disobeying him, I liked it. It was a rush, a high as such.

It was six-thirty by the time I got up and made my way downstairs. I didn't even know where I was going. I stood at the bottom of the steps, looking round the hallway at the closed doors, feeling myself getting flustered when I saw Mabel. I felt a small sense of relief swaying over me when I saw her familiar face.

"Royal," she said sternly but in a hush of a whisper, her eyes looking behind her, her head snapping back round to me.

"Mabel, help me. Where do I go?" A nervous giggle left me.

"Sir is livid." She shook her head. "Second door on the right, good luck." She placed her hand on my shoulder, giving me a small smile as she disappeared down the hallway and behind one of the many closed doors. I walked slowly towards the dining room door, my heels clicking and echoing round the large hallway. I tried to slow my breathing; my heart was racing inside my chest. I stood outside the second door on the right, closing my eyes for a moment as I grabbed the iron door knob and twisted it, hearing the latch open as I pushed the door slowly, my eyes meeting his angry ones instantly.

"Well, well, well," he bellowed across the large dining room table, his fingers pressed into his chin, his elbows on the table. The room was duck-egg-blue and gold; very dated. There was a huge gold chandelier hanging down over the dining room table, which was a dark oak. It had twelve chairs seated around it, and two large gold candelabras sitting proud in the middle of the table. I swallowed the large, apple-sized lump down my throat.

"Decided to finally join me, did you?" He dropped his hands as he pushed his plate away from him in temper, standing from the table as he sulked his way over to me, his hand pushing through his blonde hair. He stopped, his body towering over mine as he looked down at me, his hooded eyes were so dark. But yet, I couldn't stop looking deeply into them.

"I didn't realise how disobedient you were," he growled at me as he grabbed my chin, tipping it up to him, his perfect lips lowering closer to mine. "Yet, you have proven to me that you can't follow simple instructions." A small, evil grin spread across his face. "And all I wanted was a nice dinner with you, to talk, to get to know you a little better and you couldn't even turn up on time," he spat.

My breathing fastened, my chest heaving up and down from his words. He was vicious and spiteful, but my body betrayed me once again. His spare hand ran around my back, pushing me closer to him. His breath hitched, and I watched as his eyes softened for a moment. His grip round my face wasn't as hard. My heart skipped in my chest, a warmth smothering me before his beautiful eyes changed back to cold and calculating in a second.

"If you were more *experienced,* I would bend you over that table, pushing your pretty little dress up your body and exposing you completely, then I would grab a fistful of your fiery-red hair and fuck the living day lights out of you," he growled. "But I would stop you from coming. Every. Single. Time. Just as a punishment, because you don't deserve it." He dropped his hand from me as he walked back towards his seat, sitting down at the table as he looked at me. I was still frozen to the spot, my insides melting. My brain was trying to get me to register what the fuck had just happened.

"You going to join me?" he asked, holding his hand out towards the seat next to him. I nodded as I walked over.

I took my seat, a waiter appearing and lifting the silver lid to my plate. Chicken Parmo, crushed potatoes and steamed vegetables. My belly growled.

"It would have been hot if you would have been here on time." He tutted as he continued eating his dinner.

I didn't say anything, just picked up my knife and fork and started eating. After a few minutes, I pushed my plate away before wiping my mouth with the white, linen napkin.

"Eat some more, please," he ordered, his voice harsh but soft.

"I can't, I'm too full." I shook my head.

"Royal," he said my name sternly.

"I'm not forcing it down me," I said firmly, my eyes narrowed on him.

"You have hardly eaten anything, no wonder you are

so skinny," he hissed. I rolled my eyes. I couldn't even be bothered to answer his arrogant-self back. A few moments of silence passed, and I took in a deep breath before speaking.

"Thank you for the dress." I smiled as I took a sip of the cold white wine that was poured into my glass.

"You're welcome, it looks good on you." A small smile graced his face as he looked at me before looking away. I sat fiddling with the corner of my napkin as I waited for him to finish his food. I let out a sigh of relief when he nodded towards the waiters to come and clear the table.

The tension was thick in the air, the silence deafening. I wanted to excuse myself, but I didn't want to be rude by getting up and leaving. The minutes slowly ticked by, the silence becoming too much.

"How old are you Xavier?" I blurted out; I couldn't take the silence any longer

"Why?" His curious eyes bored into me.

"Just because..." My voice trailed off, my eyes meeting his. "You know my age, it's only fair." I gave him a little smile.

I watched his lips twist into a smirk.

"Thirty-five." His voice was flat, dull.

"Oh, you're like my own sugar daddy." I stifled a laugh as I took a mouthful of my water. I watched him stiffen, his hand tightening around the stem of his wine glass.

Shit. He didn't like that comment.

I dropped my eyes into my lap, pressing my lips into a thin line and wishing the ground would swallow me up. After a few moments, I heard him let out a deep sigh.

"In the next couple of days, we are going to rectify your little *issue*," he said as he wiped his mouth then dropped the napkin on the table. "Once you are used to me, I will have you when and where I please, do you understand me? Every part of you would've been filled by me." His eyes burned into me.

I nibbled my lip, trying not to cry before nodding.

"Then, once we are married, I am going to fuck you until you're pregnant with my baby. The next Archibald." He ran his index finger across his bottom lip.

"My *little* issue is quite a big deal to me," I mumbled which received a deep, throaty laugh from Xavier.

"Oh, baby, it really isn't that big of a deal. I could take it right now if you want me to show you that it's not worth the hype." He bit his bottom lip as he looked me up and down. A small smirk appeared as he focussed on my chest. "You like that idea; your nipples are hard and showing through your dress." He groaned as he stood up from his seat and walked behind me, wrapping his fingers round my neck and pulling my head back to look up at him.

"Are you thinking about it?" he questioned me as he lowered his face over mine. "Are you thinking about my fingertips trailing up and down your naked body, my lips planting wet kisses all over you," he said quietly, his voice humming through me. My breathing fastened, a dull ache burning in my stomach. His sickening smile appeared again as his hand glided across my collarbone and down to my breast as he rolled one of my hard nipples between his fingertip and his thumb, causing a small moan to leave my lips.

"Are you thinking about having my hard cock so deep inside you, making you cry out my name again and again?" he teased as his lips now moved to my neck as he bit softly on my skin, his grip around my neck tightening as I heard him groan.

"Oh, princess, I am going to fucking ruin you," he promised. "And I am going to enjoy every single minute of it." He laughed before dropping his hand, my body felt sluggish as I sunk into the chair before he walked out of the room, slamming the door behind him. It took me a moment to register his words.

I was doomed.

I pushed myself off the chair, and I wasn't sure if it was humiliation or anger that was coursing through me. How dare he speak to me like that, as if I was nothing but a toy to him, merely a plaything to get himself off with. I would do anything not to give into him, not to give him the one thing that meant so much to me.

I walked towards the heavy doors, hoping to see

Mabel on my travels. Not sure where I was going, I just carried on down the hallways. I moved to the back of the large house, walking through a glass conservatory that was built onto the back. It was filled with finished and unfinished paintings and a few empty easels. The house didn't make sense, it didn't flow. It confused me.

I pushed through the other side of the conservatory, which now had me in the complete other side of the house. This side was more my taste, high ceilings with white coving around the top of the walls. The room that I walked into had soft grey walls, thick plush white carpets and two big grey velvet sofas facing the fire place, which had a large flat-screen television above. I was in awe. How could one side of the house be so run down and derelict, yet this side be so beautiful and modern?

I furrowed my brow as I continued walking through the lounge area, my wandering eyes taking everything in. I stepped through a small corridor when I noticed a door ajar, and my curious mind wanted to explore. I pushed it open, my mouth dropping open in surprise as my wide eyes took in the beautiful library in front of me. I strolled in, standing in the middle of the floor and spinning round, looking at the painted ceiling of winged cherubs playing harps. The walls were floor-to-ceiling with books, upon books. There was a stunning, deep green sofa sitting in the middle of the floor, a couple of gold floor lamps and a huge window looking onto another large garden. The walls were a warm cream, with hints of gold accents around the room. I was in heaven. The smell of the old paper books was intoxicating.

I had found my favourite place.

I was startled when I heard a groan coming from outside the room I was in. I panicked, running towards the door and into the hallway, my eyes searching up and down the long, skinny corridor. I let out a sigh of relief when I noticed no one was there. I heard a grunt come from behind me, my head spinning quickly around when I noticed another door ajar on my way back to the lounge area. I stood outside, my eyes moving towards the gap, when I saw Xavier standing there, hunched over his desk. He stood upright but looked at the ceiling, then threw his head back as he called out my name in a moan.

"Oh, Royal, baby. Fuck." His voice was raspy.

Then it dawned on me.

He was getting himself off.

I gasped loudly, which caused his eyes to turn towards the door. The pure hatred in his eyes in that moment was too much. I ran away as fast as my feet could take me. I heard him banging about in the room as his footsteps ran towards me, a growl coming from his throat as he tried to catch up with me. I continued through into the gardens, looking behind me as I saw him catching up to me.

"Royal!" he shouted out.

I didn't stop, I just kept going. My legs were getting tired and heavy. I looked behind me again, then focused in front of me, when I tripped over in my heels, falling to the ground. I moaned where my body hit the ground, the impact harsh on my skin. I sighed, drawing in a deep breath when I felt his hands round my ankle as he fell to the ground with me. I rolled over onto my back, scurrying away from him through the dirt.

"You can't escape me," he growled as he pulled me down towards him by my ankle.

"Now you've gone and ruined that pretty fucking dress." He shook his head, a sickening smile creeping on his face.

"Did you enjoy yourself, baby?" I cooed at him, so desperately wanting to get a rise from him. I was petrified but I didn't want him to know that. His hand grabbed my thigh, pushing my legs apart as he lay his body in-between them, his lips over mine as his other hand grabbed my cheeks, squeezing them. My hands tried hitting him away, but it was no use, he didn't let go. If anything, his grip only got tighter.

"Please, get off me," I pleaded with him as he hitched my dress up, his hand skimming up my thigh.

"Can't do that, angel." He shook his head as he bit my bottom lip harshly then suddenly let it go, his lips brushing against mine.

My belly flipped, butterflies swarming my chest from

that small bit of contact from him. I didn't want him to know, I didn't want him to sense what I had just felt.

His hand stopped travelling when it got to my knickers, his breath stilling. His eyes penetrated mine so deeply, yet I couldn't read him. He pushed himself off of me, dragging me up with him.

"Not tonight." He shook his head. "Not here." His voice was low and husky. He re-adjusted his suit, his hand running through his hair. He turned on his heel and started to walk away. My heart was leaping out of my chest, I felt so overwhelmed and confused. My heart screamed, my body betrayed me, and my brain told me to stay well clear of that man.

"And, Royal," he mumbled as he turned around slowly. "If I catch you in this side of the house again, I won't be so polite next time," he stated. His voice was a little louder, and more assertive than before. I didn't say anything, just glared at him and gave him the best death stare I could. Because, trust me, if looks could kill, he would have just dropped to the floor dead. He let out a small chuckle, his back facing me as he strolled away, his hands back in his pockets.

I just wanted out; I didn't want to be here. I have been imprisoned by him for a couple of days and already I feel myself breaking underneath him. Which is exactly what he wants.

To break me, in every way possible.

Chapter
Five

The next few days passed relatively quickly without much drama. I didn't leave the room the day after my run in with Xavier, I thought it was best just to keep out of his way. I didn't want to have to deal with seeing him.

I had spent most of the morning in the garden, tending to the flowers and cutting them back. I kept a few back for myself, laying them beside me. I wanted to take them back to my room, just to put a bit of colour in there. I stood up from my knees, smiling as I saw Mabel walking over to me.

"Afternoon, Royal." She smiled, her eyes looking at my grass-stained knees. "You okay?" Her voice was a little hesitant as she continued gazing down at me.

"Hi." My voice was high-pitched and a little over enthusiastic. I smiled back at her. "I am, I'm in my happy place. I love gardening." I sighed happily, my eyes scoping across the flower beds. "How are you?"

"I'm okay, just having my break. I made a picnic, would you like to join me?" she asked, and I now noticed the wicker picnic basket swinging from her arm.

"I would love that." I smiled as I dropped my gardening tools and put my cuttings in my gardening bucket.

"Perfect, happy to sit here?" she asked. "I don't have long."

"Of course, sit, sit," I said a little excitedly as I fell back onto the grass, resting my arms behind me on the floor and watching her sit opposite me, placing the picnic basket in the middle of us.

She leant forward, opening up the basket and handing me a cucumber and soft cheese sandwich. I thanked her, taking it from her before taking a small bite, my tummy grumbling in appreciation.

"You've caught the sun." She smiled as she looked at my bare shoulders. "Did you not put any sun-cream on?" She frowned as she took a bite.

I sighed deeply. "No, it was quite cloudy when I came out this morning and I got so engrossed, I just didn't realise." I shook my head.

"I'll drop you some cream later, help take the redness down." Her eyes were kind, her voice soft.

"Thank you, you're too kind." I nodded slightly.

"Anything for you, you're my friend."

"As are you, Mabel. It's nice to have someone to talk to and have lunch with." I laughed, finishing off my sandwich.

"Maybe we can have dinner together one night? I normally get off about seven. All depends if me and my family have got everything done." She shrugged.

"Well, I don't have any plans. I just sit in my room every night; it could be worse I suppose..." My voice trailed off.

"Are you happy here, Royal?" she asked as she handed me another half of a sandwich.

"I wouldn't say happy." I scrunched my nose up. "But I'm not completely unhappy either."

"Do you think you will be here forever?" she asked.

"I think so." A sad smile graced my face, realisation kicking in.

"Do you miss your parents?" Her voice was small, her sandwich still in her hand, her head cocked to the side.

"I do." I nodded, biting on my bottom lip. "But I am also so angry with them." I shook my head.

"Sir calls them every night, letting them know you are okay." She reached forward, putting her hand on my knee and smiling.

"He does?" My heart warmed slightly at the thought.

"Yup, I always hear him just as I am clocking off." She nods.

"Well, I didn't expect that." My mouth dropped open

slightly.

"He isn't all bad, I promise." She bit into her sandwich. "He is a good boss, kind when he wants to be." She let out a little giggle.

"How do you get home?" I asked, changing the subject, my mind racing with questions. Did she like him as more than a boss?

"We live over there." Her head moved to the side, so she could look behind me, her hand pointing to a beautiful thatched-roof cottage in the distance.

"Lovely." I smiled.

"Yeah, it's not bad." She shuffled up onto her knees. "Thank you for eating with me, I've got to go," she said, looking at her watch. "There are some strawberries in there, enjoy them. Once you're done, just pop the basket back in the kitchen." She smiled.

"I don't know where the kitchen is." I laughed nervously.

"Oh." She looked at me confused. "Okay, just walk through the French doors, first door on your right. I'll collect the basket from there later, time to change the beds." She rolled her eyes. "Let's have dinner tomorrow, I will try and get off a little earlier. I'll knock on your room for seven." She smiled as she walked away. "Bye, Royal," she called out.

"Bye." I waved to her back, instantly feeling like an idiot.

I untensed my shoulders as I reached for the picnic basket, grabbing the punnet of strawberries and taking a couple of bites of one. Oh my God, they were delicious. I devoured six, licking my lips then put the punnet back in the basket. I stretched my bare legs out, my arms resting behind me as I tipped my head back, the sunshine beating down on my face. I loved the sunshine... My skin not so much. I was wearing chino navy shorts with a white bandeau-top tucked inside them and flip flops. I frowned when I felt a shadow over my face, letting out a small groan that the sunshine had disappeared. I snapped my head forward and opened my eyes, seeing a familiar pair of black brogues by the picnic basket, an impeccable pair of tailored navy suit trousers which were tightly fitted in all the right places. My eyes kept wandering until they met his, a little smirk on his face, his hands in his pockets. His blonde hair flopped forward onto his face as he looked down at me.

"Enjoying the sunshine, angel?" he asked.

"I was," I said with a hint of sarcasm, rolling my eyes at him. "Until you ruined it."

I watched as he crouched down, his arms resting on his thighs as he balanced himself on the balls of his feet, his eyes level with mine, his breath brushing across my lips.

"The sunshine won't be the only thing getting ruined." He winked at me.

"You don't scare me with your empty threats. If you wanted to *ruin* me, you would have done it already," I challenged him, my voice steady even though my insides were knotting with anxiety.

"Don't challenge me," he growled as he dropped forward onto his knees, pushing my thighs apart with force. I panted, my eyes firmly on him. "I don't make empty threats, Royal. I'm looking forward to fucking that smart mouth of yours." His voice was low, his face close to mine as he moved his hand in-between my legs, running his index finger down my core, through the material of my shorts. My chest dipped, my body flushing at his touch before his hand moved under my bum, his four fingers digging into my bum cheeks, his thumb firmly pushing against my most sensitive spot. "This is mine and tonight is the night I am going to claim it, I'm not playing games with you anymore, Red. I'll be at your room at eight p.m. Don't keep me waiting," he growled as he took my bottom lip in-between his teeth and pulled it slightly before letting it go and smiling at me, his thumb now pressing harder into my sweet spot. "You're so ready." He licked his lips before rocking back onto the balls of his feet and standing up.

"See you at eight, angel." He rubbed his thumb across his bottom lip, his eyes dark. I watched him walk into the house, full of arrogance. As soon as the door was shut, I let out the breath I had been holding.

Once he was clearly out of sight, I grabbed the picnic basket and my gardening tools and ran towards the kitchen. I dumped the basket and bucket down on the marble floor of the kitchen before I ran towards my bedroom.

After I had a bath, washing the dirt and grass stains off of me and washing the sweat out of my hair, I slipped into a cool, light-coral summer dress and white sandals. I brushed my long hair, then ran the hair-dryer over it. I opened the door to my bedroom, always hesitant as to whether it would be locked or not, but lucky for me, it was open. I knew where I was heading, I had a few hours until my fate was to be sealed. I knew what the deal was now, I knew it was happening and I just needed to close my eyes until it was over, then hopefully he would be bored with me and move onto his next victim.

I walked through the cluttered conservatory, walking quickly to get to my destination. I picked up the pace as I ran through the other lounge and into the brightly lit hallway and down towards the library, my heart racing as I closed the door behind me. I got here; I was safe. For now.

I walked into the room, in complete awe of everything around me. I smiled at the ladders that were sat against the high bookshelves, I ran my fingers along the edge of one of the book shelves before my fingertips wandered down the spine of Wuthering Heights. I loved this book with everything I had. It was a classic. I pulled it out of its place on the bookshelf and dusted it off by blowing on the cover, then continued to wipe the dust off softly with my hand. I walked towards the large window that overlooked the gardens when I found a little snug that I hadn't noticed when I was in here the other day. I smiled, holding the book to my chest as I sat in the green, bat-winged chair, bringing my knees to my chest, then opened the book, the smell of the old paper intoxicating me. I closed my eyes for a minute, enjoying this moment of pure silence before I bowed my head down and opened the first page of the book, my heart skipping as I read the first line. I forgot how much I loved this story, and just like that, I was lost in Catherine and Heathcliff.

I heard commotion outside as I lifted my head and groaned from a stiff neck. I rolled my head back, stretching my neck, my hand rubbing the kink out. I stretched my arms above my head, trying to stretch my spine out. I leaned forward, looking round the wall that I was tucked behind as I heard his voice getting closer. I looked at my watch... Fuck, it was past eight o'clock. I had been so consumed in my little book bubble that I hadn't realised the time.

"Have you found her yet, Alan?" I heard him ask, he sounded worried. "Keep fucking looking," he growled at him as I heard the library door open. I froze in my seat, but I couldn't pull my eyes from the door when his eyes met mine. His face instantly relaxed, his eyes wide, his hand still firmly on the door handle.

"She's in here," he shouted out, dropping his head forward slightly but keeping his eyes on me.

He let go of the handle as he stalked over to me. He did things to me that I couldn't explain, like making my hairs stand up on the back of my neck. I closed my book and clung onto the spine tightly, my knuckles turning white.

"Do you know how to tell the time, *Royal?*" My name slowly left his mouth as he came closer.

"I do, yes."

"Oh good. I was starting to think I needed to get you a private tutor as this is *twice* that you have made me wait for you, and you don't show up on time." He tutted, rolling his eyes as he stood in front of me.

"We had plans, you defied me. Again. Do you like making me angry, Royal?" he asked as he cocked his head to the side.

"I lost track of time," I said, my voice small.

"Did you? Doing what?" He raised his eyebrows as his hand stroked his beard.

"Reading," I mumbled as he snatched the book off of me.

"I should have guessed you would be reading this." He scoffed. "You do know it's just a story, sweetheart, there is no such thing as a fairy-tale ending. Even

Heathcliff and Catherine didn't choose each other in the end. People don't deserve happily ever afters." He tossed the book to the floor, my heart breaking as I saw it land on the glossed, oaked floorboards.

"As much as I want to fuck you, to brand you with just me, I am so fucking angry, and if I did go ahead with my plan of taking your purity, I would destroy you." He leant down so his face was in front of mine, one of his hands on the arm of the chair, his long fingers wrapping round it. The other hand tucked a loose strand of my hair behind my ear. "If I did carry on as we planned, I would tear you apart in anger." His finger ran over my bottom lip now, and I sat frozen. "And what I would do to this pretty little mouth," he said in a low voice as he pushed his finger in-between my lips, his breath hitching as I sucked it. I don't know what came over me. He whipped it out quickly as he stood, grabbing the top of my arm and pulling me up, turning me quickly as he pushed me against the wall. I winced as my back hit the cold, hard wall.

"Don't fucking tease me, Royal. Are you even a virgin or are you trying to scare me off?" he growled at me, one hand next to my head resting on the wall, the other in his pocket. His eyes burned into mine.

"Because, angel, that isn't going to scare me off. I don't give two shits if you are a virgin or not. I will still fuck you, I will still ruin you, and I will still make you mine." He groaned as his hand came out of his pocket, his fingers barely touching my skin as he glided them up my thigh before he cupped my sex, making me gasp.

"Don't be a cock tease, it doesn't suit you, princess. And if I find out you're lying about being a virgin, well..." He trailed off as he pulled his hand away. "Let's just say, you'll know about it." He banged his hand next to my head on the opposite side of the wall to his other hand before he turned on his heel, stamping on my book as he did, and stormed out the room.

I let out my breath once I was behind a closed door, walking over to the book and brushing it down, making my jelly legs move towards the door. I put Wuthering Heights back where it belonged, running my finger down its spine before letting out a deep sigh and closing the library door behind me. I dragged my sorry self all the way to my bedroom, opening the door to find a tray on my bed with a pot of soup, fresh crusty bread and another one of his red roses along with a note.

You infuriate me. I'm growing tired of your behaviour. Eat.

X

I didn't want to take the soup, but I was so hungry. I climbed onto my bed, lifting the little lid of the soup pot. The scent of tomato soup filled my nostrils, my belly groaning in appreciation as I took the first bite of warm, crusty, buttered bread covered in soup. It was so good.

Once I had finished, I stripped off, slipping into my pyjamas and climbing under my covers. A full belly and a day in the sun had wiped me out. As soon as my eyes were closed, Xavier's beautiful, intriguing eyes darted round in my head, his voice whispering before I was in a deep sleep.

Chapter

Six

I woke heavy-headed, I wasn't sure if it was the deep sleep or if I was coming down with something. I begrudgingly pulled myself out of bed and walked towards the bathroom. I splashed my face with cold water and brushed my hair into a messy bun, pulling a few strands of red hair down then brushed my teeth. I rubbed some lip balm onto my lips and flicked my lashes with mascara before walking back into my bedroom to find the soup tray gone, and a new tray on the bed. I picked the rose up and placed it in the vase with my growing collection. I couldn't help the feeling of disappointment coursing through me when I didn't see a note. I lifted the lid on the plate to see scrambled egg on toast. I devoured it, when I heard a knock at the door. I grabbed my silk dressing gown off the back of the door and wrapped it round my slender frame, frowning at my clothes on the bed. I wish I would have gotten dressed before stuffing my face. I opened the door, full of hesitance, gripping onto the handle tightly as I revealed Xavier. A cool shiver ran up my spine, and my hairs stood up on the back of my neck.

"Good morning, Red," he said, his voice low so it sounded more like a growl. He didn't wait to be invited in, he just barged past me. I rolled my eyes at his rudeness when I heard his voice boom, "Something interesting on the ceiling?" His brows furrowed as his eyes burned through me. I ignored him. Letting go of the door and walking over to the bed, I sat down on the end, trying to cover myself as best as I could with my dressing gown. I was even more aware that I was naked underneath, worried that he could tell.

"Don't hide your body for my benefit," he said quietly as he stepped towards me, stopping at the foot of the bed. He pulled his hand out of his pocket, brushing his thumb across my bottom lip, a soft groan leaving his throat. He pulled my bottom lip down to my chin before grabbing my chin harshly. He dropped it as quickly as he grabbed it, then he ran his index finger down my bare throat. My breath hitched; my heart raced. I kept my steady eyes on his the whole time, not wanting to show how petrified I was in this moment. He continued his slow trail as his fingers brushed between my breasts. My eyes fluttered shut and closed for just a moment. He pushed his hand into the inside of my dressing gown, stopping his trail abruptly, giving my breast a gentle knead.

"Your body is mine, do you understand, Royal?" His voice was a little louder than a whisper, and his lips formed a smile as my eyes were back on his. He slipped his hand out then ran his fingers across my hard nipple that was constricting against the tight silk of my dressing gown. His fingers rolled it delicately, and I couldn't help the small whimper that slipped from my lips. I couldn't believe my body reacted under his touch. I didn't want it to.

"Seems your body also agrees it's mine," he growled as he dropped his hand suddenly then walked away from me, towards the door. I sat there panting, trying to gasp and catch my breath.

"We have a ball to go to tonight." I heard him sigh as he grabbed the door handle. "I will have a dress sent up for you. Be ready for seven." He turned around to face me as I stood. "And, Royal, don't you dare make me fucking wait," he growled as he opened the door.

"I have plans tonight," I said brazenly, walking towards my dressing table.

"Excuse me?" he said deadpan, slamming the bedroom door. I swear I felt the walls shake. I turned around to face him, gripping onto the dressing table and wrapping my fingers round the edge as he stormed over, standing in front of me. I wanted to edge back, but I couldn't. I saw the anger on his face, and it scared me. He pushed his knee in-between my legs as he forced his way between my thighs, his lips hovering over mine. His distinctive eyes burned into mine. "Plans with who?" he growled.

"Ma… Mabel," I stammered out, trying to remember to breathe.

"The servant?" He scoffed, laughing softly as he ran his hand through his beard before it flew to the base of my neck, his lips now by my ear.

"You don't hang out with servants, Royal. The only plans you adhere to are the ones with me. And tonight, we are going to a ball. You are going to smile, hold my hand and play the fucking part that I need you to play of being my doting fiancée. Don't make this a game, Royal. You will always lose." His hand dropped from my throat, and my hand flew up to my neck as I panted, him still very firmly in-between my legs. His eyes dropped from mine as they focussed on my parted, pink lips. He took his bottom lip in-between his teeth before sucking in a hiss. "If you act like a good girl, I may let you see your parents for an hour this weekend." His finger ran down the side of my face. "It's up to you, princess, good behaviour gets rewards, bad behaviour gets punishments." He shook his head slightly as he dropped his hand from my face. "Do I make myself clear?" he asked as he stepped away.

I couldn't speak, it was like he took my voice. I just nodded, like a stupid nodding dog that you see in the back of cars.

I was so weak around him.

"Good. I'll see you at seven. And don't forget, Red, don't make me fucking wait." He slammed the door as he left, leaving me to crumble onto the floor, bringing my knees up to my chest as I stared forward. My mind racked with a million thoughts.

I was never getting out of here.

It's only a matter of time before he forces his way onto me, taking everything sacred from me. Everything I was hoping to give Christopher. But it was going to be bitterly taken. I couldn't even stop him.

I was a prisoner.

After a pity-party for one, I pulled myself up off the ground and dusted myself off. I slipped for a moment, forgetting who I was and what ran through my blood. I was born royalty, born to wear a crown and have people bowing on their knees in front of me. I felt an inner strength radiate through me. A strength I thought had left me. I made a promise to myself. I was going to bring Xavier Archibald to his fucking knees.

I threw on an old, loose playsuit and ran down to the garden to see if I could find Mabel. I didn't want to cancel our plans tonight, but I didn't want to feel the wrath of Xavier again today. I needed to play the part, play along with his silly games. I sighed when I didn't see her out there, so I made my way to the kitchen and saw her rummaging through the cupboards.

"Mabel," I called out.

"Royal." Her little face lit up with her smile. "You okay?"

"I am." I smiled back at her. "But please don't hate me, I have to cancel tonight." I let out a deep sigh.

"Oh what? Really?" she said, her eyes dropping to her hands.

"I'm sorry. Xavier has told me I need to go to a ball with him." I shook my head. "But trust me, I would much rather be spending the evening with you than going to an uptight, stuffy ball with the beast himself. I would rather be burning in hell than have to spend another minute with him." I giggled, my eyes searching Mabel's blank expression before her eyes stared behind me. My skin covered in goose-bumps. Shit.

I wanted the ground to swallow me up there and then, to take me down to hell. I turned on my heel slowly, my heart jack-hammering in my chest as my eyes met his icy, cold glare.

"Is that so, *Royal?*" My name fell off his tongue slowly, his eyes narrowed on mine. I gulped.

"It is," I said nonchalant.

"Really?" He stepped towards me, and I stepped back, bumping into Mabel.

"Really," I said flatly, my voice quivering slightly. My subconscious the whole time reminding me I was born to be a queen, to lead a country. I could take on Xavier.

I crossed my arms over my chest, standing my ground and furrowing my brow.

"Leave," he barked to his staff, including Mabel. They all scurried away like sewer rats, his voice still echoing around the large kitchen.

"Red," he said deadpan, his eyes not leaving mine. I stepped back again, groaning as my back hit the worktop. "I'll be honest..." He trailed off as he pushed himself up against me, cornering me. "I am getting sick and tired of your silly little games." He dropped his head for a moment before he tilted it up slightly, his eyes looking at me, a cruel grin appearing on his face. "But not enough to let you down easy. Not enough to let you go." He laughed coldly, his hand running round the back of my neck before grabbing it and tipping my head back to look at him.

"Do you know how angry you make me?" he asked as his eyes focused on my parted lips.

"I can take a guess." I smirked at him.

"Go on..." He was goading me. *It's okay, baby, I can goad you too.*

"I make your blood boil, and you try to tame me, don't you, beast? But you can't. You will never tame me or break me. You can do what you want, I will fight you every single time."

"Is that so?" he growled, tightening his grip.

"Yes," I said in a whisper, not taking my eyes off him.

"I'm not scared of you, Xavier. You can threaten me all you want, I would rather die than lay down and take orders from you. Your threats are empty, just like your life and your heart," I spat at him bitterly. I saw the fire ignite in his eyes, something in him switching. His jaw clenched before his lips twitched as he leant his head back and let out an almighty roar of a laugh before his head snapped back at me, his forehead pressing against mine. His breathing was ragged. He didn't say anything for a moment, just burned his eyes into mine. I wasn't going to break the contact, I wasn't going to back down to him anymore. I could numb him out. Completely blank him out.

"You're poison, Red, do you know that?" he asked me, his voice chillingly cool.

"I don't actually." I ran my tongue across my top lip. "But do tell me," I said a little too excitedly.

"Like the apple that Snow White bit. You are rotten to the core, laced in a thick poison," he said through gritted teeth. "I want to hurt you, hurt you so bad just so I can hear you scream my name," he growled at me. "And I can't wait for the moment that I fuck that smart fucking mouth of yours, then once I've ruined your mouth, I'll continue to ruin every inch of you." His grip on the back of my neck was so tight.

"Was that another empty threat, Xavier?" I sung his name as I bit down on my bottom lip. Adrenaline now pumped through my veins. "You're all mouth and no show," I said loudly before laughing in his face, which clearly sparked even more anger.

He pushed me back onto the work surface, his hand moving round to the base of my throat, his other roaming down my body before his fingers grabbed the hem of my playsuit, pulling my shorts to the side and exposing my underwear. His eyes flicked up at me, I couldn't even see the colour anymore. They were so dark and hazy. I had gone too far, pushed and goaded him to this moment. I placed my hand over his as I tried to pull his large hand off my neck.

"Not going to happen, princess. Still think this is an empty threat?" he roared as his fingers circled over my sex, through the material of my knickers, before he cupped me down there. Something was burning inside of me, I didn't know what it was. Rage maybe? Humiliation? I had gone too far but I couldn't help goading him.

"What you waiting for?" I spat at him. His hand dropped from my throat and grabbed the top of my playsuit, pulling me up to look at him, his other hand still firmly cupping me.

"You," he growled.

"You've got me," I said breathlessly, my chest rising up and down fast. I felt wet in my knickers, not quite sure why I reacted this way to his harshness. He ran his hand up my spine, grabbing my hair and pulling my head back to expose my throat. Was it wrong that I wanted him? Wanted him to take me here and now. His lips hovered over my bare throat before he placed his lips on me ever-so-softly as he brushed them against my skin before they moved up to my ears.

"Stop pushing my fucking buttons, Red," he whispered.

I couldn't help my panting, the burning in my stomach growing inside and moving down in-between my legs, now becoming a dull ache.

"You have just given me the green light, princess, you're fucking soaked for me," he whispered in my ear as he let go of my hair, my head tilting up to face him.

"I might be a beast, Royal, but don't belittle me to force myself on you. When we fuck, Red, and we will fuck, it will be with you willing and begging for my touch." He winked at me. "Your pussy is already mine," he growled as he dropped his hand from in-between my legs, leaving me alone as he walked down the hallway.

I sat for a moment, completely dumbfounded.

How the fuck had he won over my innocence before he had me?

Chapter Seven

I spent the rest of the afternoon trying to read, but I couldn't. Xavier was invading my mind and soul; the dull ache was now a throbbing sensation between my legs. I couldn't concentrate. He used me like a play thing, but the truth was, I wanted to be used. I shook my head at my thoughts, angry that I let him affect me like this. I didn't even like him, he just knew how to push my buttons, to get me to react. I heard a knock on the door, and I sighed as I pulled myself up. I opened the door to see Xavier's little bitch standing there with a dress bag.

"This is for you." He smiled as he handed me the dress, then a note with a rose. Of course.

I snatched them out of Alan's hands before slamming the door in his face. I was irritated. I threw the dress bag on the bed, holding the note whilst smelling the rose.

You are poison, Royal, but a poison I can't wait to taste.

X

I screwed my nose up and threw the note in the drawer with the others, the rose being placed in the vase with the rest he had given me, along with the fresh flowers I cut from the garden. I let out a little sigh. I stood at the foot of my bed, unzipping the bag and revealing a stunning emerald-green dress. I would have never chosen this colour for myself, but it really was beautiful. I couldn't help but feel my heart sing. Had he chosen this for me? I ignored it, shutting it down in a moment.

I ran my finger over the silk skirt, smiling at the feel of it between my fingertips. The neckline was sweet-heart-necked, dipping lower than I would have liked. I dropped my clothes to the floor before stepping into it, pulling it up my hips and around my chest. I managed to do my zip up myself after fighting with it for five minutes. I readjusted myself as I looked in the mirror, gasping slightly. The green made my eyes pop and my red hair stand out against my pale skin. I pulled my hair out, letting its natural wave settle down my back. I skimmed my hands down my hips where the dress clung perfectly, a thigh-high slit sitting mid-thigh. The dress had a mesh netting where the neckline sat a little lower. I had a satin ribbon around my tiny waist that had a tulle train attached which fanned out behind me. I was in love. I slipped into the champagne-coloured high heels that came with the dress then sat down to do my make-up and hair.

I brushed my cheeks with a small amount of bronzer before flicking my lashes with thick mascara and dusting my lips with a deep-red lipstick. Rubbing my lips together before removing any smudges, I sprayed my Chanel no.5 perfume then pulled a small amount of hair up off of my face and tied it into a messy bun before curling the rest of my hair. I gave myself a little smile in the mirror before standing up slowly, taking a breather. I really didn't want to go tonight, but I didn't have a choice. I looked at my delicate gold Rolex on my wrist. It was ten to seven. I grabbed the door handle, turning it slowly as I walked out of my room. My safe haven.

I walked cautiously as I made my way to the sweeping staircase when I saw Xavier standing at the bottom, looking handsome in a stunning black tuxedo. His eyes looked me up and down, taking in my appearance from my head to my toes, making me blush. His little bitch was standing next to him, also running his eyes up and down my body.

"Royal," he said with a hint of a smile.

"Xavier." His name rolled off my tongue like satin, and a sweet smile graced my face as I stood in front of him. I saw him lean towards Alan, his lips close to his ear as his eyes stayed focused on me. "When I told you to choose a dress, I thought I made myself clear..." His voice trailed off. "I don't know if I want to kiss you or fucking strangle you, Alan."

I let out a small giggle.

"Something funny, Red?" His head snapped back to me before his little bitch stepped back.

"Nope, nothing." I shrugged, still not able to lose my smile.

"Good," he said sternly, but he smiled at me. Why couldn't he always smile? He looked so handsome when he smiled.

"You ready?" he asked me as he held out his hand.

"Ready as I'll ever be," I admitted, a shot of electricity coursing through me as I touched him. I pulled my hand away, jolting it towards my chest as my breathing fastened.

"Royal? What's wrong?"

"Nothing." I shook my head. "Don't be nice to me now. I know you are only doing it to play the part, as am I," I said boldly.

He stopped to look at me. "Good," he snarled. "Just do as your told." He slid into the car that his little bitch had opened the door to, me sliding in next to him.

"May I just say, I didn't choose that dress for you. I would have never chosen a dress as pretty for a prisoner," he admitted.

"Noted," I said bluntly before nibbling on my bottom lip. I know I made my comment, turning cold on him, but I couldn't cope with him, with the niceness. He was acting, putting on a show for his audience.

Our relationship was a fraud, as was our engagement.

"Seeing as you are *technically* my fiancé, I want you to have this," he said as he reached inside his tuxedo jacket, producing a black velvet box and tossing it onto my lap. "I'm sure it will suffice for you, princess," he growled.

I furrowed my brow as I stared at him, his hand moving to his beard.

"I am so lucky," I said sarcastically.

"Don't rattle my cage, Red," he snapped at me as his eyes were on me.

"Why's that, baby? Don't want me to make a scene tonight?"

"Just keep your mouth shut while we are in there, nod along and fucking smile." He shook his head as his hand ran down his leg and he placed his hands on his knees.

I opened the box, my heart skipping a beat when I saw a princess-cut diamond. It looked huge. I took it out of the box, sliding it onto my ring finger delicately, letting out a small sigh as I looked down at it.

"Thank you," I muttered. "It's beautiful." My eyes flicked up from the ring to him, his eyes on me but his mind elsewhere.

"Do you miss him?" I asked, a pain shooting through my heart.

"Every day," he mumbled, his eyes darting back and forth to mine.

"I bet," I muttered, my voice small.

"I miss him more than *you* would ever know, I feel like half of me is missing." I heard him sigh. He pulled his eyes from me and looked out the window as we pulled into the driveway of a huge manor house. I felt nervous, apprehensive.

"Remember, Royal, don't fuck this up. We won't be here long," he said as he stepped out the car, doing the buttons of his tuxedo jacket up, holding his hand out for me to take. I did, even as everything in me didn't want to, but I did. He grasped it tightly as he pulled me into him for the photo opportunities. I looked up at him as he smiled the biggest grin I had ever seen. It made me feel uneasy.

"Look at the cameras and fucking smile," he said through gritted teeth. My smile was small as he clung to me, his hand tightening around my waist. After a few minutes, he held his hand up and told them enough. They dropped their camera lenses as we walked into the ball.

"What is the ball in aid of?" I asked as we climbed the steps.

"Just charity, that's all you need to know. For

someone like me, and someone in your title, it's good for us to attend events like this. It's all about the money, Royal, and I have enough to give. We won't be here long. Stay close, stay smiling and keep quiet. Only speak if spoken too, and if not, then I don't want to hear a word leave your lips," he muttered, his voice soft.

We walked into the lavish ballroom. It was airy and light. The windows were floor-to-ceiling, arched with long burgundy floor-length curtains. My eyes wandered to the ceiling, the chandeliers glistening from the light bulbs, the crystals chiming softly from the breeze. I couldn't help but swoon slightly. I was a sucker for a stunning room. The more character the better. I was brought back round when I felt a pinch on my skin. I looked down and Xavier's hand still tightly clung to my hip. We walked towards an older man, and I knew instantly who it was.

"Mayor Whittaker." Xavier took his hand from my hip, and I instantly missed the connection, the feel of his hand on my body as he reached his hand out, shaking the Mayor's hand.

"Xavier Archibald." He smiled as he shook his hand before his beady eyes moved to me. "Ah, and the beautiful Royal." He pulled me in for a kiss on each cheek, a small growl leaving Xavier's throat. My subconscious was screaming excitedly that this bothered him.

"I must say, I was shocked when I heard about your engagement from your father, the king. This was one none of us were expecting." He let out a little laugh, the light shining off of his bald head from the chandeliers, his hands going to his little round belly as he continued to chuckle.

"I'll be honest, Mayor, I'm still shocked that my father agreed," I said, my lips spreading into a huge grin, which caused an evil glare from Xavier.

"You're a very lucky man, Archibald, having such a rare beauty on your arm."

"Am I?" he taunted. "I wouldn't say I was the *lucky* one, if anything, it's her that is lucky. If you wouldn't mind, I have more people to speak to. Not sure I want to waste any more of my breath speaking to you." Whittaker flicked his eyes at me then moved them to Xavier. They were volley-balling between the both of us. He went to speak but stopped himself. He just took a step back, nodding his head and bidding me farewell. It annoyed me how much people felt threatened and scared of him. He was nothing but a bully.

"No need to be rude," I said in his ear, rolling my eyes.

"There is when you don't fucking listen." His voice was a rumble that vibrated through me.

"I do listen, I was just making conversation with an old family friend. Or am I meant to be a mute as well tonight?" I asked, my brows raising. I wanted to look at him, but my eyes were focused on the busy room in front of me.

"If you could, I would appreciate it." His voice was flat, blunt.

"Fuck you," I spat as I went to walk away when I felt his hand wrap round my wrist, pulling me back, my body turning to face him, our faces close. His eyes looked down at me, but it was like he was looking straight through me.

"Don't you dare show me up," he growled.

"Wouldn't dream of it. Now, let me go before I do make a scene," I growled back at him. *Two can play that game, baby.*

He dropped my wrist as I stormed off towards the bar. I couldn't stand the man. I loathed him.

After my fifth glass of champagne, I spun on the stool, sighing as I watched the lord of the manor himself laughing and joking with his little puppets. I didn't know what they saw in him. He was vile, and they were probably just using him. People like him didn't have real friends. I shook my head as I started sipping my fresh glass of champagne, it was going down far too easy. My wandering eyes scanned the room. I knew most of the people here, but I didn't like any of them, they were all street rats who were looking for their next leg up in the world of elites. Pathetic if you asked me.

I downed my glass before spinning back on my chair. "Another one, please," I said to the bartender, pointing my finger to my empty glass.

"Certainly, your highness." The bartender smiled at me as he took my dirty glass, producing a clean, full one in seconds.

"Thank you," I muttered. I took another sip. I spun back round, looking into the ballroom. I was watching him the whole time, like a hawk. He didn't look at me once, which made sense really. I was just an accessory tonight. He didn't want me here, he needed me here to make it look like we were the perfect couple.

I pulled my eyes from him when I saw Christopher standing in the corner, looking devilishly handsome. His eyes met mine. My heart raced in my chest, I couldn't slow it down. I leant my arm back, placing the champagne glass on the bar behind me as I slid off the bar stool and sauntered towards him.

The rest of the room blurred out around me as I approached him.

"Christopher," I breathed.

"Royal," he said quietly, his eyes leaving mine and flitting towards Xavier, who still hadn't looked over.

"What are you doing here?" I asked. "Why are you not at home?"

"I didn't just work for you." His eyes narrowed, his tone clipped.

"Can you take a break?" I asked, looking at his deep hazel eyes.

"I'll meet you outside in five," he said quietly. I

nodded, my eyes wide, my heart thumping. I started walking for the door, looking over my shoulder to make sure Xavier hadn't noticed I had gone. Luckily for me, he was still too engrossed in conversation with a leggy blonde. I let out a sigh of relief as I ran down the steps of the manor house, the cool air hitting my lungs, the effect of the alcohol hitting me. Shit. My head felt hazy, dizzy. I shook my head, putting my hand to my forehead, trying to take a moment.

"Royal, are you okay?" I heard Christopher's voice wash over me.

"I'm fine, just too much to drink." I sighed before breaking into a smile as I stood against the cold wall.

"How have you been?" he asked as he moved closer to me, his black hair pushed back away from his beautiful face.

"Not bad for a prisoner." I let out a small giggle. "You?"

"The palace is lonely without you," he admitted.

"I'm lonely," I muttered, biting my bottom lip. I fluttered my eyes down, looking at my interlocked fingers.

"I miss you, Royal." He sighed. "I should have acted on my feelings."

"I miss you too." I looked up at him. "But it wouldn't have changed anything. I wouldn't have been allowed to be with you," I choked out. He stepped towards me, his hand cupping my face as his lips were inches from mine.

"Let's just run away together," he whispered.

"Wouldn't that be amazing?" I whispered back as I looked deep into his eyes, longing for him to kiss me.

"Am I interrupting something here?" I heard Xavier's voice boom through me, my head turning to look at him, my heart thumping.

"Do you like peasants, Royal?" he asked as he stepped towards me, Christopher stepping away and bowing his head. "You would never be allowed to be with such scum, Red. You know that, baby." He stood close to me, his hand on my chin, gripping tightly. "You belong to me, or do I need to remind you?" he asked.

"No," I whispered, my eyes glistening with unshed tears.

"Do you like making me angry?" he growled.

"Yes." The word was out before I could register. His eyes lit with fire. "I love nothing more than making your blood boil, beast," I said through gritted teeth.

He dropped my chin from his grasp as he turned to face Christopher, his hands fisting in his pockets. "You," he called him forward. "You are working for me. Nothing like watching two people want each other, but it's even better when they can't have each other." He let out a small laugh.

"Say goodbye to lover boy, we're going home," he snapped as he disappeared inside, me following him, not looking back at Christopher.

He was cruel.

Vicious.

Savage.

Chapter
Eight

I burst through the front door of my prison, my throat burning, my eyes bulging from the unshed tears that I was holding onto.

"Royal, don't sulk. It doesn't suit you," Xavier said as he followed me.

"Oh please, just stop, will you?" I shouted at him, my voice constricted, turning on my heel. "You got what you wanted, I didn't show you up, I played by the rules. You ignored me all night, Xavier, all night! But as always, I had a moment of freedom to see an old friend and you sought me out, like always. You don't even like me, why can't you let me just go and be happy?" I cried. I didn't realise but the tears were falling.

"Because you don't deserve happiness, just like I don't," he said deadpan. He stood tall, his hands in his pockets as he looked down at me.

"You're a monster. What happened to you to make you so savage? To make you so cruel? Who broke your heart to make you like this?" I shouted out as the tears fell quicker.

He didn't say anything for a moment, just ran his hand under his chin and through his beard. After a moment his lips parted. "I have work to do, Royal. Go to your room. You're making a scene, it's not very *Royal-*like," he snarled at me.

I had never been happier than I was now to leave him and do as he said. But before I did, I stormed into the kitchen, my heels clicking along the floor as I walked towards the wine cabinet and grabbed two bottles of white. Xavier was still standing, his hands so deep in his pockets as I walked towards him, my eyes on him the whole time as I kicked my shoes off, kicking them in his direction before I stormed up the stairs to my room, slamming the door behind me.

My blood was boiling, rage was burning deep inside of me. I had never felt as angry as I did now. And from tomorrow, I had to have Christopher here with me, knowing I could never have him, which was torture in itself. I screwed the top of the wine off, bringing it to my lips, drinking as much as I could before I gagged. My eyes stung. But it didn't stop me. I took a breather before taking another big gulp. I threw myself on the bed. He was such a prick. A handsome prick, but nevertheless, he was an arsehole. A horrible, vile arsehole. I sat back up, huffing, taking another big mouthful of the wine, this time continuing to swallow until I couldn't swallow any more. I shuddered, the acid after-taste burning my tongue and throat. It wasn't even nice and probably cost him a pretty penny. I couldn't see Xavier buying a cheap wine. I placed the bottle on the bedside table, standing from the bed and tumbling slightly. I sat back down, shaking my head as I took a moment to try and compose myself. I pushed myself up again, walking to the bathroom and looking at myself in the mirror. I was a shadow of myself, empty, hollow. And it was all because of him.

I sulked back to my bed, my mind wandering back to last night in the kitchen. I couldn't deny the small pull I felt from him in that moment. It was pure lust, nothing more than that. A small burn appeared in my belly, a dulling ache between my legs. I let out a moan of frustration. I picked the bottle up and took another two big mouthfuls before opening my bedroom door like the disobedient princess that I was and sauntering down the stairs, swaying my hips. I knew where his office was, it was the room I caught him pleasuring himself in a few days ago. I rushed through the conservatory and into the lounge before I was out in the hallway. I took a deep breath, one more mouthful of wine and winced as I placed the bottle on the floor. I could hear the quiet muffle of his voice on the phone. I took a moment, counting to three before I pushed his door open and strutted towards him.

"Royal." His voice was low as he looked up and over his computer, holding his phone away from his ear. I stopped at the side of his leather chair, reaching for his phone and cutting whoever it was off he was talking to, dropping it on the floor. I pulled his chair back to give me some space before I pushed his computer screen and keyboard off his mahogany desk, listening to it crashing as it fell. I saw his eyes hood over, and I knew I had pissed him off, but that only riled me up more.

"What the fuck do––" I stopped him, shaking my head, giving him a small smirk.

I sat on the edge of his desk, close enough but just not close enough for him to touch me.

One hand curled around the edge of the desk, the other trailed up my bare thigh before I hitched my dress up around my waist, exposing my lace thong. I heard a small growl leave his throat as he shuffled in his seat. I slipped my hand down the front of my knickers. I started touching and rubbing myself whilst keeping my eyes on him the whole time. I was feeling brazen, bold, wild. It was definitely the wine, but I couldn't stop. Watching him watching me pleasuring myself was a turn on.

He pulled his bottom lip in-between his teeth, his throat growling louder now as I started to moan, my fingers stroking my clit faster as I felt the sweet build-up of my orgasm. I may be a virgin, but I knew how to take care of myself. I spread my legs further, making sure he had the most perfect view as I came, moaning out loud, my body trembling. I stilled for a moment, dropping my head forward before I flicked my lustful eyes up to him. I pulled my hand out my knickers then stood in front of him, his breathing was fast as his eyes penetrated through me. I hooked my fingers round my knickers as I slid them down my legs and off my feet, holding them in my fingers and dropping them into his lap. I bent down, looking him dead in the eyes as I ran my fingers over his bottom lip.

"That's as close as you will get to tasting and touching me," I whispered, winking at him before turning on my heel and walking out the door, closing it behind me.

My heart was jack-hammering in my chest.

What the fuck had I just done?

I had taunted the beast.

I felt sober in that instant.

I heard his footsteps coming from the office as I froze on the spot. My back was against the cold wall. My brain was trying to decipher what had just happened. My eyes pulled from in front of me, shock rattling through me as I saw his angry eyes seeking me out.

"Xavier... I..." I said breathlessly as he stormed towards me before he stood in front of me, my eyes looking up at his as his hands clasped round my face, his eyes closing for a mere moment, his breath ragged and harsh. My heart was drumming in my chest, constricting against my rib cage. I didn't know what he was going to do, I didn't want to know. I pushed all his buttons and more tonight.

I pinned my eyes on him as his flicked open. His eyes were stormy as his lips crashed onto mine. Butterflies fluttered around my body, my skin prickling with goose-bumps. His lips were soft, his tongue stroking mine. My eyes were wide, and I wanted to push him away, I didn't want his lips on me, but then again, I did. So bad.

Just as I was getting into it, he pulled away from me. He dropped his hands as quick as he put them on me before stepping away, his eyes looking me up and down.

He let out a little laugh, and my eyes narrowed on him.

"Something funny?" I asked as I crossed my arms across my chest, feeling slightly humiliated.

"I'm laughing at you." He ran his thumb across his bottom lip, his eyes looking at his feet before he flicked them up to me.

"And why's that?" I asked deadpan.

"Your little show. And I must admit, Royal, it was a pretty good show. But all you've done is made me realise that you are nothing but a cock tease. I should technically take you back in that room and get you to sort out how hard you have made me. You have caused this; my cock is throbbing." He shook his head as he grabbed at his crutch. "But I won't do anything until you are begging for me to touch you, begging for me to give you a real orgasm and not one brought on by yourself." He licked his lips. "All you've done is drive me to want you even more. You know your body, and from the little taste you gave me, I know I won't be disappointed when I finally get to have you. But let it be known, Red, your time is almost up... Tick tock." He chuckled again as he walked away. "Thanks for the kiss, but it wasn't all that. You need some practice," he muttered as he slammed the door to his office shut.

***

I woke in the morning after the worst night's sleep I think I have ever had. I had heart palpations most of the night, anxiety ripping through me. Not only did I have to face Xavier after what I did last night, but I had to now face Christopher. Every. Single. Day. It was going to be torture.

I let out a deep sigh before rolling on my side, staring at my phone. I was desperate to call my mum, to hear her voice and ask for her advice. I didn't know how I was going to get through this. I reached for my phone... It was time to call her. I had ignored her for long enough, trying to punish her for my father's mistakes. It wasn't hers. Sure, she let me go without putting up much of a fight, but she was doing her queen's duties by standing by his side. I wanted to know so much more of what happened on that night with Xavier and my father, but not yet. I'm not ready to feel or hear the betrayal of my father again. I was pulled from my thoughts when I heard her hushed voice.

"Royal," she said into the speaker.

"Mum," I choked out. Hearing her voice brought my emotions out.

"Are you okay? Xavier has been calling us and keeping us updated. I wanted to give you a call so many times, but I wanted to let you have your space as such..." Her voice trailed off.

"I'm okay, I think," I stammered over the last two words.

"Royal, talk to me," she begged, her voice still low.

"I'm lost, Mother, broken and confused. I am feeling things for a monster that I don't care for, and now he has brought Christopher over to work here, to taunt and tease me." I sighed.

"I'm sorry," she sobbed out. "I'm so sorry."

"You don't have to be sorry." I shook my head as if she could see me.

"I do," she mumbled as I heard her heels click along the tiled floors.

"Just help me, Mum, I feel like I am drowning," I said quietly.

"You have royal blood pumping through your veins, my darling, you don't need help. Do what you have to do, this is all a game to him. I will do everything to get you back home with me. I promise."

"Mum," I cried out to her as I heard a banging on the

door before cutting the phone off, dropping it into my lap when the knocking on the door came again. I palmed the tears off my cheeks as I stood from the bed and went over to the door, pulling it open quickly before flicking my eyes up to see Xavier standing there.

"Good morning, Royal," he said as he stood against the door frame, his eyes looking up and down my body before they focused on my eyes. His face softened, his mouth going lax slightly. "Are you okay?" he asked as he stepped towards me, which made me step back and away from him.

"Not overly, but I'll get over it." I bit my trembling bottom lip as I knotted my fingers for a moment.

"What's happened?" His eyes weren't as intense as he asked me the question.

"Nothing, just not feeling very well," I lied before walking back to my bed and sitting on the edge.

"Serves you right for drinking all that wine last night," he hissed, his eyes darkening again in an instant.

"Yup." I sighed with clear exhaustion showing.

"Breakfast is being served downstairs today, no hiding in your room this morning, princess," he snarled at me.

"Brilliant." I nodded as I pulled my eyes from him, staring at the photo of me and my parents.

"I will wait for you to get dressed. Now, get up and make yourself look beautiful," he muttered before sitting down on the end of my bed in his pristine suit. Did he not get sick of wearing them all the time? As soon as he was seated, I darted up and ran towards the bathroom. I couldn't be near him. I was still disgusted with myself. I turned the over-bath-shower on, because as much as I wanted a bath, I didn't want to keep Xavier waiting. I'm pretty sure he had something horrid up his sleeve.

Once I was showered, I wrapped my towel around my body and walked out anxiously to my wardrobe. I didn't look at him, but I felt his eyes on my back, looking me up and down. I was doing everything in my power not to look at him. I pulled my towel tighter around my body as I looked at my clothes. I pulled out a light grey smock dress before darting back into the bathroom, pressing my back against the wall and letting out the breath I didn't know I had been holding. I held the dress up to my chest, my head tipping back, my eyes closing for a moment.

"It's fine, Royal," I muttered to myself.

I felt my skin prickle with goose-bumps before I heard his voice boom through me like thunder. My head turned slowly as I drank him in. He walked slowly towards me. He was so handsome. I let out a giddy sigh before I clammed up, frozen again.

"I must say, you look delicious soaking wet." His voice came out in a low growl. I swallowed hard, keeping my eyes on his the best I could. He stepped closer to me, his finger running across my bottom lip, sparks coursing through me from his touch.

"Now, hurry and get ready. I don't want to wait much longer," he said in a growl as he walked out the bathroom. I dropped my head, taking a couple of deep breaths before dropping my towel and getting myself dried. I threw my hair up into a messy bun, pulling a few loose strands down around my ears. I looked up at myself in the mirror, my pale skin illuminated slightly, the light dusting of freckles scattered across my nose and cheeks. I gave myself a small smile before walking out of the bathroom. I slipped my sandals on and sprayed my perfume, completely ignoring him as he sat on my bed.

I walked towards the door, turning the door knob and opening it before stepping out. "You coming?" I asked, looking back over my shoulder, drinking him in.

"I wish." He groaned as he stood up, fisting one of his hands in his pockets as he stepped up behind me. His scent filled my nostrils and intoxicated me in that moment.

We sat down at the large dining table, Xavier's hazy eyes on me the whole time as I sat nervously waiting for breakfast to be served. I saw his eyes flick up, a twisted grin on his face as he watched our breakfast being brought up by none other than Christopher and Mabel. My heart jack-hammered in my chest, my breathing was fast and harsh as I dropped my eyes to my lap.

"Royal, don't be rude." Xavier tutted at me, shaking

his head before his hand stroked his beard. "Thank Christopher, please," he ordered as he watched Mabel with beady eyes as she placed his breakfast down. He sat back, his eyes now watching Christopher's every move. I watched as he placed my breakfast in front of me with shaky hands, his eyes not connecting with mine at all. I felt broken and humiliated.

"Thank you, Christopher," I muttered quietly. Christopher bowed his head as he stepped back and stood against the wall with Mabel.

"You may be excused." Xavier dismissed them both, waving his hand as if they were a nuisance. I looked at both of them, my eyes darting back and forth.

"Oh, and, Royal," he said as he swallowed his food, Christopher and Mabel still in the room. "Don't even think about fucking the servant boy," he growled as his dark eyes burned into mine. I gasped, trying to catch my breath as the air was knocked out of my lungs, my head turning over my shoulder so I could see Christopher, but he dropped his head and walked out the door, slamming it behind him. I felt the anger bubbling inside me, and I snapped my head round quickly to look at Xavier.

"Why are you being such an arsehole?" I said blasé. "Was this the only reason you wanted me to come down here and have breakfast with you? So you could dangle me like a new shiny toy in front of Christopher?" I banged my hand down on the table.

"Don't be silly, Red." He shook his head as he smirked. "I didn't do that for Christopher, I did it for you. Just to remind you that you are mine. You will always be mine." He nibbled his bottom lip before popping a strawberry into his mouth. "Well, and a little bit for Christopher. He needs to know that you are a no-go. He isn't to even sniff your perfume. He is to keep his distance," he said sternly. I was still clutching my fork tightly, my knuckles turning white from my grip.

"Anyway, the reason I wanted breakfast with you was to let you know that I need to go away next week for a few days for business. I was going to say about you coming with me, but after your attitude this morning, I think it's best you stay here, with Alan. He will keep a close eye on you and report back if need be. So, just let it be known, Royal, I will have eyes on you the whole time. I will know your every move." He wiped his mouth with a napkin, dropping it on top of his plate before pushing himself away from the table as he walked towards me and stopped.

He leant down, so his lips were close to my face. "Now, eat your breakfast, don't waste my food, Royal. And keep the fuck away from Christopher." He stood tall as he walked out the dining room, leaving me on my own to sit and eat my French toast and fruit. I had, all of a sudden, lost my appetite. I pushed my plate away, throwing my napkin on the table and storming out of the room, slamming the door behind me, hoping that he heard it.

I stormed through the kitchen, past Mabel and Christopher who were in the middle of a conversation and collapsed on the grass, the sun beating down on my bare skin before the tears began to fall. I didn't know how much longer I could keep this up, being his prisoner. Part of me would rather die than spend another second with him.

I felt a shadow over me, and I spun round, ready to shout at Xavier, but I found Christopher standing above me.

"Royal..." His voice trailed off.

"Leave me alone, Christopher, please. We shouldn't be talking. If he sees, if he finds out..." I choked. "It doesn't bear thinking about."

"I don't care, he can do what he wants to me. I am your friend; you're my friend and I won't see you upset because of that beast." He dropped to his knees, pulling me into an embrace. Mabel ran up behind him and threw herself over both of us. In that moment, I felt more love than I ever had in my life.

"Thank you," I muttered as they both pulled away from me, now sitting on the grass next to me.

"Don't worry about him, Royal, he is all mouth," Mabel said in a whisper, but not before looking over her shoulder to make sure he wasn't there.

"I know." I sighed. "But it's still not nice having to live here with him. I just want to go home. I don't want to be his prisoner anymore." I dropped my head back and let the sun beat down on my face.

"I should run. He goes away tomorrow, for a few days, so I could get away... Maybe," I said as I lifted my head up to look at Christopher and Mabel.

"He will find you," Mabel said deadpan.

"That's true," Christopher agreed with her, nodding his head.

"This is going to be my life now. Stuck in this prison with a man I hate," I spat. It was true I hated him, but I couldn't deny the fire that he set off deep inside me.

"It won't be forever, babe. Plus, you've got us," Christopher said as he leant across and rubbed his hand softly up my arm. His hazel eyes were warm as he smiled at me.

"Get your fucking hands off of her," I heard as Xavier's voice ripped through me. "Now, peasant, before I pull you off her myself," he growled. Christopher froze before his eyes widened. I felt tears spring to my eyes. Christopher's hand dropped from me before Xavier dragged him up by his white shirt and marched him into the kitchen. I looked at Mabel, panic all over my face, her eyes fixed on mine. I pulled my eyes from her before looking at the double doors of the kitchen, waiting for Xavier to re-appear. Within minutes he was back, stomping over to me, his eyes hooded and dark as he pinned them to me. I took a deep breath, ready for his attack.

"Get up," he said sternly and bluntly.

"No. I don't want to." I shook my head before crossing my arms across my chest.

"Get the fuck up, Royal, I am already angry, don't make it worse," he threatened through gritted teeth before he pushed his blonde hair away from his face.

"I won't get up until you tell me Christopher is okay." I crossed my legs underneath me, scowling at him.

"Your peasant is fine. Now, get up," he said exasperated.

"He has a name." I glared at him, my voice strong but quiet.

"Royal, don't push me," he growled, looking to the side to see Mabel still standing there. "I suggest you leave, Mabel, before I fire you and your whole family and put you out on the streets," he snarled at her as she scampered away.

"Why are you such a heartless, cruel man?" I asked, confusion lacing my voice, my brows furrowed.

"Because I am. Now get up, I won't ask again." His hands pushed into his pockets. I rolled my eyes and sighed as I unfolded my arms. Before I knew what was happening, I was being dragged up by Xavier and thrown over his shoulder as he marched me into the house and up the stairs.

"Put me down!" I screamed.

"Not a chance, Red," he said with a laugh, but his voice was still angry. He tightened his grip around my waist as we walked towards my bedroom. He kicked the door open and dropped me onto the bed. I pushed myself up towards the headboard, and he followed as he kneeled in-between my legs, pushing them apart as he sucked in his breath. I pulled the skirt of my dress down as well as I could to stop his hungry eyes. His full bottom lip was pulled in by his teeth, his eyes staring down at me.

"Do you know how infuriating you are?" he asked as he rocked back onto the balls of his feet.

"Nope. But I am sure you are going to tell me," I answered sarcastically.

"I want to hurt you." His eyes narrowed. "I want to hold you. I want to kiss you. I want to pleasure you. I want to claim you." His voice was low. "But I can't. My senses tell me to stop, you're a poison to me, Red. Like a drug. I crave you, every minute of every single day. You are like a type of heroin, made just for me." His voice was soft, his eyes glistened with a shimmer of kindness, and I dropped my guard for a moment, a small smile gracing my face. "But I also despise you. I loathe you like you wouldn't believe, and all I can think about is punishing you, hurting you and degrading you. Because that's how you make me feel." I felt my heart drop from my chest and into my stomach, the bile rising up my throat. My eyes stung from his vicious words.

"I would never love you. How could someone ever love a beast?" I spat at him.

"Good job you'll never have to find out," he chastised back. "I leave at six a.m. tomorrow morning for three days; Alan will be keeping an eye on you. You will join me for dinner tonight at seven p.m. Make sure you wear something decent," he said as his eyes trailed up and down my body. "You're a princess, not a peasant, so don't dress like one," he said as he stood from the bed.

"I won't be there for dinner," I admitted, my eyes focussed on my hands that were in my lap.

"When did I say you had a choice?" He turned on his heel to face me as he stood at the door.

"I——" He held his finger up, cutting me off.

"When will you realise you don't have a choice in anything? See you at seven," he said in a loud voice as he walked out the door and slammed it behind him.

Chapter Nine

After spending the rest of the day in my bedroom, lost in my books, seven p.m. was fast approaching. I didn't want to go down to spend the evening with him, and I didn't want to have to deal with him either. I just needed to get through dinner, then I would be rid of him for a few days. And I couldn't wait.

Okay, so I would have his little bitch, Alan, watching my every move but I didn't give a fuck about him. He was nothing to me. I would do what I wanted, when I wanted, and I wasn't going to be dictated to by him.

I opened the wardrobe and grabbed a silver satin floor-length gown. I held it up against my body as I looked into the mirror and smiled. I dropped my smock dress to the floor before I stepped into the silky material that slipped up my skin. The dress was stunning, it had cuffed arms that sat just under my shoulders then clung to my body as if it had been made for me. The back was completely open before re-joining just above my bum. I slipped into a silver pair of open-toed sandals and sprayed some perfume, then flicked my lashes with mascara and applied a matte-red lipstick across my lips.

Happy with the way I looked, I walked out of the bedroom, my head held high. I flicked my wavy hair over my shoulders as I stepped carefully down the stairs. I walked towards the dining room, the door ajar. I froze when I saw my parents sitting at the table, massive grins on their faces. Before I could say anything, Xavier was by my side, his arm snaking around my waist as he pulled me to him, his lips pressing against my ear. "Smile, show them just how happy you are to be with me, baby," he cooed.

My breathing fastened; I was intoxicated by him. "Also, that dress is criminal. You look fucking stunning," he said before he pulled away from me. I couldn't help the swoony feeling that consumed me, but I know now that everything he says is part of a game.

"Royal, baby," my mum cried out as she stood and swooped me into a cuddle. "I have missed you." She nuzzled into me before kissing me on the cheek. She wiped her eyes before taking her seat next to my father, smiling at him before she faced me again.

Xavier held my hand as he walked me over to the long table, pulling my chair out for me to sit down then planting a soft kiss on the top of my head as he took his seat next to me. I felt myself blush from the small bit of intimacy he had shown.

"Oh, Royal, you look positively glowing and so happy." She beamed.

"I am." I nodded, my eyes telling a different story and she could tell. But I did my bit, I smiled and played the part. I didn't say two words to my father, I couldn't believe he had actually showed his face here. I leant forward for my wine glass before taking a big mouthful, Xavier's hand giving me a gentle squeeze on the top of my knee, his eyes on mine as he watched me swallow my drink. I darted my eyes to him, narrowing them on him before I turned to face my parents.

"So, Daddy, missing me?" I asked with a snarl.

"Royal..." He started to talk but stopped, dropping his head.

"What's wrong? Can't muster the words? Or is the guilt eating you alive now you have seen me in the flesh?" I shook my head, disgusted with him before taking another mouthful of my wine. I could feel Xavier staring at me, and I side-eyed him, a small smirk started to form on his lips.

"Royal, I'm, I..." he stammered.

"For fuck's sake, Dad, spit the words out, will you? If only you had struggled this much with gambling me away." I couldn't sit here any longer. I pushed my chair back and walked towards the door when I bumped straight into Christopher, sending his tray flying, the food spilling down my dress. My mouth was wide open with shock, Christopher's eyes were on Xavier who was behind me, his hand pushing round my waist to my stomach, pulling me back towards him.

"I suggest you get yourself a towel and clean up this fucking mess," he growled at Christopher, who bowed his head like a submissive and ran towards the kitchen. I was still slightly shocked. I grabbed his hand, ripping it off of me as I walked out the door, moving as quickly as my heels would allow, when I stood at the bottom of the stairs, gripping onto the newel post as I tried to steady my breathing. I felt him behind me, my skin prickling with goose-bumps.

"Are you okay, Red?" he asked as he stepped closer to me, his breath now on the back of my neck as he pushed my hair to the side. I tried to quieten my breathing, my head dropped slightly, my eyes closed.

"I'm fine," I said with a quivering voice. I turned to face him, swallowing the hard lump down my throat as I looked into his mesmerizing eyes.

My lips parted slightly, drinking every inch of him in. "Take me," I said in a whisper.

"Sorry?" he asked, snapping back to his old self as he stepped away from me.

"I want you," I mumbled out, feeling the blush

creeping onto my face.

He laughed a deep laugh as he threw his head back. "Oh, Royal... Baby..." He snapped his head up to look at me. "I don't want you. Not like that anyway. I only want to fuck you to get you pregnant with my baby. Not for pleasure, you don't do it for me." He chuckled before he walked back towards my parents.

"Don't flatter yourself, baby," he called out before going into the dining room.

***

I sat at the dining room table by myself, feeling a little lighter than I did yesterday. It was knowing that he was gone, only for a few days, but he was gone. I felt like I could breathe. I smiled when Mabel sat down next to me. "Morning, Royal." She smiled at me as she tucked her chair in.

"Good morning," I said, a little chipper.

"Someone is in a good mood." She nudged me.

"Well, you would be if your captor had left the house for a few days." I smiled.

"I get you." She nodded as she drank her water.

"Have you got much work on today?" I asked.

"Hmm, not too much." She leant back on the chair, bringing her knee up to her chest. "Why do you ask?"

"Wondered if you wanted dinner with me tonight? I was going to ask Christopher as well, if you don't mind? I miss him so." I sighed.

"Yes! Yes to dinner, it will be so nice. And of course I don't mind." She clapped her hands a little too excitedly. "Can I ask you something?" she said as she dropped her leg, resting her elbows on the table.

"Of course." I nodded as I placed my knife and fork down.

"Was... Well... Is there something going on between you and Christopher?" I saw her cheeks blush.

"Was, is, I just... I don't know." I shook my head. "But it doesn't matter, because I can't ever be with him. Not while I am locked to Xavier, and he isn't going to let me go," I said quietly as I saw little bitch walk in.

"Royal, Xavier has asked me to take you to the library for a couple of hours," Alan said as he stood, holding onto the door knob.

"I am quite capable of walking to the library by myself, thank you." I shot him a glare over my shoulder. "Besides, I don't want to go to the library, I am going into the garden," I said as I stood. Mabel stood with me, by my side. "And don't make any plans for dinner, I am having dinner with my friends, in my room." I nodded at him as I got to the door, standing next to him. "Clear the plates." I smiled a fake smile at him. "Please."

I walked past him and towards the garden, I wanted to be outside, not trapped inside whilst the weather was glorious. Who did Xavier think he was telling me what to do? All so he could keep an eye on me? I sat under the pergola, looking over the gardens, the sound of the waterfall trickling in the background from the water feature, when I saw Mabel and Christopher walking towards me with a jug of lemonade.

"Hey." I smiled as they placed the jug and cups on the table.

"Hey, mind if we join you?" Christopher asked.

"No, of course not. Sit," I said excitedly. They both scooted to the side of me, sitting next to me as Mabel reached across and poured the lemonade into the glasses.

"Thank you," I muttered as I took the glass off of Mabel before taking a sip. It was delicious. "Why don't you both just take the rest of the day off?" I looked at them both, pulling my brows together.

"Because Xavier would have my arse." Christopher laughed.

"But Xavier isn't here..." My voice trailed off as I tried to contain my smile.

"I know, but fucking Alan will grass me up," Christopher said a little apprehensive.

"Fuck Alan. I'm his fiancé, if anything, I am in charge and I am giving you the day off. If Xavier has a problem, he can talk to me about it." I cheered out loud as we all clinked glasses.

I looked over my sunglasses to where Alan was standing, his eyes glaring at me. I just laughed and enjoyed the rest of the day with my friends.

It was what I needed.

***

The evening was in full flow, and we were all sitting in our pyjamas with bottles of wine and endless snacks. We sent little bitch out for supplies, and after a bit of a protest, he happily skipped out the door to fetch our goodies. The evening was getting on and Mabel decided to call it a night. She said her goodbyes before walking out the door, closing it softly behind her. I knew Alan was standing outside the door, and the thought that me and Christopher were here on our own was probably pissing him off, meaning that he would no doubt text Xavier and let him know.

"How are you?" I asked as I turned the music down.

"I've been better." He shrugged his shoulders.

"Mmm, me too." I nodded in agreement.

"I've missed you, Royal. Honestly, not knowing if you were okay was driving me insane." He let out a sigh as he leant towards me, stroking a loose piece of hair out of my face. I felt his breath on my face, my eyes closing slightly as I tried to control my breathing.

"I've missed you too," I muttered before I pulled back away from him, my hand resting on his chest as I pushed him away gently. "But we can't." I shook my head. I couldn't believe the words were even coming out of my mouth. A few weeks ago, I wanted nothing more than to be with Christopher, but now, things were different. I couldn't risk him getting hurt or punished because of my feelings. I did like him, more than he would ever know.

I saw the hurt flash in his eyes as he let out a sigh, moving back away from me, his head dropping. "But I know Mabel likes you." I dipped my head, smiling at him, bringing his face up to look at me by tipping his chin up.

"She was asking about you... Plus, I think you two make a really nice couple." I gave him a small smile, my heart obliterating in my chest that I was actually letting him go. I couldn't describe the pain that was searing through me, but I knew it had to be done. It was the right thing to do, for me and him. I had to let him go. I wiped a stray tear away before I embraced him in a tight hug, his arms wrapping around me. I didn't want to let go, I just wanted to stay in his arms for as long as I possibly could.

***

I woke startled, lifting my head off of a hard chest and looking around the dark room before I fixated my adjusted eyes on Christopher. *Shit.*

I scrambled up, gently nudging him to wake up. "Christopher, wake up," I whispered. "Please, wake up." I nudged him again, this time with a little more force.

"What? What's wrong?" he asked as he reached out for me before trying to doze back off.

"You fell asleep in my room, I need you to get up. Fucking Alan is going to have a field day with this. Please get up."

I saw his eyes go wide as he shot up, running for the door and opening it to be faced with Alan's cold stare. He didn't say anything, just ran down the hallway as quick as he could.

I rushed to the door to see Alan smirking at me, his phone up to his ear.

"Sir," he snapped as his grin grew wider. "Christopher has just left her room." He nodded. "No, and no he wasn't either. Okay, bye." He hung up the phone before sliding it in his back pocket.

"Xavier is pissed," he snarled at me as he folded his arms across his chest.

"But nothing happened!" I raised my voice at him.

"He doesn't know that though, does he? He isn't here..." His voice trailed off as he looked me up and down.

"But you do, you are here," I said, my voice small, instantly feeling uneasy around him.

"That's true, but he will believe me over you. Especially because he thinks you were both undressed when Christopher scarpered out of your bedroom."

"Alan, no, you didn't," I said with a gasp, my eyes going wide before my hand came up to my mouth. "Yeah, I did," he snarled at me with a growl. "Because you fucking deserve it." He laughed before slamming my bedroom door. I turned, resting my back against it as I slid down. My body was covered in a cold sweat, the blood pumping in my ears, my heart jack-hammering against my rib cage. I wasn't scared for me; I was scared for Christopher.

What the fuck had that little bitch done?

I stood from the ground before swinging the door open and flying at Alan, hitting my balled fists against his chest in anger.

"What is wrong with you? Why are you playing silly fucking games?" I screamed at him. He didn't reply, just grabbed my tiny wrists with one hand, the other grabbing my throat as he pushed me back into my bedroom and onto my bed. He raised one knee and rested it on my bed.

"Don't fucking touch me. You caused this, not me." He growled as he released his grip around my neck before standing up and readjusting his tee and stepping back. "If you play with fire, you silly girl, you'll get burned." He laughed before he walked out of my room and slammed the door behind me, and I heard the lock slot across.

Chapter

Ten

I jolted up in my sleep, my heart thumping, my eyes puffy, my throat sore from crying myself to sleep. I had nightmares of Xavier plaguing my dreams, his eyes invading my thoughts. I turned the lamp on next to my bed to have a drink of water, when I saw him, sitting in the corner of the room, at my dressing table chair. He was wearing one of his signature suits, his shirt undone slightly and a bottle of whiskey in his hands. His eyes were hazy, hooded.

"Xavier," I gasped out, my voice raspy.

"Royal." My name rolled off his tongue, his eyes pinned to me.

"You've been gone a day, why are you here?" I asked as I pulled my duvet up under my chin, clinging on to it tightly.

"Well, after a little call from Alan, and being told that

that prick came out of your room half naked, I had to come home and see to you, didn't I?" He scowled at me before taking a big gulp of his whiskey, running his bow-tie through his fingers.

"But I didn't do anything, and he wasn't half naked! It's fucking Alan!" I protested.

"I don't believe you, just like I don't believe that you're pure like you claim to be. I believe that you have been fucked by Christopher, over and over again." He growled as he stood up, his whiskey bottle still tightly in his grip as he stood at the side of my bed. I could smell the alcohol on his breath.

He leant down as he placed his whiskey bottle on the bedside table. He grabbed my chin and tilted my face up to look at him, his lips close to mine as he tightened his hold. His free hand travelled up my bare thigh, pushing my nighty up round my hips. He didn't pull his eyes from me. I pushed his hand away but that didn't stop him. He gripped my thigh as he let out a growl.

"Stop fighting me, you told me the other night that you wanted me..." His voice trailed off before he let out a deep sigh. "So let me have you," he muttered as he continued his slow trail up my leg. A pant left me, a small smirk on his face as my body reacted to his touch. He moved his face closer to me, his fingers loosened up on my chin before he pressed his lips to mine, kissing me slowly, pushing his tongue into my mouth. I could taste the poison on his tongue, but I wanted more. His kiss deepened, his fingers tightening again as he reached the apex of my thighs and groaned as he brushed his fingertips over my sensitive skin. He pulled away from me, sinking his teeth into his bottom lip and biting down on it before he dropped to his knees in front of me. I kept my eyes on him, my chin feeling bruised from his touch. His hand splayed against my stomach as he pushed me back slightly, then spread my legs before he flicked his tongue on the most intimate part of my body. His fingers dug into the skin on my stomach as he pushed his tongue further into my folds, licking and flicking over my sensitive bud. I sucked in my breath; the feeling indescribable.

He glided his other hand up the inside of my thigh, teasing my opening before pushing two fingers inside me. I cried out, my fingers gripping onto the bedsheets, and the sting that I felt started to burn.

"Xavier," I called out breathlessly. "You're hurting me," I admitted, my eyes looking down at him. He pulled his fingers out of me, but kept his tongue moving over me before he moved his mouth from me. He stood, his dark gaze beating down on me as he undid his suit trousers, kicking them down to his ankles as he fisted his hand into his boxers, pulling out his hard, thick length. My eyes widened and I swallowed hard, my mouth going dry. The sheer panic was ripping through me.

He leant over me as he grabbed me round the throat, pushing me back forcefully, his hand gripping the base of my neck as he pushed my legs wide apart, then nestled between them.

"Now, I am going to see if you really are a virgin," he snarled.

"Please, Xavier, don't do this. I wouldn't lie about this. I didn't sleep with Christopher; I haven't slept with anyone." The panic was apparent in my shaky voice. He ignored me, lining himself up at my opening, his eyes looking down at how close he was to me.

"Please." I let out a silent cry, pleading for him not to do this. Not like this. I wanted him, but I wanted him to take me tenderly and make love to me.

His eyes flicked up to mine as a tear rolled down my cheek, my hands trying to pull his from my throat before his eyes glazed over, a glisten of light shooting through them as he pushed himself off of me, falling to the floor, his gaze on me as I moved up the bed as quickly as I could.

"Royal." His voice was barely a whisper.

"Leave me alone," I cried, my hands shaking, my stomach flipping and churning.

"Please, Royal… Let me," he pleaded as he got on his knees, crawling towards me.

"Just fucking get out, Xavier. I hate you," I said through choked tears. "I hate you," I managed to mumble out before pulling the covers over my head and letting out my held-in sobs.

"I'm so sorry," he said calmly as he collected his things and walked out of the room, closing the door gently behind him before I let out a loud cry.

Xavier

I stood outside the room, clutching at my chest, feeling like my heart was being torn apart. What the fuck did I do? The disbelief turned to rage as I felt my blood boil deep inside me. She was that little bit of light left in my soul and I had completely blacked her out. I turned around, facing her door, wanting to open it and beg on my fucking knees. I wanted to beg for her forgiveness, but it was too late. I walked towards the stairs, running down them as fast as my legs would take me before I ran towards my office, slamming the door behind me and balling my hand before I threw my fist into the wall again and again, trying to relieve the hurt I was feeling.

I stopped when I saw my knuckles swelling, the blood rising to the open wounds. I screamed out in frustration as I stormed over to my liquor cabinet, grabbing the first bottle I see. I pull the lid off before bringing the thick bottle rim up to my lips, letting the poison slip down my throat, a satisfying burn following. I winced before taking another big mouthful and sitting myself down on my office chair. I sat for a moment in silence, contemplating my thoughts. I flicked the mouse on my laptop and brought the screen to life. My heart obliterated at my screensaver picture, my eyes brimming.

The bottle of whiskey rested in my hand, my grip loosening as I focused on what was in front of me, my other hand running across my scar before I completely lost it.

The anger bubbled in me as I screamed as loud as I could, throwing the glass bottle against the wall. I stood up on my feet, my hands balled into fists. I dropped my head, my eyes squeezed shut before they flicked up to look at the screen again.

"I'm so sorry," I muttered before falling back into my chair and letting darkness take over my already-blackened heart and soul.

I truly was a monster, and when she knew the truth, I would lose her forever.

***

Royal

I couldn't sleep, my eyes were dry from the shed tears. I knew he was a monster, a beast, but I never thought he would try to force himself on me. I honestly thought his threats were empty, but this wasn't to take my virginity. This was to prove a point to himself that I wasn't pure like I stated. This was revenge. He was fed lies by that snake, Alan, and he believed him over me. Even when I was begging, he still believed him. Fuck, he probably still believes him now, even once he snapped out of his drunken rage.

I kept replaying the moment over and over in my head. It was like something deep inside him clicked, I had never seen his face look so scary. His jaw was clenched, his eyes dark and stormy. A low hum vibrated from his throat as he climbed on me.

I couldn't deny the sparks that flew when he touched me, his hand gliding up my thigh, his mouth covering the most sensitive part of my body. I felt conflicted.

My mind was screaming at me, but my heart was beating like it had never beat before. And it was beating for him, and only him, but I wasn't sure I was ready for the feelings my heart wanted me to feel. I clutched at the material on my chest, trying to still my erratic heart, but it was no use. Nothing could still it.

I thrashed in the covers after trying to sleep off the dreaded feeling that was deep in the pit of my stomach, but it was no use. I walked into the bathroom before splashing my face with cold water, trying to snap myself out of this mood I was in. I dragged my feet over to the little bedside drawer that I kept his handwritten notes in, pulling them out one by one and reading them. He was so cryptic. He was the definition of smoke and mirrors.

I grabbed my silk dressing gown off the hook on the back of my bedroom door, wrapping it around my black satin nighty and tying the ribbon round my waist before slipping my slippers on. I slowly and quietly opened the door and tiptoed across the wooden floorboards. I walked down the long, narrow corridor until I got to the sweeping staircase. I held onto the bannister as I walked into the darkness, my heart thumping fast as I reached the bottom, holding onto the newel rail as I twisted to walk down towards the kitchen.

I gasped, holding my breath when I saw his office door was open. I closed my eyes for a moment, hoping that he wouldn't notice me walking past. I pushed onto my toes as I tiptoed slowly past as quietly as I could, letting out a sigh of relief as I made it to the kitchen without being noticed. I closed the door behind me then headed for the fridge, wrapping my fingers around the double handles and pulling them open, the light inside so bright, making me squint as I reached forward for the milk.

I turned to the side, closing the doors with my hip then walked over to the island in the middle as I grabbed a saucepan out, pouring the milk in and placing it on the stove as I turned the burner on. I stood stirring the milk continuously until it started bubbling. I smiled as I turned the gas off and moved the saucepan back to the island, grabbing a mug as I started to pour.

"Be careful you don't get burned, Red," I heard his

voice echo round the room, making me jump as I dropped the saucepan on the island, the boiling milk spilling and burning my hand that was resting on the worktop.

"Shit!" I cried out as I pulled my hand away quickly and ran it under the tap.

"Royal," he said in a low voice. He was by my side in an instant as he took my hand in his, bringing it to his plump lips and kissing it gently before he held it back under the water, his eyes burning into the side of my head.

"Get away from me," I snarled, turning my head to look at him before narrowing my eyes on his.

"Red, please," he said exasperated.

"No, Xavier. No," I said with a raised voice, shaking my head, my hand still under the cold tap. "Don't, '*Red, please*' me. I am done with your shit. I am done."

I turned the tap off then walked towards the kitchen door, gliding past the spilt milk and saucepan before knocking it off with my hand, not wincing when I heard it clatter on the floor. I grabbed the door handle to open the kitchen door, but before I could, I felt his fingers around my wrist as he pulled me back to him, spinning me around so I was up against his body. I bowed my head, both of my hands resting on his chest, his heart racing under my fingertips. I slowed my breathing, my insides were screaming for me to push away from him and run like I always do, but I couldn't. My feet were stuck to the ground as if they were surrounded by concrete. Completely grounded by him. His hand slowly moved up to my face, tucking a lose strand of my fiery-red hair behind my ear before his fingers trailed down to my chin and lifted it up, so I looked into his soulless dark eyes.

"Let me go," I breathed out to him.

"Never," he whispered back before he crashed his lips onto mine. My shoulders sagged slightly as I melted into him, his arms wrapping around my back and pulling me closer to him as his tongue pushed into my mouth. His expert tongue stroked and caressed mine. Our kiss was slow, intimate and wrong.

I felt betrayed by my body, my heart was singing, my mind was screaming at me to let go. But I couldn't.

Who knew poison would taste so good?

He pulled away, still keeping me close, his eyes burning into me as I looked into his.

"I'm sorry, Red," he mumbled.

My small hands were back on his chest and I pushed away, shaking my head as I stepped backwards away from him, feeling the effects of his kiss leaving me as I put distance between us.

"Sorry doesn't cut it," I muttered before turning and walking away. I heard a thump and my heart dropped as I looked over my shoulder to see him standing, one hand fisted by his side, the other in the wall. His face was pained, his jaw clenched, his eyes hooded. Then he dropped his head, his shoulders sagging before he let out an almighty scream.

I carried on walking, not looking back for fear of being pulled back to him.

And I didn't want that.

Chapter

Eleven

Once I was back in my room, I ran a bath. It was three in the morning, and after my little meeting with Xavier, I was more awake now than I was before. I slipped into the hot water, welcoming the sting from the burn. I sighed as I rested my head back on the roll-top edge, my fingers wrapping round the edge. My eyes drifted to the burn on my hand, the mark getting angrier by the minute. I sighed, pulling my eyes to the water, relaxing slightly and listening to the complete silence. I can't believe he kissed me in an effort to make me forgive him. I couldn't deny what I felt when he placed his lips on mine, I didn't want it to stop. But it was wrong, we were wrong for each other. So wrong.

After half an hour in the bath and feeling no sleepier than I was before I stepped into it, I was agitated again. I couldn't calm my mind, couldn't switch it off.

It didn't help with the anger bubbling deep inside, and it wasn't just Xavier that had angered me. It was my father, my mother, the little bitch, and of course Xavier. But he wasn't the sole reason. To be honest, my anger for him wasn't even that bad. I was more disappointed in him.

I knew he was cruel; I knew he was a monster, but I didn't think he would really show his true colours like he did tonight. But then he kissed me, throwing me all off balance again. Ripping through me and awakening my inner soul.

I crawled onto my bed, hid under my covers and lay waiting to doze, it would come... eventually.

I woke with a blurry head, a heavy heart and a groan as I heard a knock on the door. Already feeling agitated that I had been woken up, I looked over at the time, it was eight a.m. I threw the covers back in a temper as I stomped over to the door. My brows were furrowed, my face blotchy with pillow creases still apparent on my pale skin. My eyes felt like they had grit in them. I let out a deep groan followed by a sigh as I pulled the door open to see Christopher standing there with a tray of food. My heart sank.

His right eye was closed and black, his lip busted. I put my hands over my mouth, shocked at the state of him.

"Chris..." I muttered out in a concerned voice, but he held his hand up and shook his head.

"Save it, Royal, I'm not interested," he growled as he pushed past me and into my room, placing the tray down on the bed with force. The tea spilt slightly onto my plate of food, but I didn't care. What I cared about was about to leave my room in a rage I never knew he had inside of him.

I ran in front of the bedroom door, holding my hands out so they were blocking his exit.

"Move," he growled at me, his eyes piercing mine.

"No," I said in a whisper as I shook my head, my throat burning as the lump started to grow, my eyes filling with unshed tears.

"Fucking move." He stepped towards me, towering over me.

"Not until you tell me who did this, and why you are so angry with me." My voice was barely a squeak.

"Who did this to me?" He started to raise his voice. "Who do you think did this to me? Are you that fucking stupid?" he spat at me, his fists balling at his sides.

"No, he wouldn't have…" My voice trailed off.

"Last night he came to my sleeping quarters, dragging me out of bed, laying his fists into me again and again." He shook his head, his fists unbaling. "What did you tell him about us? It couldn't have just been what that little weasel, fucking Alan, said," he growled as he fisted his hands again.

"I didn't say anything! It's all Alan's doing. He knew I had a crush on you, but I thought you knew that, seeing as he caught us at the ball..." My voice trailed off as I dropped my head. "I'm so sorry, Christopher." I felt my own anger brewing now.

"Save it, Royal, I don't want to hear your apology. Just leave me alone," he snapped as he pushed through my barricade and ran out of the room. My hands started to shake; my body trembled. I was raging. I saw the note poking under the tray, then stormed over there with my shaking hands as my eyes read it.

I reacted on what I heard last night.
I'm sorry.
X

I screwed the note up, throwing it on the floor as I stormed out the room, my temper as fiery as my red hair. I flew down the stairs as I headed for his office, flinging the door open. He wasn't there. I ran towards the library over the other side of the house, pushing the door open again, to find him not there. My eyes scouted round the room, when I saw one of the bookcases slightly ajar. I walked towards it, curiosity getting the better of me. I slipped through the gap, not wanting to open it as I was scared it would make a noise. I headed down the stairs that took me to a basement where I saw pictures upon pictures of Xavier and another man. It wasn't until I got closer and noticed who it was next to him. My face paled, my blood ran cold as I felt the bile starting to rise in my stomach.

"What the fuck are you doing in here?" he bit at me as he came up behind me.

"I, er, I..." I stammered over the words, not being able to muster anything.

"Get out," he said coolly. Too coolly for my liking.

"No." I shook my head, my rage returning. "I came to find you for a reason," I snapped back at him.

"Why's that, Red? Come to kiss me again?" he said with arrogance as he walked towards me, his hands fisted in his pockets.

Yes.

"Not a chance in hell." My eyes narrowed on him. "How dare you do that to Christopher!" I shouted at him as I stepped towards him, my head tilting back to look up at him.

"He had to be taught a lesson." He licked his lips before pulling his bottom lip between his teeth.

"No, he didn't." I shook my head. "He didn't do anything. *We* didn't do anything," I shouted. "When will you get that through your thick skull?" I growled. His hand came out of his pocket as it ran round the back of my head, pulling me towards him so our faces were millimetres away from each other.

"I won't," he whispered with a smirk.

I pulled away from him before bringing my hand up

to his cheek and slapping him as hard as I could, instantly regretting it when I saw the look on his face. I turned on my heel to walk away, my heart thumping in my chest when I felt his hand round the back of my neck, pulling me to face him. My eyes darted back and forth to his before he kissed me, his lips on mine, setting my soul on fire. His hands snaked round my waist and ran over my black satin nightdress before he lifted me up, my legs automatically going round his waist, a small groan leaving his throat as he walked me over to the wall by the stairs. His hand moved under my bum while the other one rested on the wall next to my head. His muscles rippled under his skin. His fingers skimmed over my knickers, tracing up and across my core which caused a moan to leave my mouth. His tongue was invading my mouth before his hand that was near my head was round the back of my neck as he gripped on tightly. I wanted him. I wanted every single inch of him.

He pulled away, his eyes dropping to my lips before they came up to my eyes.

"Not here. Not like this." He shook his head as he put me down, still standing in front of me then leaning down and kissing me on the forehead, lingering for a moment before walking up the stairs and away from me.

I stood frozen with my heart thumping in my chest, confused and wanting.

***

I got dressed in a sage-green summer dress, the thick straps sitting over my shoulders before I plaited my hair to the side. I dusted a light pink blush over my freckled cheeks before flicking my lashes with a coating of mascara. I stroked some coral lipstick over my lips before checking for smudges. I slipped into my tanned wedged sandals and sprayed my perfume then made my way down to the garden. I walked towards the pergola when I saw a familiar face. My mother was sitting there, looking as amazing as ever. Her long hair curled down her back as she sat at the table. Her smile widened on her face, my eyes lit up, my heart beating faster as I got closer. She stood from the table, embracing me in a warm motherly hug. I squeezed her a little tighter before she let me go and took her seat back at the table before picking up the teapot and pouring out the steaming brown liquid, adding a dash of milk and a sugar cube to my china cup.

"What are you doing here?" I asked as I sat down opposite her. My eyebrows knitted together as I watched her.

"Xavier invited me over, said he wanted to surprise you." She smiled at me as she looked up at me as she finished stirring my tea then tended to her own empty cup.

"Did he now..." My voice trailed off as I felt my skin prickling as I looked over my shoulder to see him looking as devilishly handsome as ever. His hands were in his pockets, which I have come to love, as he stood broad. A small smirk was on his face as he watched me. He knocked the air from my lungs before I faced him.

"How are you doing?" she asked as she took a sip of her tea and smiled in appreciation before her eyes came up to meet mine.

"I'm doing okay... I think." I let out a little laugh as I looked over my shoulder to see if Xavier was still there, but he wasn't, and I couldn't help but feel a little bit disheartened by it.

"You think?" she asked. "Royal, darling, what is going on in that pretty little head of yours?" she asked concerned as she reached across and took my hand before giving it a gentle squeeze.

Oh, I don't know, I am being forced to marry a beast, he forced himself on me, he beat Chris up, he is hiding something and he may have been the best fucking kiss I have ever had and I can't wait for him to break me.

"Nothing, honestly. I'm fine. And yeah, I'm doing okay. Getting used to it now." I nodded, swallowing, trying to clear the dryness of my mouth and looking at my fake engagement ring before I took a mouthful of my tea. It was delicious.

"Well that's nice to hear, I want you to be happy," she said as she let go of my hand, and her eyes left mine for a moment as a big smile appeared on her face but soon disappeared when whoever was walking over got closer. I didn't have to look over my shoulder, I knew exactly who it was. Christopher.

He stood next to the table, placing a plate of scones, clotted cream and jam down as well as some finger sandwiches before he stepped back.

"Oh my God, Christopher." My mother's voice was high-pitched, shock lacing it. "What happened?" Her hand went up to her mouth as she took in the sight of him.

"Why don't you ask the *princess,*" he snarled before walking away from me.

I lifted my eyes from the table and looked at my mother, confusion was written all over her face as her eyes darted from me to Christopher, who was still walking away.

"Royal," my mother snapped at me. "Are you going to explain?" Her head tilted to the side.

"I will if you give me a minute instead of jumping down my throat," I growled at her.

"I'm waiting." Her perfectly shaped eyebrows raised as she continued to stare at me.

"Xavier beat him up," I said deadpan, my sorry eyes batting down to my hands in my lap.

"Beat him up?" she screeched. "Royal... Talk to me," she ordered.

"Okay, want me to talk to you, do you?" I said, my voice angry. "Xavier brought Christopher over to work here because he caught us getting close at a ball we had to

144

go to, so as a punishment and constant reminder that we couldn't be with each other, he made sure he worked here. Then, Xavier had to go away, so me Christopher and Mabel," I said her name a little louder so Xavier could hear, I knew he was listening, I felt him, "All sat in my room and we had food and snacks and wine and we chatted. It was the most fun I have had in a long time." I shook my head. "Then Mabel left because she was tired, me and Christopher sat and talked. There was a moment where it looked like he was going to kiss me, but I pushed him away. I went on to tell Christopher how Mabel really likes him and that I think he should get to know her a little better. Next thing I know, we had fallen asleep and knowing that Xavier's little bitch was sitting outside the door like a fucking prison guard, I had to get him up, make him go back to his own room. He opened the door to see fucking Alan standing there with a stupid smirk on his face while on the phone to Xavier, telling him that me and Christopher were both undressed. Which we weren't. But Xavier chose to believe Alan over his soon-to-be-wife, got drunk, went to Christopher's room angry and beat him up, then he came to mine and..." I stopped, rubbing my lips together to stop the verbal diarrhoea that came out of my mouth. I had to take a few deep breaths, seeing as I didn't come up for air once during that spill.

"Oh my God," she whispered, her eyes wide before she looked through me. I snapped my head round to see

Xavier standing a few yards away from me.

"What happened when he came to your room?" she asked me, but her eyes were still on Xavier.

"Nothing," I mumbled, not even able to look her in the eyes.

"Royal," she warned, her tone clipped.

I went to open my mouth when I felt his hand on my shoulder, gripping it tightly. "Baby," he cooed at me, his voice smooth and low. The hairs on the back of my neck stood.

"Xavier." My mother scowled at him as she stood from her chair and stopped in front of him, her eyebrows knitted, her eyes narrowed on him in an evil glare.

"I want you to apologise to Christopher," she said deadpan.

"And why would I do that?" He smirked, goading her.

"Because as the queen of this kingdom, I am asking you... No, I am telling you. I can take Royal as quick as her cowardly father handed her over to you. Apologise to Christopher now, and I suggest you sort that employee of yours out who is spinning lies to you to turn you against Royal and Christopher," she said with authority. Xavier didn't say anything, just tightened his grip on my shoulder, making me wince.

"Get your hands off of her, now," she bellowed at him. He dropped his hand quickly, resting it on the back of my chair. She turned slowly to look at me. "Did he touch you that evening?" she asked me.

I swallowed the hard lump that had formed in my throat before I looked up at him.

"Don't look at him, tell me. Did he lay a finger on you that night?" she asked again, her tone harsh.

I took a deep breath before my eyes met hers.

I shook my head.

"No, he didn't." A small smile crept on my face, and I felt Xavier let out the breath that he had been holding. His fingers trailed up my spine softly, gently, sending a shiver across my body.

"And that's the way it will stay until you are ready. Do you understand me, Xavier, or do we need to go and have a private chat?" She raised her eyebrows as she looked into his soul.

"I do"––he nodded––"Understand." He cleared his throat.

"Good." She smiled as she took her seat opposite me again. "Oh, and, Xavier, just a reminder that my daughter is a princess, soon to be a queen which will make you, unfortunately, a prince. She isn't a prisoner, so don't keep her like one," she barked at him as she took a mouthful of her tea out of her china tea cup. "Now, be a good boy and go fetch us a fresh pot of tea, please." She smiled sweetly at him, her head tilting to the side, her crown not moving at all.

He didn't say anything, just stepped back away from me then grabbed the teapot and walked into the kitchen, disappearing.

I let out a little giggle.

"And that, my darling daughter, is how to deal with a pig of a man. Now, let's have lunch. We have lots to talk about." She raised her shoulders slightly as she grinned her beautiful smile at me. I smiled back, picking my teacup up and listening to her as she filled me in on what had been going on.

Chapter Twelve

Xavier

To say her mother's words didn't piss me off would be a lie. She fucking infuriated me. I walked away like the gentleman she thought I was. And I was a gentleman, when I wanted to be. But something struck home with me.

I was going to be a prince. I know I said I wanted her to abdicate the throne, but the more I think about it, the more I don't want her to do it.

I shook the giddy feeling away before I carried on walking to find Christopher. I knew he was pissed with Royal, but it was nothing to do with her.

It was all me. Well, and Alan.

Alan. Shit, I needed to talk to him.

I ran my hand through my beard as I reached the pantry where Christopher and Mabel were talking, their voices hushed.

"Am I interrupting something here?" I asked, my voice booming around the room. I watched Mabel jump back, her eyes focusing on her feet.

"No," Christopher said bluntly, his fists balled as he faced me.

"Christopher," I said in a low voice, walking towards him, my hands fisted in my pockets.

He didn't say anything, he just stood there.

"Mabel, could you please give us a minute? I need to speak to Christopher, *alone.*"

She didn't speak, just scurried away, closing the door behind her.

"What do you want?" he spat at me as I stepped closer to him.

"I've come to say sorry," I said as I sat on the wood-block worktop.

"You have?" He looked confused, and his face softened.

"I have." I nodded.

"I wasn't expecting that." He shook his head, his hand running through his unruly curls.

"Can you let me know what happened that night?" I asked, my voice calm, quiet.

"Erm, yeah…" He raised his eyebrows as he shuffled on his feet before he started talking. "Me and Mabel went to Royal's room, we sent Alan to get snacks for us so we could just sit and talk." His hand pushed through his hair, and my eyes were set on his face, not moving at all.

"Then Mabel said she was tired and wanted to call it a night, so we said our goodbyes and then it was just me and Royal." He nibbled on his bottom lip; he was nervous. Good.

"We stayed talking, then I pushed my luck a little, and I tried to kiss her." His eyes flicked up to mine and I tensed, feeling the anger rising in me, but I wanted to give him the benefit of the doubt. I wasn't going to jump and react. No. I was going to listen.

"But she pushed me away, said she couldn't do it. I felt like such a prick, I knew we had our little crush on each other before she met you. But then she met you, and I don't know, she changed..." His voice trailed off, and my heart warmed slightly that he had noticed a change in her.

He snapped me back into the room as he carried on.

"Then I panicked, got up and ran for the door, *fully dressed,* just so you know. As I got to the door, Alan was standing there, the phone already to his ear. I heard Royal shouting at him and wanting to know why he said what he did. I stopped when I heard Alan say that you were pissed off, she pleaded with him, telling him that nothing happened, he replied saying that you didn't know that because you weren't here..." I saw something change on Christopher's face... Sadness maybe? Anger?

"Then he said that you would believe him over her because he told you that we were both undressed. He went on to tell her that she deserved it before slamming her bedroom door. I didn't hear if anything else happened because I carried on running." He shrugged, kicking his foot on the floor. My jaw clenched, and my lips twitched as I felt rage consume me like wildfire in the dry forests.

"Thank you, Christopher, I really appreciate it. And again, I am sorry. I hope you forgive me," I said as I hopped off the worktop, my hand running through my blonde hair, pushing it off of my face.

"Not a problem," Christopher muttered as I headed out of the pantry to find Alan.

Enough was enough.

I stood in the doorway of the kitchen, smiling at her and her mother. She looked so happy and carefree I had to change things, make her feel more at home here. After all, this was her home now.

I pulled my eyes away from her as I made my way into my office, sitting with a glass of whiskey whilst I waited for Alan to come through the door.

Ten minutes had passed, my anger was getting worse and worse by the minute. Five minutes later, he walked in.

He made me sick.

"Sir, you wanted to see me?" he asked as he crept round the door.

"I did. Shut the door," I snapped at him, my eyes narrowed on him. I wanted nothing more than to hit him again and again, but I couldn't. Not yet. I had to bide my time.

He sat down in front of me, his little sausage fingers pushing through his overly-gelled mop of black hair.

"Do you think it's acceptable to lie to me, Alan?" I asked, tapping my crystal-etched tumbler with my index finger.

"When have I lied, Sir?" he asked as he pulled down on his shirt. First sign that he is lying, he was fidgeting.

"The night you told me Christopher and Royal were undressed." My jaw clenched, even saying the words pissed me off.

"They were undressed." His eyes were on me before they darted to the side, looking at the wall. Second sign he was lying, he looked to the side.

"You've got one chance to admit that you lied; Alan. Don't fucking piss me off," I growled.

"I'm not lying to you, it's that fucking slut that you've been blind-sided by." Third lie. Royal was not a slut.

I saw red, a haze consuming my sight as I stood from the chair, dropping my glass on the desk as I stormed over to him, grabbing the back of his head and slamming it down as hard as I could on the desk. He groaned out, and a feeling of satisfaction coursed through me that I had hurt him. Oh, it felt good. I let go of his head, dropping to my knees so my face was level with his.

"Don't you ever fucking call her a slut again; do you understand me? From now on, you don't go near her, you don't speak to her and you certainly don't fucking look at her. Do I make myself clear?" I growled at him.

He made a whimper noise as he held on to the bridge of his nose that was bleeding.

"Don't fucking lie to me again," I shouted at him as I stood up, brushing down my knees and straightening my shirt before walking out to find my Red.

I had to make things better between us.

Make things right.

I walked to go and get her, but she was still in conversation with her mother and I didn't want to ruin their little lunch date. I let out a sigh before I found Mabel walking towards the dining room.

"Mabel," I called out.

"Sir." She stopped, her eyes batting down to the floor.

"Can you set the dining room, please? Not the one on this side, the one over the other side of the house, please. I need it perfect." I smiled at her before she nodded and rushed past me towards the kitchen.

Chapter Thirteen

Royal

I said goodbye to my mother, my heart breaking as I watched her drive away. I didn't realise just how much I missed her. I walked back up to my bedroom, a small smile gracing my face when I saw a single white rose and a note on my pillow. I picked it up, bringing the rose petals to my nose and smelling them. It smelt divine. I placed it back down as I picked up the handwritten note.

Dinner is at six in the main dining room, next to the library.
Don't be late.
I want to make things right.
X

My heart leapt in my chest before I placed the card

with the others in my drawer and popped the stemmed rose in the vase on my windowsill. It was already four p.m.; the day had just flown.

Once I had my bath, I was looking through my wardrobe for something to wear. I hadn't realised that a dress had been put on my bed, still on the hanger for me to wear. A light-grey, satin bodycon dress with thin spaghetti straps. I ran my hands over the delicate material, internally smiling. I dropped my towel and stood into a seamless white thong and a strapless, lace bra. I pulled the dress up over my hips and slipped my hands through the straps before pulling them up on my shoulders. I skimmed my hands down my body, my head tilting as I looked at myself in the mirror. I stepped into my black, sandaled heels. I couldn't help but smile, the light-grey looked amazing against my ivory skin. I sat at my dressing table, taking my hair out of my towel and running my brush through it, blow-drying it straight.

I did my make-up, keeping it as natural as I could but making my lips a matte-pillar-box-red. I felt nervous but excited. Normally, I felt nervous because I didn't want to see him, but this time was different. I wanted to see him. I sprayed my perfume then made my way downstairs. I walked through the kitchen and into the old conservatory before I got to the plush lounge. I loved this lounge. I wanted to spend more time over this side of the house, not the run-down side that I was captive in.

I carried on towards the library, when I saw the door before slightly open. I pushed through it, gasping when I saw Xavier standing there with a huge grin on his imperfect face. He was wearing a dark, navy two-piece-suit with a crisp white shirt underneath, with the two top buttons open, his collar open wide so I could see his beautiful neck. I wanted to place my lips over his neck and kiss every inch of his exposed skin.

"Royal," he purred as he walked towards me.

My eyes wandered round the dining room. I had never been in this room before. The ceilings were high with large gold crystal chandeliers that were glistening. The table was white marble with gold flecks that sat on thick, marble pillars. The chairs were champagne-coloured velvet that I ran my fingers over delicately. I smiled at the white roses in the middle of the table that sat pretty in the vase. Either side were two gold candelabras that were lit, which made the room look even more charming. The main lights were dimmed, so there was a certain ambience about it. Romantic maybe?

I flicked my eyes up to him, drinking every inch of him in. Something had definitely shifted between us; I just didn't know what. He snaked his hand round my waist and pulled me towards him. "You look wonderful." He spoke softly before placing a kiss on my cheek. I felt myself blush underneath his touch; my insides alight.

"Thank you, you look wonderful yourself." I smiled

at him again. He walked me towards the table, then pulled one of the high back chairs as he gestured for me to sit down. I took my seat, thanking him as he pushed me in. I grabbed the napkin and laid it over my lap, I didn't want to spill anything down my dress.

I watched as he sat down, my eyes on him the whole time. "Thank you for the dress, Xavier. Honestly, it is beautiful." My eyes fluttered down to my lap before I looked back at him.

"You are most welcome. Beautiful dress for a beautiful woman." He smiled at me before reaching for the bottle of white wine. "Would you like a glass?" he asked as it hovered over the top of my wine glass.

"Please." I nodded, my voice small. He poured me a small glass before filling his own up. I reached across and picked it up, bringing the rim of the glass to my lips and taking a small mouthful. The taste made my tastebuds explode. It was delicious.

I shifted in my chair; his intense stare hadn't left me since I walked into the room. It was making me uncomfortable. There was a thick tension in the air which didn't help.

"Am I making you tense, Red?" he asked as he placed his elbow on the table, his long, thick fingers stroking his beard.

"A little," I admitted, blushing again. *Damn it.*

"Why?" he asked.

"Because we have never done this as such, you have always been so..." I stopped talking, my breath catching in the back of my throat.

"So mean?" He finished my sentence for me as a small smile appeared on his face, his eyes glistening. Even though they were so different, they were so beautiful.

"Exactly that," I said on a sigh, my voice shaky. He dropped his hand from his beard as he reached over and grabbed my hand, running his thumb tentatively across the back. I felt tingly, my skin pricked with goose-bumps, my stomach fluttered with a thousand butterflies.

"I wanted to do something nice for you, something to show you I am sorry," he muttered as he let go of my hand.

"Why?" It was my turn to ask him now.

"Because I owe you an apology," he said quietly as he sat back in his chair, grabbing his wine glass and taking a big mouthful. I watched his lips open, his tongue darting across his bottom lip as he placed the glass back on the table. Everything he was doing was affecting me in a way it never had before. I coughed, trying to compose myself. But it was no use. He could see right through me.

"You need to be a little more descriptive, Xavi," I teased as I took my own mouthful of wine and pinned my eyes to him.

"Xavi?" He shook his head slightly and let out a

throaty laugh as he looked at me slightly confused.

"I like that little nickname for you, you gave me Red."
I shrugged my shoulders up slightly. "Anyway, back to
being more descriptive." I winked at him. I all of a sudden
felt brazen, fearless.

He laughed again, his Adams apple bobbing up and
down as he did.

"I found out the truth," he said quietly, his eyes
watching his swirling wine that he was creating by circling
his glass gently.

"Keep going, Xavi," I said gently, using his new
nickname.

His eyes lit up at my words before the fire
disappeared.

"I spoke to Christopher, I heard what you said to
your mum. So I needed to find out what actually happened
that night, and who best to ask than the boy who is
crushing on you." His eyes instantly went dark, stormy
even, his jaw clenching and twitching. His grip tightened
around the stem of his wine glass.

"You did?" I asked, a little surprised.

"I did," he growled. "And he told me everything. I
knew he wasn't lying. I have this ability to notice when
people are lying, Royal." His tone was softer now, his grip
loosening, his beautiful eyes regaining their glisten as he
watched my lips as I swallowed a mouthful of wine.

"I found out Alan had lied, and I'm sorry that I didn't

believe you over him. I heard what he said to you... Well, Christopher heard what he said to you." He sighed. "You won't be seeing much of Alan anymore, he isn't to talk to you, to look at you, nothing. He is to keep his distance. And as for Christopher, I know he isn't a threat anymore. I won't treat him like one either. He is your friend, albeit an old love interest, but he reassured me that there is nothing, and there won't be anything going on between you two," he said, a little stern, his eyes looking down at my heaving chest.

"So, yes, Red, in short, I am sorry. Sorry for that night, sorry for every other night that I hurt you or upset you. That was never my intention. Well... It was, for a while. But I am so used to being this monster, this callous, cold, vicious beast, that I sometimes have no control over how I behave. But I want to try and control it. The best I can." He swallowed hard, his voice sounding constricted, tight, small. *Was he sad?*

I didn't say anything. I pressed my lips into a thin line, drumming my fingertips on the table, trying to calm my mind and my thumping heart.

"Royal, please forgive me," he said in a plea, reaching across and grabbing my fingers, pulling them towards him slightly. "Please," he begged again. My eyes darted back and forth from his, his face breaking every second I left him waiting.

"Yes," I whispered. "I forgive you."

Chapter Fourteen

Once dinner was finished, Xavier pushed himself up from his seat, walking to my side and taking my hand in his as he pulled me up.

"Come," he muttered as he walked me out of the dining room and towards the lavish lounge. I sat on the sofa as he walked over to a huge black and grey globe. I watched him like a hawk, how he moved, his little quirks that I was growing very fond of. He flicked a small lock over, then opened the top half of the globe up. There were four crystal decanters in there, all filled with different spirits, and one was filled with a deep red wine.

"What would you like?" he asked as he turned to face me.

"Surprise me," I breathed out, pressing my thighs together to try and relieve the ache that was building. He hadn't even done anything, but his presence was getting a little too much for me.

"Oh, Red, baby, I am going to surprise you alright," he said in a threatening manner, his voice low and slightly intimidating.

"Is that another empty threat, Xavi?"

His eyes burned into mine as he strolled across to me, owning the room like the God that he was. His hand reached down and grabbed my face as he tilted my face up towards him, his neck craning slightly as he stood over me. "Don't push me, baby," he growled. "You know my threats are far from empty." Before I could answer him back, he pushed his lips onto mine, his hand still firmly holding my chin as his tongue pushed its way through my cushioned lips. I let him, I wanted him to consume me. I wanted to be consumed by him. A throaty groan left him as my tongue danced with his. Our kiss was hungry, his mouth covered mine. I leant back slightly, wanting him to follow, but as soon as my back was against the sofa, he pulled away. His fingers ran through his hair in a frustrated manner as he stepped back away from me and moved back over to the drinks globe. He pulled the lid off the crystal decanter that was filled with an amber liquid then poured it into matching crystal tumblers. He walked over, his whole demeanour slightly off. His big strides closed the gap between us almost instantly.

"Here," he said as he held out the glass.

"Thank you," I muttered, taking it off of him and

bringing it to my lips, slightly hesitant. I hadn't ever had a drink like this before. I watched him as he drank it, smiling down at me as he swallowed. My stomach flipped. He darted his tongue out, running it across his top lip so slowly. My jaw laxed as I brought the glass away from my bottom lip and rested it on my lap.

"You're a tease," I stated confidently before taking a mouthful of the liquid amber. As soon as it hit my taste buds, my stomach churned. I wasn't going to show him that though. I kept my eyes steady on him, swallowing it as smoothly as I could and ignoring the burn in my throat. He threw the rest of the liquid down his throat before placing the cup on the mantlepiece, then he took my hand and pulled me up. He took my glass off of me and placed it on the floor next to me.

"You think I'm a tease?" he said in a low voice before laughing. "So naïve." He shook his head as he walked me back down the hallway and past the dining room. I was a little confused as to where we were going. We continued down a narrow hallway before coming to a halt at a large sweeping staircase. He turned to face me.

"Would you like to spend the night with me?" he asked, his eyes shining like stars under the ceiling lights.

I didn't say anything; my mouth was dry. I could just about managed a nod.

He led me up the stairs and onto a gallery landing. This house just kept getting bigger and better. This must be the nice side; I must live in the servant quarters. I screwed my nose up, my head screaming at me to get away from him.

"What's wrong?" he asked as he stopped outside what I assumed was his bedroom door.

"Just a little confused about your house. You're over here, living like a king, and I am over the other side, being kept as a prisoner in the servants' quarters."

"Well, you were my prisoner," he said with a smile as he pulled me closer to him. "Now, can we go inside?" he asked with a silly smirk on his face. I wanted to run from him, but my heart was already in too deep. I was a goner, a sucker who was falling for the beast.

"Yeah," I whispered, nibbling my bottom lip. I was nervous, so fucking nervous. I knew I wanted this, I just couldn't keep up with the battles between my head and my heart. I was sure I wanted it to be with him... No, I was certain. Did I love him? No, but what I was feeling was getting a whole lot stronger. I liked him more than I hated him, so that was something. He pushed the door open, a strong scent filling my nostrils. It smelled of him. His cologne, the crisp linen and a hint of mint. It made my mouth water. Once I had come back round from my Xavier hit, I looked at his lavish room. The walls were white, the floors a dark wood. His bed sat in the centre of the room, a thick grey duvet covering it, with matching pillows. The wall behind had a huge picture of a beautiful jungle, with a tiger striding towards us, it's mouth open.

I couldn't help but lose myself in it.

"What's the story behind the tiger?" I found myself asking.

"It reminds me never to turn my back on someone I don't trust." He winked at me. "I like to always keep my eye on the enemy," he whispered as he snaked his hand around my waist, breathing my scent in. My breath stilled; my heart raced. I tipped my head back, resting it on his solid, hard chest as my eyes wandered to the ceiling. My mouth went dry when I saw a huge mirror above his bed. I swallowed hard, a small gulp coming from me. Xavier chuckled. "I like to watch where I can." He nibbled on my earlobe before spinning me around, our faces almost touching before his hand glided up my body, pushing me down onto the bed. A small scream came out my mouth as he took me by surprise. My skin was tingling.

"Red, are you ready?" he asked me as his eyes looked down at me, burning through me.

"I am," I whispered. I was sure he could see my heart thumping through my chest. He pushed his suit jacket off of his shoulders, folding it over his arm and laying it on the chest of drawers beside him. My eyes were on his body, watching him. I was hypnotized.

He unbuttoned his shirt, and my eyes went wide when I saw his body underneath. He was chiselled to perfection with a small dusting of blonde hair across his chest.

"Did your parents ever tell you it's rude to stare?" he chastised me.

"They did." My mouth was as dry as the Sahara Desert. "But I can't help myself," I admitted, a crimson blush spreading over me. He stepped closer to me, taking my hand and pulling me up to my feet. His left hand pushed round my back, pulling me to him. His right hand slowly pushed my strap off of my shoulder. I was panting, my chest heaving with anticipation and nerves. My stomach was being swarmed by butterflies. He slipped it down my arm before he worked on my other strap. Taking both of his large hands and pulling my dress down to my hips, he sucked in his breath as his eyes focused on my bare skin. I kept my eyes on him the whole time.

His hands gripped my hips, his hips pushed up towards me. I could feel how hard he was. My insides were squirming with delight.

I hooked my fingers inside my dress as I pushed it down my hips, then held his hand whilst I stepped out of it. My hair fell over my shoulder, sitting over my breast. His eyes were alight with desire and hunger. He used two fingers to push my hair over my shoulders, away, so he could look at every inch of me.

"You're beautiful. Perfect. So pure." He groaned before pressing his lips on my neck. Small, gentle kisses were being trailed down my neck and to my collarbone before he dropped to his knees, his eyes looking up at me. I was so turned on, seeing this powerful man on his knees in front of me. Waiting for me.

My greedy hands reached out, touching each of his shoulders before pushing his shirt off, so I could marvel at his body. *Fuck.*

His jaw clenched tightly, his lips twisting into a smirk before his hands started their glide up the backs of my legs, slowly, teasingly. And still, his eyes were on mine. Not taking them off me for a moment. He stopped when he got to the under creases of my bum, running his index fingertips along them before growling.

"I am so fucking hard, Royal, and it's all for you." He groaned as he placed a kiss on the top of my thigh before moving his luscious lips over to the other one. His hands roamed before coming round to the front as he gestured for me to open my legs more. I did. I thought I would have been self-conscious standing here in nothing but my underwear and heels, but I wasn't. I had never felt more confident.

"I'm going to make you come like you have never come before, Royal. Your legs will be fucking trembling by the time I am finished with you." He winked before his index finger stroked across the front of my underwear, making me gasp and shudder at the same time. The hairs stood on the back of my neck from that small bit of contact, a current of electricity coursed through me. He smirked before hooking his finger around the lace of my thong, pulling it to the side to expose me. I heard his breath suck in, a throaty growl left him as his finger glided between my folds, slowly, so slowly. My curious eyes watched, and his lips parted as he started exploring me. He circled his thumb gently over my clit, my breathing heavier as I continued to watch him.

"Does that feel good, baby?" he asked as his beautiful eyes flicked up to me.

"Mmhmm," I moaned out, that's all I could manage.

"Good." He smiled. His thumb continued its gentle, slow massage before his index finger teased at my opening, his tip circling around in my wetness, softly stretching me.

He slipped his finger in a little further, the feeling of him filling me was delicious. My hands flew to his hair as I grabbed it.

"Oh," I moaned quietly. I couldn't explain the feeling of what this felt like. I felt overwhelmed by him. His thumb still continued its slow teasing manner, his finger now slowly pumping in and out of me

"Xavier," I whispered, my head tilting back slightly before I looked back down at him, my fiery-red hair falling forward.

"I'm going to taste you now," he whispered as his thumb stopped, his finger pulling out of me before he sucked on it, groaning in appreciation. "So much better than I expected," he admitted. His long fingers trailed up my tingling skin, then hooked around my knickers as he pulled them down my long legs, and off my feet. Bringing them up to his nose, he inhaled them then shoved them in his back pocket.

"Open your legs, baby," he demanded in a soft voice. I did as I was told.

"Lean back onto the chest of drawers, support yourself," he ordered.

I leant back, the chest of drawers hitting me in my lower back before I pushed my arms behind me and wrapped my fingers round the edging of the drawers.

"Perfect." He grinned.

He trailed his finger up the inside of my leg, then his finger slipped into me again, causing me to moan at him.

Before I could take a moment to regain my thoughts, his mouth was on me, his tongue flicking across my already sensitive clit which caused me to cry out. His strokes were slow, but forceful. Every flick made me crumble that little bit more. His free hand was on my hip, holding me in place as he continued to taste me. His finger started to speed up, pumping in and out of me, his tongue now matching his strokes.

"Oh... I'm... Fuck..." I moaned. He sucked on my clit before massaging me with his expert tongue again, his finger pushing deeper into me now. My walls tightened; I could feel myself clamping around his finger. He pulled away, his eyes looking at me. "Come for me, angel, I want to taste you." His mouth was back on me, sucking and licking over me, and my eyes watched him as he made me come undone.

My head tipped back, one of my hands in his hair. I grabbed it tightly, my orgasm ripping through me. I moaned out his name, making sure he could hear how good he made me feel. My legs were trembling, shaking beyond my control. He didn't stop, his finger was pulsing in and out of me, his tongue still vibrating on my sensitive clit as I came down from my high. I pulled his head away, shaking my head. He stood, my arousal all over his lips. He stood close to me before he crashed his plump lips to mine, his tongue invading my mouth, my heart pounding in my chest.

He pulled away. "You're an angel." He grinned before covering my mouth with his once more.

Chapter Fifteen

He laid me on the bed, pushing his trousers down to his ankles. His tight boxers were constricting across his cock. He was so hard. My hazy eyes were pinned to him, I couldn't look away.

"Like what you see, angel?" he asked me as he stepped towards me.

"I don't know, Xavi, I can't see anything yet," I teased. He took another stride, so he was standing literally in front of me.

"Take them off," he said.

"Sorry?" I blinked up at him.

"Take. Them. Off," he said again, slowly but over-emphasising every word.

I shuffled to the edge of the bed, leaning down and ignoring his hard cock in my face as I undid my shoes before kicking them off and laying back on my elbows.

"Done." I winked at him as I looked up through my lashes, licking my lips.

"Oh, you trying to be smart, Red?" He growled as he bent down, wrapping his right hand round the back of my neck and pulling me up so I was sitting upright on the bed again.

"I won't ask again. I'm waiting." He groaned as he grabbed his bulge with his left hand, tipping his head back slightly but his eyes stayed down, looking at me before he dropped his hand from my neck.

I hooked my finger and thumb into the sides of his boxers, my heart hammering in my chest as I started pushing them down his thick, toned thighs. My jaw laxed as I saw him, standing to attention. *Oh dear God.* I swallowed hard.

"Now do you like what you see?" he said proudly, his pretty fucking face smiling at me.

I just looked up at him, I couldn't even speak.

He reached around and unclipped my bra, pulling it off and throwing it over his shoulder as he winked at me. He dropped to his knees, wrapping his arm around my waist and pulling me closer to him as he nestled his body between my legs. His grip tightened round my waist as he took my hard nipple into his warm mouth, sucking and licking. I felt the pleasure ripping through me, making me instantly wet again. With no warning, he slipped his finger into me, this time a lot harsher than the first time as he started pumping himself into me. I groaned, my head tipping, my back arching up so he took more of my breast into his mouth.

He let go of my back suddenly, his mouth popping my nipple out as his left hand reached down between my legs as he grabbed himself. I whined at the loss of his mouth on me before I watched him look down, his finger still pumping into me fast, I leaned back, propping myself onto my elbows to watch. I was so horny watching his finger slipping in and out of me as his spare hand wrapped around his thick girth, his hand pumping up and down himself. I felt confused, but the feeling soon left once I felt myself building, my belly bubbling with pleasure.

"Touch yourself, like you did on my desk," he grunted, his eyes flicking up to mine, hooded and dark.

I reached down in-between my soaked core and started rubbing my finger over my clit, matching his thrusts into me.

"You feel so good, angel, so tight and all mine," he moaned out as his eyes watched what was happening between us.

"I'm getting close." I moaned as his fingers pushed into me deeper, my head tipping back to look at the ceiling. Holy fuck, seeing him in-between my legs, my naked body laying out in front of him was so hot. He let go of himself, grabbing my hand away before his mouth was on me. His hungry tongue massaged my clit, his fingers pumped into me and his other hand wrapped back around himself as he growled out. I couldn't stop my legs trembling again, my back arching, my hands grabbing and fisting the duvet underneath me as I came undone again from Xavier's expert tongue. His name left my lips on a loud moan. He pulled away from me, his fingers slipping out as he crawled over me and pumped himself faster until he found his own release, coming over my stomach, his head looking at the ceiling, smirking into the mirror before he was back looking at me, his lips pressing into mine softly before he pulled away.

"Fuck, that felt good." He shivered, then shook his head lightly. "Little steps, Red, little steps," he said smoothly before standing up and heading to the bathroom. I watched his glorious, naked body walk away from me. I couldn't help but stare.

Once the door was closed, I let out my breath and lay back on the bed, looking at myself in the mirror.

I had my first hit; my first taste and I was already addicted. I was high off of him and I wasn't looking forward to the comedown.

I needed him constantly.

My heart was hammering in my chest, my mind replaying how he worked my body, making my orgasm so intense. I trailed my fingers across my lips, smiling at the tingling I was feeling. My moment was cut short when I heard him padding over to me, holding a wet flannel. My eyebrows raised as I watched him step forward and clean himself off of my stomach. The cloth was warm against my sensitive skin. I smiled at him, my eyes watching his face. His jaw was soft, his eyes glistening. I loved everything about his face. His eyes, his scar, his beard. I sighed, which caused him to look at me.

"Are you okay, Royal?" he asked as he finished wiping me.

"I am," I said with a happy sigh.

"Are you happy here, with me?" he asked, his voice a little cold as he came and sat next to me before pulling the duvet open, wrapping his arms around me and lifting me to move me under the duvet. He wrapped his arms around me, pulling me in close to him as I snuggled under the covers. The warmth of his body melted my insides.

I took a moment to contemplate his answer... I was happy. Blissfully happy, believe it or not.

"I am. I just miss my mother, I miss my freedom," I said in a whisper. I felt him tense, his arms tightening around me.

"Go to sleep, Royal," he ordered, his head nuzzling into my neck.

My eyes were heavy, my mind hazy and my body in post-orgasmic bliss. I was asleep within seconds, dreams of Xavier invading me.

This was where I wanted to be.

With him.

Chapter

Sixteen

Two Weeks Later

Xavier had moved me over to his side of the house. After our night together, he thought it was right that we lived like a real couple; eat together and spend time together. The only thing we didn't do was sleep together. I had my own room, he had his. I was growing more and more angrier as the days passed. It had been two weeks since he sent me to seventh heaven and he hasn't touched me since. He doesn't even kiss me on the lips. I get small kisses... on my forehead. Like a child.

I want him, I want him completely. I sighed as I finished applying my lipstick, then ran my fingers though my tight curls, giving my hair the wavy look that I have come to love. I stood from the dressing table, looking around my huge room. Our rooms were interconnected, but Xavier locked his door most nights, unless he wanted to come into my room and sit for a while. It was bizarre. He was so guarded with a huge fortress around him. Every time I got close to knocking it down, something would happen, then within minutes he would push his walls so high that I didn't have a hope in hell.

I sat on the edge of my bed, looking around the room once more. The walls were a warm cream with hints of gold throughout. It was similar to my old room over the other side, but more luxurious.

I had a huge en-suite with a free-standing roll-top bath and a separate walk-in shower. I had a walk-in wardrobe with clothes that Xavier had bought for me and shoes that every girl dreamt of. I was still his prisoner. But things are starting to change... I think.

I was wearing cropped navy trousers with a seam running down the centre of the leg. They were high-waisted. I had a cream blouse tucked inside of them, the neck a plunged V. The sleeves were quarter length with small ruffles. I wore tanned moccasins, comfortable and practical. I didn't know where we were going, Xavier just told me to be ready for eleven. It had gone eleven and he was late. I rolled my eyes. If that was me who was late, I would know about it.

My heart started skipping when he walked through the door, a smile on his face as he walked towards me.

"You look lovely, Red." He leant down, kissing me on the forehead. Butterflies swarmed in my stomach from his touch.

"Thank you," I muttered as I stood. "You don't look too bad yourself." I smiled at him. Who was I kidding, he always looked good. Smelled good. Most likely tasted good. I let out a little sigh as I started walking towards the door. He was wearing a dark grey suit with a light pink shirt underneath. His honey-blonde hair was swept over to the side, his eyes dewy and bright.

"We are having dinner with your parents tonight," he said as his hand found my lower back as we walked down the hallway and to the stairs.

"We are?" I asked surprised. I hadn't seen my mum since our afternoon tea and my stand-off with Christopher.

"Yes." He breathed heavily. "But I thought we would go out for dinner tonight, if that's okay with you?" His eyes looked down at mine, and my eyes met his gaze.

"That would be lovely, thank you, Xavi." I beamed at him before looking ahead and walking down the stairs, him still close to my side.

Xavier opened the front door, letting me out first before following behind me. I was grateful not to have seen Alan for the last two weeks, and glad that he had listened to Xavier's warning.

There was a red Porsche sitting outside on the gravelled driveway. I furrowed my brows before stopping and looking up at Xavier. "What is this? Where are we going?" I asked confused.

He smiled at me, his eyes creasing slightly in the corners as he wrapped his arm around my waist and pulled me towards him. "This is a gift, from me to you. A Porsche Carrera 911. And obviously, I had to get it in red." He let out a soft chuckle, his fingers swirling in a tickling manner on my hip.

"Do you like it?" he asked.

"I do..." My voice trailed off; I was speechless.

"Yeah?" He crooked his head down to look at my face, my eyes were welling. "Then why are you upset?" he asked, and this time, he was the one that looked confused.

"I'm not upset, I am overwhelmed with happiness." I looked up at him, my lips pressed together in a smile as I begged with my eyes for him to kiss me. To make this moment even more amazing than it already was. His eyes flickered with heat, I felt it burning through me. His right hand came up to my face, cupping it and he leant down to hover his lips over mine. "Don't forget your manners now, Red," he whispered.

"Thank you," I said breathlessly. As soon as the words were off my tongue, his lips were on mine, kissing me like I have wanted for the last two weeks. I melted into him, his hand still firmly cupped round my face, his arm tightly round my waist as he held me up. My knees were weak.

His tongue pushed through my lips as mine followed

his strokes. A groan left his throat before he pulled away. I hated that he had stopped, but I was also grateful that he had kissed me.

"As much as I want to kiss you all day, we have something to do. Get in the car, Royal," he ordered as he dropped his arm from my waist, and I instantly missed the connection. I walked round to the passenger side when I felt him watching me. I looked up and he was shaking his head.

"No, baby, go get in the driver's side," he said softly. Now I was even more confused, I couldn't drive.

"But I can't drive, Xavi," I protested, shaking my head at him.

"I know, but why not learn now? Perfect timing... That way, you can have the freedom you asked for." He smiled sincerely at me.

My heart thumped in my chest.

"Don't I need to have a real test or something?" I stammered over my words.

"You will. Now get in the damn car." He growled, his eyes hazing over. I walked quickly round to the driver's side, sliding in and adjusting my seat. My eyes were darting all around the car, my anxiety building when I saw the gear stick. I had only ever sat in the back of a car, never in the front.

I was sweating. The nerves were too much.

"Royal, baby," he cooed as he sat next to me, his

hands reaching over to mine. "You can do this. It's not hard. Just think of where you could go once you learn to drive." His smile was small. "You could even leave me..." His voice trailed off; his eyes stormy. "But you wouldn't get far, I would always find you, always come after you," he said in a slow, low voice. As if he was warning me.

"You don't need to warn me, I won't be leaving. Ever," I said as convincingly as I could.

"Good." He nodded, his eyes pinned to me. "Don't ever leave me." His voice was quiet, desperate even.

"I won't," I whispered, my eyes flicking down to my lap before bringing them back up to meet his intense stare.

"Start the car, Red," he said candidly.

"You haven't given me the key," I replied baffled, my eyes darting around looking for them.

"You don't need a key," he said with slight humour in his tone.

"Sorry?"

"You don't need a key," he repeated himself. "There is a small stalk where you would normally have a key. Turn it clockwise, foot on the clutch and it'll start." He smiled.

I looked down between my legs, looking at the three pedals.

"Sorry, which one is the clutch?" My voice quivered slightly, my ivory skin blushing at my naivety.

"It's okay, don't apologise," he said softly as he leaned across the centre of the car, his scent enchanting my senses. "It's the pedal to the left, that's the clutch. You press that down to start the car, and to also change gear." His eyes were on mine now, and my eyes were wide with panic.

"You can do this, Red, stop being such a little girl," he snapped as he sat back in his chair. "The pedal next to the clutch is your brake, the one to the right is your accelerator. Your left foot is only used for the clutch, you don't need to turn into Michael Flatley to brake and change gear, okay?" He smirked.

"Left foot only, no Michael Flatley. Got it." I nodded. I pressed my foot on the clutch, turning the stalk and smiling when the engine roared.

I pushed the car into first gear as I slowly lifted my foot off the clutch, when the car started jolting, throwing me forward in my seat. Panicking, I lifted my foot off of the clutch which caused the car to stop. I looked at Xavier, dumbfounded. A stupid grin spread across his face.

"You have to accelerate, Red. If you take your foot off the clutch with no acceleration, you are going to stall it. Which you just did."

"Fuck's sake." I sighed as I tipped my head back and looked at the ceiling.

"It's fine, I stalled loads of times." He laughed. "Don't tell anyone, but I still stall it now occasionally." He shrugged.

"Well, that's made me feel slightly better," I grumbled.

"Now, put the car back into neutral, push your foot down and restart the car," he said as he ran his fingers through his beard.

I did it again, pushing the clutch down, starting the car and pushing into first.

"Find your bite, Red. Once you feel it, which you will, push on the accelerator then lift your foot off completely." He nodded.

I nodded back and followed his simple instruction, the whole time worrying I was going to stall it again.

And I did.

Again.

And again.

And again.

"Fuck's sake, Red, honestly. Last time," he growled, pushing his hand through his hair in frustration.

"Do you want to do it, Xavier?" I shouted at him, hitting my hands on the steering wheel.

"No, I don't, but we have been sitting on the drive for best part of forty minutes."

"So? Are you in a rush to be anywhere?" I snarled at him, my eyes narrowing and focussing on his.

He sighed, dropping his head then rubbing his temple with his fingers.

"Just start the fucking car," he barked.

"No, fuck this shit, I would rather die than spend another second with you," I spat out at him, unplugging my seatbelt and opening the door, slamming it as hard as I could as I stomped my way towards the house. I heard his car door shut, his feet on the gravelled driveway as he closed the space between us. He reached out and grabbed my arm to pull me round to face him.

"Don't think so, Red, no running, remember? Funny how when the going gets tough, you run," he sniped.

"Go away," I muttered. He protested as I tried to pull my arm from his constricting grip.

"No." He shook his head.

Before I could argue back, he pulled me into his chest, his hand coming round my waist, lifting me up and putting me over his shoulder as he walked back to the car. I protested, slapping his back and kicking my legs like a spoiled brat.

"Stop hitting me, Royal," he warned as he dropped me to my feet. "Now, get back in the car, I can do this all day. Get in, and fucking drive."

I sulked back into the car, plugging myself in again and starting the car before he was sat in the passenger side. I tightened my grip on the steering wheel, my foot on the clutch, sitting at my biting point. Just as he opened the door, I pushed my right foot down on the accelerator and drove forward, his hand still gripping the door handle.

"Royal, stop the fucking car," he shouted out as he started running along with me and I slowly increased the speed. Of course I was going to stop, I was just having a little fun. As I got towards the gates, I slowed before stopping. A red-faced, out of breath Xavier glared at me through the open door before he sat down next to me, pushing his hand through his hair.

"It's on," he growled as he slipped in the car, the electric gates slowly opening.

"What's on?" I asked him, confusion lacing my voice.

"You'll see," he said in a growl. I swallowed hard before I pulled away and out of the gates. My mind was going into over-drive. I had poked the bear, when would I learn?

***

After three hours, a few more bickers between us and some stalls along the way, we were finally pulling back onto the drive. I had the hang of it now, but it's not something I would rush to do again.

I cut the engine, relaxing my shoulders and tipping my head back. I closed my eyes for a moment feeling mentally exhausted.

"You did well, Red," Xavier complimented me. "You really did." He reached over and took my hand in his, rubbing his thumb across the back of my knuckles.

"Gee, thanks," I gushed sarcastically. "I would say it was the teacher, but I would be lying."

"Ouch, you wounded me." He slipped his hand out of mine and clutched at his pink shirt over his heart, pretending to be hurt by my truthful words.

"Better actor than you are teacher." I sniggered before letting out a sigh and opening the car door, closing it behind me as I stalked towards the front door. I heard him getting closer, the sound of his Oxford shoes getting louder as he clicked over the gravel.

"Where you running off to?" he asked, slight concern lacing his husky voice.

"Indoors," I answered him, slightly confused as to why he had asked me.

"I know that, but you're running from me." He took my hand in his and pulled me back towards him.

"Xavi, I'm not running. I am simply going into the house, I need a drink. I'm hot," I admitted, my eyes flicking towards his.

"Okay," he said with a sigh of relief, leaning down and planting a soft kiss on my forehead.

"Okay," I muttered back, smiling at him as I held onto his hand, leading him into the house. I didn't understand the feeling that kept creeping over me, the thought of him thinking I would leave him. I could feel the anxiety penetrating through him. I didn't know what I could do to make him see that I'm not going anywhere. Not now. Not ever. I hadn't said the words out loud, but I was infatuated with him. My soul had completely and utterly fallen in love with him.

Chapter Seventeen

The sun was setting in the distance. I smiled as I watched it begin to hide behind the clouds. I don't know what it was that captivated us all when it came to the sun setting. Another day of our life was ending, but yet, we all loved watching it happen. I sighed as I spun round and walked towards my en-suite, running the hot water of the gold, ornate tap. I put some lavender bubble bath in and topped it with rose petals from the flowers that Xavier had given me yesterday. I was a little nervous about going out tonight, we had been out once and that was when Xavier took me to the ball, to play the good, doting fiancé. I let out a small giggle at the thought of how far we had come... Little steps, but still far for me and Xavier.

I undid my silk gown and dropped it to the floor as I stepped into the bath, covering myself completely in the bubbles. The smell was divine. After spending far too long in the bath, I reluctantly pulled myself out, wrapping the towel around me and picking my dressing gown up off the floor. I padded over to the sink, looking at myself in the mirror. It was like my skin was glowing, and I smiled at my reflection.

I walked into my bedroom, another big smile gracing my face, my heart fluttering in my chest when I saw a dress bag on the bed, and a note lying next to it with a peony on the top. I missed his notes. I didn't get many anymore.

I practically skipped over, picking the flower up and smelling it, letting out a heavenly sigh as I brushed the petals against my lips. My other hand flipped open the note, eager to see what he had written today.

My lady in red, you're simply breath-taking.
X

I dropped the note and the flower on the bed, my hungry hands pulling on the zipper to reveal a silk red dress. It had one shoulder cuff, and a split so high I was worried I would expose myself. I shook the thoughts away as I dropped my towel and wrapped my gown around my body. I sat at the dressing table and dried my hair before curling it in loose waves then ran my fingers through to break up the tighter curls. I applied a light layer of foundation before running a thin line of eyeliner across my top lid, finishing with a small flick at the end. I brushed a dusting of blush over my cheekbones and finished with a bright red lipstick. I flicked my lashes with a thick coating of mascara, making my eyes pop. I hung my dressing gown up before walking towards my underwear drawer in the walk-in, rummaging through and finding a seamless nude thong. I slipped it up my long ivory legs then chose a strapless nude bra. Not the prettiest, but I didn't want any lines or bumps from my underwear. I carefully took the dress from its bag before stepping into it and pulling it up over my little curves. I slipped my right arm through the cuffed sleeve and did the zip up at the side, where my left bare arm was out. I looked down at the split on my left leg, it sat just a little under my groin. It was a little revealing, but Xavier would never have chosen it if it was too much. I slipped into silver heeled sandals, one hidden under the floor-length dress. I sprayed my perfume before looking at my watch, it was time to go. I knocked on the interconnecting door, waiting for him to call out. But he didn't. I tried my luck at the handle, pushing it down then pulling it open. I scoped his room, my heart racing in my chest. I was nervous to see him.

He wasn't here.

I couldn't help the pang of disappointment that shot through me. I let out a sigh as I walked towards his bedroom door that took me to the landing that led to the sweeping staircase. I took each step carefully, my hand gliding down the solid oak bannister. Then there, standing at the bottom looking as handsome as ever, was my Xavier. Standing in a black suit with a crisp white shirt buttoned up underneath, with a red single stemmed rose in his hand.

"Royal," his voice purred my name.

"Xavier," I said silkily back to him.

"You look…" His voice trailed off as he sunk his teeth into his bottom lip, his eyes looking me up and down.

"So do you." I smiled at him as I took his held-out hand, clasping it gently before he placed a soft kiss on my cheek. I blushed under his lips, my eyes fluttering shut for a moment.

"You ready?" he asked as he handed me the rose, which I took and held straight up to my nose.

"I am." I nodded as he clung to my hand and walked me towards the driveway.

"Happy for me to drive?" he asked as he unlocked the Porsche.

"Yup," I said a little quickly. "I have done enough driving for one day." I winked at him.

He opened my door, standing tall as I slipped past him and into the passenger seat, smiling as he closed the door behind me. I crossed my bare leg over the other and rested my head on the plush leather seat. I turned my face to watch him slide into the car, my heart thumping from just the sight of him. I loved everything about him, but most of all, I fell for those eyes. His perfectly imperfect eyes.

He strapped himself in, leaning over and placing a quick, soft kiss on my lips before starting the car, the engine purring. He pulled away slowly as he approached the gates.

We were only in the car a short while, and not one of us had spoken. My mind wandered to Alan. I was grateful that I hadn't had to see him, I just hoped that Xavier got rid of him for good. But I couldn't work their relationship out. Xavier was clearly his boss, but Alan got away with so much. He spoke to Xavier like dirt sometimes and I couldn't work it out. Xavier only rose a few times to him, but it was as if Alan had some sort of hold over him, and I didn't know why.

My mind was rattling with questions to ask him. I took a deep breath before speaking. "How's Alan?" I asked, my eyes on him. His jaw clenched, his fingers tightening round the wheel.

"Fine," he snapped. "Why do you ask?" His face turned to mine for a moment, his eyes narrowed.

"Just wondered. Is he your boss? Like, secretly?" The words were out before I registered.

If looks could kill, I would have been dead. Right there and then.

"What the fuck, Royal?" he bellowed across the car.

"Of course he ain't. He works for me. Me. I am the fucking boss. I work for no one. What sort of question is that? Why even ask me?" He shook his head, his face turning a slight scarlet. I couldn't work out if it was from embarrassment or anger.

"I... Well... I just..." I stammered for a moment, my eyes looking down to my lap.

"Spit it out, Red," he growled at me.

"I just feel like, that sometimes, he treats you like his employee, not the other way around." I winced as I said it.

"He is my employee," he said bluntly. "Do you want me to *prove* that he works for me?" he questioned.

"And how would you prove it?" I asked, my eyes now back on him.

"I'll fire him. Right now." He clenched his jaw tight again.

"No, don't fire him." I shook my head.

"Are you sure? Do you need to see me make him jobless for you to see that I am his fucking boss?" he barked.

"No." I pressed my lips into a thin line, shaking my head again.

"Do I need to show you that I am the boss? Because believe me, Royal, I know just what to do to show you how much of a boss I am. Don't ever fucking question me again. Anything else you want to ask?"

"Nope." I looked out the window as I answered him.

"Good," he huffed out. A few minutes passed before I started talking again.

"I'm glad I don't have to see him much anymore..." I trailed off.

"Can we stop talking about fucking Alan? I am already pissed off, I don't want to hear his name again tonight, do you understand me?" he asked, raising his eyebrows.

I didn't say anything, just nodded.

I felt a tightening in my belly, my stomach knotting over and over itself.

The rest of the car journey was in an uncomfortable silence, which made me uneasy. Xavier's jaw stayed clenched, tight. His eyes focused on the road ahead. I felt like I had fucked the evening up.

I let out a small sigh of relief when we pulled up to a small, cosy restaurant just on the outskirts of my father's kingdom. I had never been this far from home; I had never eaten in a restaurant before. I had only ever been allowed to balls and galas, I was never allowed out just to have something to eat. Fuck, I couldn't even go out of my castle grounds. I shook the thoughts from my head as I opened the car door, Xavier standing there, holding his hand out for me to take. I didn't take it. I knew I was being petty but how he snapped, how he changed when I asked him about Alan... I just needed a moment, a moment to breathe.

I felt his eyes burning into me. I could feel his anger

penetrating through me. But I didn't look at him. I kept my eyes forward towards the ivy-covered restaurant in front of me. I smiled a big fake smile as I reached the doorman.

"Princess Royal," he cooed, his smile as big as mine as I nodded my head softly, walking past him and into the cosy restaurant. My heart glowed when I saw my mother and father. They both stood in the empty restaurant, arms out wide as they welcomed me. I practically ran towards them, throwing myself into them as they wrapped me in an embrace. At that moment, I didn't want to leave. I wanted them to take me home, far away from Xavier. But as soon as the thought was out there, my heart broke. I felt constricted, torn.

I pulled away from my parents, looking over my shoulder as he stalked into the restaurant, one hand fisted deep into his pocket, the other resting down his side. He was beautiful.

"Xavier," my father boomed across the small room.

"Patrick," he said sharply.

"It's *King* Patrick to you," my father corrected him. Xavier let out a throaty laugh, shaking his head, then his head dropped slightly before he looked up and through my father. "You don't deserve that title after what you did," he snarled.

"Don't test me," my father warned.

"What you going to do, Patrick? Gamble your wife

away next?" he teased.

My father stepped forward, puffing his chest out like some sort of alpha. He was pretty pathetic; they both were if I was being honest. I shook my head, turning to face Xavier.

"Can we stop this? You both need to grow the fuck up," I snapped, looking Xavier up and down then firing a glare in my father's direction.

"Mother, I am hungry. Would you like to join me for dinner whilst we let the children play?" I asked, my voice loud but slightly playful as I ran my tongue slowly over my top lip, my eyes pinned to Xavier the whole time. I was revelling inside, a fire alight so deep within me. His stunning eyes narrowed on me before he pushed his hand through his swept-back hair, a low growl leaving his throat.

"Yes, certainly." My mother nodded, walking away from my father, giving him a loud tut as she walked past him, shaking her head in pure disgust. I stifled a laugh as she stopped by Xavier, giving him such a filthy look from his shoes right up to the top of his head before rolling her eyes and walking towards the only dressed table in the middle of the empty restaurant.

Xavier was quick on my heels, pulling my chair out and letting me sit down. He pushed me to the table before leaning down, his hands on the top of the chair before his lips were next to my left ear. "You want to play like that do you, baby?" he whispered. The hairs on the back of my neck stood, goose-bumps spread over my skin like wildfire. "It's on," he muttered before standing back up and taking his seat next to me on the left. His eyes trailed down my body, and he licked his lips before he reached forward and took a mouthful of his water that was on the table. I swallowed hard, my mouth suddenly dry as I watched my parents sit opposite me.

"Royal, darling, you okay?" My mum had a puzzled look on her face and my eyes flickered slightly as I watched her.

"I'm fine." I smiled, reaching for my water and taking a big mouthful before placing it down in front of me. Xavier moved his chair closer to mine, so the chairs were touching. He faced me, giving me the fakest smile I think I have ever seen.

"So, darling, tell me, what have you been up to?" my father asked, adoration in his eyes as he looked at me. I felt the bile rise in my stomach. Was he fucking stupid? I watched him for a moment, the complete ignorance over his beetroot face.

"You're looking a bit red in the face, *Daddy*. Are you ashamed and embarrassed?" I asked him straight out, my head cocking to the side slightly as I glared at him. His hand reached up to his collar, his finger running inside it as he pulled it away from his neck. I heard Xavier let out a low chuckle as his right hand reached across to my bare thigh, his hand squeezing gently. I felt a sizzling sensation as his fingers gently stroked up and down my skin.

"Royal." My father's voice came out strained, as if he was pleading for me to stop.

"Father?" I questioned him. He didn't say anything. He just gulped his water down, my mum giving him a repulsed stare.

"I have been held a prisoner, I have been lonely, angry, upset..." I started, and I felt Xavier's eyes on me. "I haven't always been happy... But I am now. Because of Xavier. And I suppose, I have you to thank. But you won't hear the words come from my mouth. Because you don't fucking deserve them," I said through gritted teeth. "Because you didn't fight for me, you didn't stop what was so wrong." I shook my head, my fists balled as I dropped my head, taking a few deep breaths.

I felt Xavier's lips on my ear. "Don't lose it, Red. You are better than that." His voice was slow, quiet. My heart slowed; my breathing calmed.

"Why don't you tell us what you've been up to, Patrick," Xavier said as he watched the waiter pour a glass of whiskey into a crystal-cut tumbler. A young lady was at mine and my mother's side as she poured us both a glass of white wine.

"Thank you." I smiled at her as I reached for my glass and brought the rim to my lips before taking a small mouthful and letting out a small moan at the taste.

Xavier's grip tightened on the top of my thigh before his finger started tracing small circles on my blazing skin.

"Sorry, Xavier, you were asking what I have been up to?" My father watched Xavier's every move. Xavier had such a smug look on his face.

"I did," he admitted as he took a mouthful of the amber poison that sat in his glass.

"Well, I've been doing trades with the next kingdom along, trying to get as much revenue for our kingdom as we can. To be able to pay off debts, so I can get back what belongs to me." My father burned his stare into Xavier, but Xavier didn't even falter. He just sat with a tightened jaw.

I went to speak but I felt his fingers glide into the slit of my dress, his hand pushing my dress over, so I was exposed to him. He didn't look at me, my eyes were focusing on his mouth as he drank his drink, not showing any emotion.

His fingers continued to skim over my over sensitive skin, each time getting a little higher than before. They trailed along the top of my thong, stopping for a moment as he sucked in a breath. I slipped my hand under the table, grabbing his big hand as I tried to push it away, my eyes on him. He let out a small throaty laugh and shook his head ever so slightly before he continued his trail down between my legs. I automatically opened my legs, welcoming him.

His finger circled over my sensitive clit, which was already soaked from his touch and caused a breathless moan to leave my lips.

"Xavier," I said hazily, my voice consumed and spellbound my him.

"I don't think you understand, Patrick." He cut me off, completely ignoring me. "I will never, ever let Royal go back to you," he said sharply as he continued to massage me before his finger glided down my folds and straight into me. I couldn't help the small gasp that left my mouth. My hand gripped the edge of the table as I tried to stay focussed. The pleasure was ripping through me as his finger continued its slow pumps into me. His thumb brushed over my clit which sent shockwaves through to my core.

"You don't have a say," my father threatened.

"Oh, I do," he purred. "She is mine. Always mine." His expert finger stroked my walls, building me up to my sweet release. I tightened around him as his fingers moved quicker in and out of me.

"I will fight you to my last dying breath." My father's voice sounded desperate.

"Good luck, Patrick. You will lose. She belongs to me. I own her, in every single fucking way," he said in a slow, husky voice. He slowed his fingers to match his voice as my orgasm ripped through me. I wanted to cry out his name, tip my head back and show him what he did to me.

But I couldn't. My fingers wrapped round the table edge tightly, my breath slightly heavier as I rode my orgasm out, his fingers slowing but still pulsing inside me. I flicked my eyes over to him, a small smirk on his face as I noticed the waiters walking towards us with our food.

He slipped his fingers out slowly as he shuffled in his seat before reaching into the centre of the table for the salt. His grin widened as he looked at my father. "Salt, Patrick?" he asked as he handed my nodding father the salt pot with the same hand that had just made me come.

I blushed crimson before excusing myself from the table.

"Everything okay, Royal?" my mother asked, concern lacing her voice.

I went to speak but Xavier spoke for me. "She is fine, Mya, she's just *come...*" His voice stopped for a moment as he looked at me, giving me a wink. My eyes were wide, humiliation masking my face, my jaw laxed. His silky voice continued. "She's just come over a little hot." He bit his bottom lip before pressing his finger that was just inside me to his lip, his smile getting wider as he licked the tip before his eyes were back on my parents. "Anyway, Patrick, where were we?" I heard him ask as I ran towards the bathroom.

Chapter Eighteen

We said goodnight to my parents as Xavier opened the car door for me. I felt heady, dizzy as such, but I couldn't work out if it was from the one too many glasses of wine or the little game Xavier played at the dinner table. The burning ache that was in my stomach was almost too much for me to bear. I felt frustrated.

I thanked him, then sitting and crossing my legs, I tried to dull the sensation that was increasing between my legs.

"You okay, Red?" he asked as he strapped himself in.

"Mmhmm." I nodded, not looking at him.

"Sorry about your father's behaviour tonight, I didn't expect that. I just wanted you to have a nice meal with your parents." He sighed.

"It's fine. Thank you for trying." I shrugged, still not making eye contact with him.

"You sure you're okay?" he asked as he started driving towards home.

"I'm just a little frustrated," I admitted, my eyes moving to look at him.

"Why are you frustrated?"

"Just because of your little game." I huffed.

"But you came... Or did you fake it?" He was now looking at me, his eyes pinned on my face, one of his eyebrows rising.

"No." I blushed.

"Sorry, I'm confused, why are you frustrated then?" he asked.

"Because of how you did it. Am I just a game to you? Are you just playing me?" I asked curtly, my voice raised slightly. "I feel like a fool. Maybe I'm blind, maybe I am just a silly, young, naive little girl who thought you actually liked me?" My eyes filled with unshed tears. I didn't even know where this was coming from, everything that had been bubbling up inside for weeks was finally surfacing. I pushed the stray tears that had managed to escape off of my cheeks.

"Royal..." he said, pulling the car over in a small layby down the country lane we were driving down. He cut the engine, leaning across the car and cocooning my face with his big hands as he pulled me towards him slightly, his eyes on my lips before they came up and penetrated straight through me and into my soul.

"This isn't a game. It was never a game," he said in a murmur. I closed my eyes for a moment, breaking the connection between us. It was too intense.

"Look at me," he requested. And I did, like a puppet who was being controlled by her puppeteer.

"You were always going to be mine. I played your father; he was the game. I wanted the best prize, and that was you, Red. It was always you." His thumb rubbed across my cheeks, wiping the mascara-stained tear marks away.

"I knew from the moment I saw you five years ago, when we danced, that I needed you, I wanted you. God, Royal, if only you knew just how bad I was..." He bit his bottom lip, his eyes back on my mouth. My lips had parted, I was slightly breathless.

"Every piece of me ached for you, it still does. I fell in love with your beautiful soul before I even got the chance to touch you. I can't imagine my life without you, Red. You are it for me. Today, tomorrow, always." He gasped as he took a breath. "Trust me, Red, you were never the game. Ever. Only the prize, the end game. Only you."

"Xavier," I breathed.

"Our love is savage, toxic, poison, I know that. But it's love. We have no control over it. It shouldn't work, we shouldn't work. Fuck." He pushed his hand through his hair, frustrated as he dropped one of them from my face. "But this is it, Red. Me and you. I'm your savage love, and you are mine," he whispered before he crashed his lips onto mine. His tongue caressed mine, stroking softly, our kiss slow, sensual. I pulled away suddenly, closing my eyes to try and take everything in that he had just said and done.

"Take me, Xavi, make me yours," I breathed out. "Take me home," I whispered. He let go of me completely, turned the stalk for the engine and booted it all the way home.

I was trembling, nerves consuming me, but excitement soon took over. He opened my door, leaning down and swooping me up in his arms as he walked towards the front of the house. He didn't put me down, just gripped around my waist tightly as he opened the door then placed his hand under my back as he walked to our bedroom. No words were said, I just had my hands round his neck, holding on tightly as we got closer and closer.

As we approached his bedroom door, my heart was racing in my chest. I jumped slightly as he kicked the door open, strolling over to his bed and putting me down gently.

He stood back, his eyes wide and watching me as he smiled. I smiled back, trying to mask how nervous I was. I wanted this more than anything, but I couldn't help the feeling of anxiety ripping through me.

He stepped back, reaching down to his bedside table

and grabbing a square, foil packet, placing it on the bed next to me. I swallowed down hard, not wanting to break my eye contact from him.

"Stand up, baby," he asked softly, extending his arm and holding out his hand for me to take. I stepped up, my legs shaky. "I want you to undress me first, please," he uttered.

I nodded, rubbing my lips together. I stepped one step closer to him, his arms sat by his sides as I ran my trembling hands up his white shirt, making my way towards his shoulders as I pushed his suit jacket back and over. He shrugged it off, letting it fall to the floor. I watched my fingers fumble with his buttons as I began to undo them, when I felt his hand grip my chin, tipping it up to look at him.

"Don't shy away from me, Red," he said softly.

"I won't," I whispered as I continued down to the bottom button. I couldn't help myself, touching his hard stomach, running my hands up over his pecks then over his shoulders as I pushed his shirt away.

My fingers trailed down his stomach and towards his belt buckle as I rushed to get it undone, pulling it through the hoops and discarding it to the floor. I couldn't help the small bit of excitement that pulsed through me. This was finally happening.

I popped his button through the hole in his trousers then pulled his fly down as I pushed his trousers down to his ankles. I stood back, watching him kick them off and put them with the rest of his clothes. I took a deep breath, marvelling at him, looking at him from head to toe. He really was beautiful. Perfectly imperfect, but perfect for me. I could see the arousal already showing on his boxers, his erection constricted.

"You've missed a vital bit of clothing," he teased. "Take them off, you've seen it before," he reminded me as he closed the gap between us. He towered over me, his eyes looking down at me as he gripped my chin, tilting my face up to look at him again. "Undress me, Red." The swarm of butterflies were evident in my stomach, fluttering away.

I hooked my fingers in the inside of his waistband of his tight boxers as I rolled them down his thick, muscular thighs. My eyes widened as I saw his cock spring from his boxers, my mouth going dry. I knew what it looked like, but seeing it again just reminded me of how big and thick he was. I started to panic, worrying about how much it was going to hurt. As if he could read my mind, Xavier started talking, reassuring me. "Baby, it will be uncomfortable, it may even hurt, but I will do everything I can to make it as pain free as I can. Trust me, please?" he asked.

"I do." I nodded as I stepped away from him.

"My turn." His voice was low, husky. He grinned at me, his tongue darting out as he licked his top lip before pulling his bottom lip between his teeth, his eyes undressing me before his hands could.

He stepped towards me, his hands on my waist as he craned his neck down to cover my mouth with his. I welcomed his kiss, taking my mind off of what was about to happen. His hand ran around my waist and to my back as he pulled me closer. I could feel his hard erection pressing up against me. He wrapped his fingers round the back of my neck, tightening his grip as his kiss intensified. I melted into him, swooning in his arms as I heard the delicious groan leaving this throat. He pulled away as his spare hand gripped the zipper on the side of my dress before he started pulling it down to my hip, his hand running inside the soft material of the dress. He slowly trailed his finger from the side of my rib all the way down to my hip where my knicker line was. I drew in a deep breath, my breath catching from his delicate strokes on my already burning skin. His hand that was round my back now moved to my breast as he started pulling the dress down my body and letting it pool to my feet as I stepped out.

"You are breath-taking, Royal, and all mine. Mine completely," he whispered before his mouth covered mine again. He walked me backwards towards the bed, the bed hitting the back of my knees which caused me to sit, my body falling onto the mattress. He spread my legs before kneeling in-between them, his eager eyes wandering down my body and looking at my knickers that were stopping him from getting what he wanted. What we both wanted. His hand moved up towards my bra and around my back as he unhooked it in one swift movement before gliding his fingertips down the side of my ribs, across my hips then down in-between my legs as he stroked them across my clit, causing a gasp to leave me. It felt amazing, and he wasn't even touching me properly yet.

"You sure about this, Royal?" he asked as he focused on me.

"Yes. So sure." My voice was quiet as I nodded. He leaned in to kiss me, his fingers wrapping round the side of my thong and pulling it to the side to expose me. I heard him suck in his breath as he looked at me before his finger glided up and down my core, swirling the tip of his finger at my soaked opening, then gliding them back up my folds again and slowly circling over my clit.

"I'm going to make you come first. It's very rare you come with your first time. I won't last five minutes with you, I have been dreaming of this day, every day, for five years," he admitted, his eyes alight with lust and desire. He moved over me as his lips were on my neck, kissing softly and sucking as his finger trailed down my centre before he pushed into me, deep but slow. I moaned, the feeling consuming me. His thumb started massaging my sensitive clit, building me up slowly to my orgasm. His finger continued slowly, pumping and stretching me, ready for him to take me. My hands were gripping onto the white bed sheets underneath me as he continued his rhythm. I felt his weight shift from on top of me as he planted kisses down the middle of my breasts, then to my navel before his mouth was over me, his tongue flicking and swirling over my clit as his finger pulses sped up, pushing me closer to my impending orgasm.

"Xavier," I moaned out as I clamped around his finger. I heard him moan, his tongue still tasting and licking me. One of my hands moved to his hair, fisting a handful as I felt my orgasm ready to tip. He slowly flicked his tongue across my clit before sucking which sent me over the edge as I spiralled out of control, riding out my orgasm as he tasted every part of me, making sure he didn't miss a single drop before he was back over me, kissing me and pushing his tongue in-between my lips so I could taste myself. He broke our kiss as he reached over for the foil packet, sitting back on his knees as he tore it open then rolled it down his thick, hard cock. I bit my bottom lip, still completely drunk off of him.

He repositioned himself between my thighs, pushing them further apart as he lined the tip of himself at my soaked opening.

"Tell me if I hurt you, okay?" he said softly as he started edging in.

"Okay," I said breathlessly as I tensed.

"Relax, baby, it'll hurt less if you untense," he said, his hand on my face as he pushed my hair away. He edged himself in slightly, and a burn and a sting followed which made me wince, my voice choked for a moment.

"You okay?" he asked.

I nodded, unable to speak.

"I'm going to push a little more, okay? Once I am in all the way, it'll ease slightly," he mumbled as he pushed his hips forward.

The burn increased, and I closed my eyes for a moment, trying to focus on not tensing up and making it so much worse.

"Look at me, baby," he said, almost begging. "I need to see you."

I did as he said. I opened my eyes and focused on him as he edged in a little more, the stretching more apparent now, the burning starting to ease but the sting still there.

I couldn't help but look down in-between my legs, the sight of him inside me made me feel things I had never felt before, then I moved my eyes back up to his face. I couldn't help but notice how clenched his jaw was, the concentration on his face was so apparent. His hips started thrusting into me again, still very slow until I felt how full I was. He stilled for a moment. He was holding his breath, his arms trembling as he held his weight over me. His eyes didn't leave me for a second, I felt so complete.

"Baby, I am going to start moving, I need to move." He let out a slight chuckle, his breathing getting slightly faster.

"Mmhmm," was all I could manage as I felt so content and love-drunk at that moment.

His hips started moving slowly as he pulled out of me slightly, he sucked in a deep breath, like he was trying to control himself. After a moment, his hips pushed back towards me. The sting was back as he moved himself out. I heard a moan leave him, his head tipping back, his eyes closed as he focused on his thrusts into me. They were slow but hard. Each time he moved back in me it felt a little better.

"I'm going to speed up, I am so close," he mumbled as he picked his speed up a little, pushing himself in and out of me. His eyes watched, a moan leaving him each time he was inside me.

"Fuck, Royal," he growled. "I'm going to come."

With that, his hips moved a lot quicker, his movements fast as he found his own release, the most delicious moan leaving his throat as he pumped himself inside me before he stilled.

"Red, baby, fuck," he whispered as he laid on top of me, his hands round my face as his lips hovered over mine. "It's always been you, Royal," he mumbled before he covered my mouth with his.

***

We had been laying for what seemed like forever, neither of us talking, both of us just enjoying this moment.

His fingers were tickling up and down my spine, my head on his chest listening to his steady heartbeat. I never wanted to move.

"Royal, sit up," he said in a hushed voice. I reluctantly pulled myself up, grabbing the bed sheet to cover myself. He threw me a look, his eyebrows furrowed as he leant forward and pulled the sheet off of me. "Don't ever hide yourself," he muttered in a warning tone. He climbed out the bed, taking my hand and walking me towards the bathroom. He turned the shower on, letting it run for a moment before he stepped under it, pulling me into the burning water.

He reached behind him, grabbing a wash cloth, lathering it up with soap before he washed all over my body before tending to my most intimate area.

"You sore?" he asked as he swooped me up in his arms, pulling me close and embracing me, the water cascading down over us.

"A little, but I'm okay, more than okay," I muttered. He craned his neck down, pressing his lips to the top of my wet hair and inhaling deeply. I felt so consumed and wrapped up in his love at that moment that I didn't want anything to take it away from me. But we couldn't stay under here forever, as much as I wanted to.

He wrapped me in a fluffy towel, then wrapped himself in one. He led me back to his bedroom. I stopped at my pile of clothes, bending to pick them up and started strolling towards the door that connected our rooms.

"Where you going, Royal?" he asked, his voice hushed. His face was full of confusion, his brows furrowed, and his eyes narrowed on mine.

"To my room?" I answered back a little confused. This is what happened right? We didn't sleep together.

"No, baby, no." I felt his hand on mine as he pulled me back into him. "Stay with me."

It wasn't a question; it was another order. I dropped my clothes back to the floor as I wandered back over to the bed with him. I watched as he towelled off his wet hair then rubbed it through his beard. He ran it over his toned body which had me gawking like a school girl at her first crush. He walked over to the bathroom, his peachy bum in my eye line before he disappeared. I stood for a moment, drying myself off and folding the towel up and hooking it over the tall radiator. I stood for a moment, completely naked as I looked round his pristine room to put something on. I couldn't see anything apart from my dress and underwear. I padded over to my bedroom door, opening it and closing it gently as I let out my held breath. I stopped and looked at myself in the mirror, my cheeks were flushed, a glow almost. I felt different, my heart felt warm pumping in my chest. I knew I loved Xavier, but this felt like so much more than just love. We were connected, our souls entwined and bonded with each other's. Like we were always meant to find each other. I felt whole, complete. I reached for my drawers, pulling a light pink nighty out and slipping it over my head. I strolled into the en-suite of my room, grabbing my toothbrush and running it under the tap for a moment as I stared back at the girl in the reflection. I didn't recognise her anymore. She looked happy, glowing, free. I squeezed a strip of toothpaste onto my brush before popping it in my mouth, my hand wrapping round the china sink top when I heard an almighty bang which made me jump. I froze for a moment when I looked in the mirror to see him standing there in low-hanging cotton shorts. His eyes were blazing, his jaw tight.

"I thought you ran," he admitted, his voice low, husky.

"No," I whispered as I rinsed my toothbrush before putting it back in its holder.

"Then why––" He went to continue but I stopped him, shaking my head and pressing my index finger up to his lips.

"I went to get something to wear, Xavier, how many times do I have to tell you I'm not going anywhere? Never." I dropped my finger, giving him a small smile. "What do I have to do to prove it to you?" I asked as I stepped back, but as soon as I put space between us, he wrapped his arms around me, pulling me back towards him. His head buried in my hair, his breath on my bare neck. He didn't say anything, just calmed himself down, his grip tight around my waist. Within minutes he let me go, grabbing my hand and walking me back towards his room. He dropped my hand as he opened his bed. "You belong here, with me. Every night." His voice was small, quiet. I always felt slightly anxious when I saw the vulnerable side of Xavier. I could never work out what was going on in his head and that frightened me. I couldn't help the massive grin that was now on my face. I climbed in, feeling utterly exhausted in that moment. He wrapped his arms around me, pulling me towards him as he nuzzled his face into the crook of my neck.

"Sleep, Red," he mumbled before I felt him go heavy, he was gone already.

I took a moment to reflect on how things had changed so suddenly, but I wasn't complaining. Because I was happy... Blissfully happy.

Chapter Nineteen

I woke, jolted. It took me a moment to realise where I was, relief sweeping over me. I turned over to find Xavier gone. I knitted my brows together. I pushed the duvet off of me, climbing out of the bed and making my way to the door. I quickly stepped down the stairs, walking towards the office, when I heard his voice. The door was ajar, and I stood just outside for a moment, about to push the door open when he said something that made me freeze on the spot.

"Xander, she is it for me. I can't believe I finally have her. After all this time," I heard him say.

I waited for a response, for another voice, but there was nothing.

"I know, brother, I know. You will never know how sorry I am." His voice was tight, constricting. I stepped back from the door, my blood running cold.

"I just had to come and tell you about her, to tell you how much I love her."

I turned on my heel and flew for the stairs, I didn't want to be caught eavesdropping. I would speak to him about what I heard, but not yet. No. I had to bide my time.

I crept back into bed, but now I was wide awake. I couldn't sleep. I kept my eyes pinned to the clock; it had just gone three a.m. when I heard him walk in. I shut my eyes quickly, pretending to be asleep. My heart was racing in my chest. He wrapped his arms around me, pulling me closer to him before he kissed the back of my head. As much as I didn't think I was tired, I fell asleep quicker than I thought I would.

***

I woke groggy, I hadn't slept well. I felt like I was tossing and turning all night. I'm not used to sleeping next to someone either, and Xavier made me hot. I felt like I was stifled, suffocating. I rolled on my back, turning my head to face him. I watched as he slept, so peaceful and beautiful. His lips parted slightly, the breath leaving so quiet. I propped myself up on my elbow, my other hand resting on his bare chest. My eyes moved from his throat, up to his beard covered mouth. The mouth that was on me last night. My breath caught, the thoughts replaying over and over in my mind. I wanted him again. I wanted to enjoy him this time. I focused on his scar that sat under his left eye. I wanted to ask him how it happened, but something always stopped me. I froze when his hand moved, coming up to my wrist and grabbing it. His eyes looked pained, but within seconds they relaxed, a small smile gracing his handsome face.

"Morning, baby," he said softly.

"Morning." I smiled at him.

"You look tired, Red, did you not sleep well?" he asked as he sat up, pulling me onto his lap, his legs opening slightly which made me dip lower onto him. His hand moved slowly up to my face, cupping it before pushing my fiery hair away and over my shoulder.

"I am tired," I admitted. "But nothing to do with not sleeping well," I lied.

"Maybe you should get some more sleep?" His voice was hazy, thick and gruff. I felt him hard underneath me.

"I don't want to sleep," I said quietly, my eyes looking at his lips.

"Good, because I want you," he mumbled before his hand wrapped round the back of my neck, pulling me down towards him, pressing his mouth onto mine before his tongue invaded my mouth, stroking and massaging me. A soft groan left his throat, his lips coming away from me. I sat up, still straddled over him as his hands travelled slowly down to my hips, his fingers brushing over the silk of my night dress. He pushed it up round my waist, a wicked smirk spreading across his beautiful face. His eyes moved slowly from my eyes to my lips, then down to my chest before they focused on the apex between my thighs, his breath sucking in.

"I want you so bad, Red," he whispered.

"Take me then," I begged, seduction lacing my voice. He lifted me up as he pushed the covers away between us. He dropped one of his hands from my hip, grabbing his thick cock as he lined it up at my already soaked entrance. His breathing stilled for a moment before he rocked his hips up into me slowly. A gasp left me as my body accepted and adjusted to him. I stilled, slightly frozen. As did he. He was giving me a moment to stretch around him. I dropped my head, nodding softly, giving him the silent go ahead to begin. I could feel the pull between us, the air thick with sexual tension. Both his hands were back on my hips as he slowly pushed himself into me, the animalistic growl that vibrated in his throat sent a shiver through me. His thrusts were so slow, torturously slow. It felt different this time, a good different. I kept my eyes on him, one of his hands cupped my cheek again, his rocks up into me still slow and soft. I felt a burn, but a delicious burn. I wanted him to show me how good it could be, I wanted to feel him even more.

"I want more, Xavier," I pleaded, my voice a whisper.

"Baby..." he protested as he stilled.

"Please," I said hushed. The hand that was on my hip moved round my back as he swiftly moved me underneath him. He was nestled between my spread thighs before he pushed himself back into me, deeper this time. I let out a deep sigh, one of my hands round the back of his neck, pulling his lips closer to mine so I could kiss him. His lips pressed into mine, both of his hands either side of my head as his hips began to move faster into me, his thrusts hard. After a few minutes, he lifted his head back, pulling the contact from our lips. He dropped his head to look at himself moving in and out of me, his movements even slower now as he watched himself filling me. He groaned; the feeling was too much. I felt a tingling in my stomach, my walls clamping down around him.

"Does that feel good, Royal?" he asked, his voice low.

"Mmm," I moaned out, his hips rocking into me faster again. His hands fisted the bedsheet, he started grunting and growling. His hips began to swirl, his cock pushing deeper into me. His lips were on my neck, and he trailed them down to my breast, licking my nipple slowly before taking it into his mouth and sucking. I moaned, the feeling of his mouth on my sensitive breast, his movements slow as he pushed in and out of me again. I felt myself ready to explode, it was getting too much. His mouth was still attentively focused on my hardened nipples, his thumb moving in-between my legs as he started massaging my clit whilst his hips rocked into me faster now, harder. I was in paradise.

"Xavier, I'm close, I'm so close," I called out, my head lifting to watch him. My eyes focussed on his expert tongue, rolling around my nipple. He stopped, looking up at me, my eyes wandering down to his hand between my legs, and the sight of him pushing himself in and out of me was just too much for me to bear. I threw my head back, my chest rising, my back lifting as it arched. Pulling his thumb away suddenly, he reared up, both his hands now gripping tightly onto my thighs as he spread them further apart, his eyes on mine, his bottom lip pulled in by his teeth. His eyes moved down, his head cocking to the side slightly before his eyes fell in-between my legs. The sound of his skin hitting mine was such a turn on. He was pounding into me hard, his breathing ragged and harsh.

"Fuck, Royal," he gasped out, his head tipping back before he looked back down. "You feel amazing, so fucking tight. And all mine."

"Xavier, it's too much... Oh, I'm going to... Fuck, Xavier," I called out as my orgasm ripped through me, his hips rocking into me fast as I rode out my explosive orgasm.

"Always. Fucking. Mine," he growled through gritted teeth as he came, his hands tightening their grip on the inside of my thighs. I watched him, a small shudder shooting through him before he stilled, falling down on top of me.

We didn't speak for a moment, his head was on my chest, my heart thumping in my ribcage, his arms wrapped around my back.

"You feeling okay?" he asked. "Sorry I got a bit carried away," he admitted as he looked at me.

"I am amazing, Xavier." I nibbled my bottom lip, blushing. "I want you to get carried away with me more often," I said, nerves crashing through me.

"Oh, baby, you don't have to ask. I'll be getting so carried away with you. Your body and soul are mine. I can't wait to explore every inch of you, I want to hear you sing my name. Always." He smirked as he kissed me.

***

The next few months flew, mine and Xavier's bond grew stronger and stronger and we had more good days than bad. He still had his moments where he was a complete arsehole, but he was my loveable arsehole.

I had lunch plans with Mabel and Christopher today and I couldn't wait. We were going to sit by the lake that was on Xavier's land. There was a beautiful little boat house that overlooked it. It was nothing special, but I had become very fond of it.

I finished making our bed, smirking at the events that had unfolded last night. Each time we had been together, it just kept getting better and better. He claims me, owns me, dominates me. Last night I was cuffed by soft, leather wrist cuffs. Attached to them was a long, soft strap that was tied to the posts on each side of his bed. I was restrained and completely bound to him. He had full control of my body. He teased me, bringing me to breaking point and then stopping. It was torture, but a torture I wanted. I didn't want him to stop. I liked being his plaything. He invaded all my senses. The fact that I couldn't stop him or hit him away just made it so much better. I closed my eyes for a moment, retracing his fingers over my skin with my own fingertips. My breath caught, the memories swirling round in my head as he made me come like I had never come before. My whole body trembled, a layer of sweat covered my naked body as I came undone beneath him. Just when I thought he was done, him bringing me back down from heaven, he sent me straight back up there again. I hummed as I flicked my eyes open, staring at the now-made bed. I radiated, he made me glow. My stomach flipped in a delicious way at my thoughts. I just wanted him all the time. I could never get enough of him. He was my addiction, drug and release, all-in-one.

The weather had started to turn, the autumn air nipping at my skin. But I loved the autumn, the leaves crisp and auburn. The days shorter, the sun not as bright. I felt like I radiated in the autumn, my skin not so pale, not so transparent.

I pulled my denim skinny jeans on then grabbed a cream long-sleeved crew-neck top. I tied my long red hair into a high, messy ponytail and flicked my lashes with a light layer of mascara. Xavier had already left this morning for a work thing; I still didn't know what he did exactly. I was just told that he was a fixer. He helped people in shitty situations. I didn't want to delve too much into it, so I just nodded and dropped the topic.

I sprayed my perfume before walking down towards the main kitchen. It had already gone midday. We had a bit of a lazy morning, breakfast in bed and all that. I blushed slightly when Mabel pulled me from my thoughts as she came bounding up to me, Christopher's hands firmly in hers, their fingers interlocked together.

"Royal!" She beamed as she pulled me in for a one-armed-hug. I embraced her, wrapping both my arms around her.

"Mabel." I smiled at her. "Christopher." I nodded curtly, pulling away from Mabel. "Are you both okay?" I asked as I walked towards the kitchen island, grabbing the big wicker picnic basket and strolling towards the autumn sun. I walked slowly on the frost-bitten grass, the sun was sitting low in the sky, taking longer to melt the ice that sat on the tips of the grass.

"We are," they chimed together. They were so sickly in love, and I was so happy for them.

"Good," I said as I turned my head back to look at them, smiling before continuing walking towards the lake.

After a short ten-minute stroll, we were finally there. I laid the picnic blanket that was hooked through the handles of the basket out onto the decked pier. As I sat down, I let out a happy sigh overlooking the crystal-clear lake. There were a couple of row boats and oars sitting neatly inside them. I wanted to go on one with Xavier. Maybe I could plan it, make it a little date? I was interrupted when Mabel called me.

"Huh, sorry?" I asked as I looked at her grinning with her cute heart-shaped face. Her smile was infectious.

"Are you okay?" she asked as she reached for a breadstick from the basket.

"I am, I really am." I nodded, grabbing my own breadstick and nibbling on it.

"I'm glad," she said. "Xavier seems happy too."

"He is. We are." I nodded again. That melted me, my inner-self smiling so wide and hugging herself as the thought he was happy with me.

"Have you seen your parents much, Royal?" Christopher asked.

"I see them once a week, especially now I can drive. I don't feel so entrapped. Even though I wasn't actually trapped to begin with..." I trailed off as I looked back out to the lake.

"Well, you were, he never let you go, did he?" Christopher piped up. I felt my temper creeping in.

"If I had wanted to have escaped, I would have. I just didn't know if I really wanted to." I tried to make it right, defend him, defend myself.

"I don't believe you, Royal," he said deadpan, his lips pressing into a thin line.

"Don't believe what?" I heard Xavier's voice before I saw him. He was stood behind me, his hand gripping my shoulder. Christopher and Mabel's eyes travelled up to look at him. I couldn't help the small grin that was coming over my face, my lips curling slightly at the corners before twisting them and nibbling the inside of my mouth to stop myself.

Christopher fiddled with his shirt collar, his face sheen with sweat even though it wasn't hot, his skin turning slightly crimson.

"Nothing," Christopher said quietly, his eyes dropping from Xavier, his head bowing to look at his lap. My eyes flew to Mabel who was looking at Christopher, and I couldn't work out if she felt sorry for him or felt disappointed in him.

"Mind if I join you?" Xavier asked, his voice soft but still with a hint of abruptness to it.

"Of course not," I chimed as I scooted along the picnic blanket to make space for him. "You weren't at work long."

"I know, it was only a small matter I had to deal with. All fixed. Plus, I wanted to get home to my girl." He smiled as he leaned in, kissing me on the cheek. I blushed; I would never tire of how he made me feel.

"You two are cute," Mabel said softly. "Look, we are going to leave you two to it. Royal, we will catch up one evening, maybe just the two of us?" she suggested, firing a dagger-look at Christopher as he stood up, brushing himself down. He didn't say bye, didn't even acknowledge me or Xavier. That was fine. If he wanted to act like a child that was fine. I didn't know what his problem was. I thought we were okay. Obviously not.

"Yes, that will be lovely," I replied to Mabel, standing myself and hugging her. "What's his problem?" I whispered as we longed our hug out.

"Not a clue," she whispered back. "If I find out, I'll let you know," she said as she pulled away from me. "Enjoy you two." She smiled. "Bye, Xavier." She walked past us and into the distance. I let out a sigh of relief.

"I think little Christopher is still pining for you," Xavier said as he popped a grape into his mouth. I rolled my eyes, shaking my head from side to side softly, a little smirk on my face.

"I don't think he is. He is with Mabel." I shrugged, looking behind as I watched Mabel run after him.

"He may be, but even so, I think he is," he said as he finished his mouthful. "Anyway, enough about him. I don't want to speak about him anymore." His voice was muffled as he wrapped his arms around me, pushing me back so he was laying over me.

"Neither do I." My voice was quiet as I looked up at him, pushing his floppy blonde hair away from his beautiful face. I loved his eyes. I fell into them so deeply, never wanting to be pulled out.

"Good," he mumbled before he covered my lips with his. I felt the electric sparking through me, coursing through my veins like the blood that pumped through them.

Our kiss was only soft, light and quick. I whimpered at the loss of him, pouting.

"Oh, angel, don't pout." He laughed as he pushed himself off of me. "Are we going to eat? Or otherwise all this food will go to waste."

"I'm not hungry," I stated, annoyed that my belly rumbled at that moment.

"Red, don't lie." He let out a throaty laugh, tipping his head back. It was my favourite sound. Seeing Xavier so free, light and happy made my heart sing. I felt like I was walking on cloud nine knowing that I made him feel like this.

"Fine," I moaned, rolling my eyes and dragging the basket towards us.

We sat amongst light chatter as we ate, the food was delicious. Sandwiches, scones, clotted cream and jam. Plus strawberries and grapes, cured meat, breadsticks and a range of dips.

I sat back, my hand cradling my food bloat as I shook my head at Xavier when he offered me a strawberry.

"I am so full," I huffed, feeling uncomfortable. I groaned as I tried to move, but I was exhausted even thinking about it.

"You look so hot with a little bump," Xavier admitted. I laughed.

"It's bloat, Xavier, nothing hot about it." I shook my head, still laughing.

"I know." He nodded as he put the strawberry in his mouth, slowly, licking his lips after. I couldn't deny the burn that was deep inside my belly. I clamped my legs together to dull the ache that he made me feel. His voice interrupted me.

"But I can't wait to get you pregnant, carrying my baby." He smiled as he wrapped his hands around me and pulled me towards him.

"Slow down." I laughed. "Let's just take one step at a time, yeah?" I asked a little taken aback.

"We are, but I am just talking about what is inevitable. You will be pregnant with my baby and I can't wait." His beautiful face lit up, his eyes glistening. I didn't want to break his little bubble that he had created, but the anxiety was rising quickly through me.

I needed to stop him, the thought of having a baby scared me, crippled me. I crawled forward, climbing onto his lap and wrapping my legs around his back as my arms hung round his neck.

"What you doing?" Xavier raised his eyebrows, his eyes alight and his voice a little shocked.

"Shut up and kiss me." I breathed as he did just that. He kissed me. It was heated, hot, passionate. Our mouths were over each other's as if it was the only way to breathe. To fill our lungs.

His hands came up to cradle my face as he pulled away.

"Stop. Or I'll have to take you right here, right now," he growled at me. I dropped my head, my eyes fluttering closed as I tried to catch my breath.

"Spoil sport," I muttered before giving him a big smile. I pulled myself off of him reluctantly and started walking to the end of the decked pier. I looked over my shoulder at him, enticing him forward with my finger. He stood and stalked over to me, his hands in his pocket. His gorgeous eyes glistened under the low afternoon sun.

"Let's go out on the boat," I said, excitement lacing my voice. "I was going to arrange a date afternoon for us to do it, but seeing as we are both here now, why not?" I turned to look at him.

"Why the hell not." He smiled as he bent down in front of me, grabbing the rope that the small row boat was anchored too. He pulled it in, standing and holding my hand so I could step into the boat with his support. Once I was in, he took a long step before sitting down opposite me. He leant across, unhooking the rope and throwing it onto the pier as he sat back, grabbing the oars and starting to row. I closed my eyes for a moment, listening to nothing but the soft song of the birds in the trees and the sounds of the water hitting the oars.

"Enjoying this, princess?" I heard him ask, my eyes hesitantly opening.

"Oh, I am." I nodded. "Very much so." My voice was quiet, a mutter. I closed my eyes again. A few moments of silence passed us, when I heard him let out a heavy weight bearing sigh.

"What's wrong?" I asked as I snapped my head forward, my eyes pinned to him.

"I don't want you to abdicate the throne." His jaw clenched tightly, which I had come to realise he did every time he was uncomfortable.

"Why?" I asked, slightly confused. I kissed goodbye to being a queen as soon as he took me.

"Because it's your path. You were born to be a queen, born to be a leader." He sighed again. "You weren't born to be a prisoner." His voice was hushed, just a little over a whisper.

"I'm not a prisoner," I defended him.

"But you were."

"Xavier," I breathed out, my chest feeling constricted all of a sudden. "I don't want to be queen. I want to be with you, only you. Always."

"And you will be with me, but as a queen," he said a little more forcefully.

I wanted to argue back, but it was pointless. I wasn't going to be queen. I was going to abdicate; I just wouldn't tell him.

He took me, knowing full well what he was doing. Now I had made my choice. And my choice was to stay with Xavier.

The tension was thick, which I didn't like. It made me feel heavy, an unbearable weight crushing down on me.

"Red." His husky voice pulled me from my hypnotic state.

"What?" I asked, exasperated.

"Don't be like that," he pleaded, his eyes narrowed.

"I'm not being like anything. You have no right to tell me what to do. It's my choice, my life. End of discussion," I said bluntly, pressing my lips into a thin line as I crossed my arms across my chest. We sat in silence for a few minutes before he puffed his broad chest out.

"I'm sorry, I just want what's best for you," he said.

"What's best for me is you. As long as I have you in my life, I'll be complete." My throat was tight, my voice small.

"Okay," he said defeated.

"Okay?" I asked him, checking if he was just saying it to silence me.

"Yes, I promise." He dropped the oars, shuffling himself forward off the small bench before placing his hands on my knees, his face close to mine as he pecked my lips. I instantly melted against him, shuffling myself forward towards him. I wanted to be as close as possible.

His weight shifted slightly which caused the boat to start rocking gently. I panicked, pushing him away as I stood up.

"Xavier, stop it from rocking," I begged, the panic creeping up my throat.

"I will, sit down, Red," he said as he lunged forward to grab my arm to pull me down but all that did was cause the boat to start rocking more, and I tried to steady myself, to lower myself so I could grab on to the sides, but it was too late. Xavier shot up, stepping to the side of me to balance me which caused the boat to lean to the side, my balance completely gone and throwing me over into the cold, icy lake. I went completely under, panic rising in my chest as I heard his voice calling me. I pushed through the water's surface, gasping. His eyes were wide, his hand gripping onto the edge of the boat, the other holding onto the oar before he broke out into a wicked, deep, throaty laugh. At that moment, I wanted to pull him overboard with me, but I knew it wouldn't have happened. I tried to hold my own laughs in as I swam over towards the edge of the boat, my arms hanging over.

"Help me up before I pull you in as well," I threatened. I paddled and watched as he pulled his suit jacket off, taking his shirt off, exposing his beautiful chest and stomach. My mouth watered. He was delectable.

"Try it, angel, I dare you," he teased as he crouched down, leaning over to help me up. As soon as my arm was gripped to the top of his arm, I pulled him down with me, both of us crashing under the water. I broke to the surface, this time it was me laughing. I couldn't hold it anymore. I was frozen, but the coldness soon left as soon as I saw his hazy eyes moving towards me.

"Oh, Royal, baby, what have you done?" He scowled playfully before he wrapped his arms around my waist, pulling me into him and kissing me. My tongue invaded his mouth, caressing his tongue slowly. He groaned, the sound sending a bolt straight through me and down to my core.

"As much as I want to stay kissing you, I am fucking freezing. We can continue this back at the house." He winked at me as he grabbed onto the edge of the boat, pulling it towards us. He let go of me before his hands were on my bum, pushing me up, my arms pulling me into the boat. The soft breeze blew, causing me to shudder. It was so cold.

I held my hand out for Xavier, but he was already half pulled up into the boat.

"Why didn't I think to bring a blanket?" I said through chattering teeth.

"Because we didn't expect to go for a brisk, ice-cold swim." He laughed as he pulled me into his lap.

"Take your top off," he muttered.

"No! Not in the middle of the lake, what if someone sees?" I blushed.

"No one can see us, just take it off, will you?" He growled.

I rolled my eyes, grabbing the bottom hem of my soaked top and pulling it over my head. He reached behind him, giving me his white shirt. I slipped it on, doing the buttons up. It sat just under my bum.

"Jeans off, you'll catch your death." He sighed. I didn't argue, just done as he said.

I undid the top button of my skinny jeans as I pulled them down, taking twice as long because they were stuck to me.

"Much better," he cooed as he sat me on the little seat opposite him.

"What about you?" I asked confused, my eyebrows pulling, looking at his goose-bump-covered skin.

"I'm okay. As long as your warm, I'm warm." He smiled at me as he started rowing towards the decked pier. I was grateful to be getting off the boat. I watched as he looped the rope round the front of the boat, anchoring it before stepping off, then taking my hand and helping me off. I turned around, reaching down and grabbing my pile of soaked clothes. I watched as he sat down on the picnic blanket, laying down and masking his eyes from the low afternoon sun. He grabbed his black suit jacket, pulling it round his body to give himself something dry to wear.

"You look hot," I said silkily as I nibbled the inside of

my mouth.

He winked at me, pulling his lip in-between his teeth. I pushed myself onto my knees before crawling over towards him. I moved in-between his legs, laying down over him as I hovered my lips over his. My eyes watched his breathing as it fastened, I felt smug. I loved how I affected him so easily.

"I hope you're not being a tease, Royal," he whispered against my lips.

"Me?" I giggled then shook my head. "No, never." My fingertips glided down his torso, skimming along the waistband of his soaked jeans. My fingers continued as I felt his bulge growing against his jeans. I rubbed gently, causing a deep throaty groan from him which turned me on even more than I already was. He leant up, pushing me back onto my knees as he grabbed my wrist. Shaking his head, his eyes were heavy and hazy, full of want and desire. He let go of my hand then placed his hands on my waist, pulling me down onto him, legs either side.

"I'm going to fuck you, right here, right now, in my shirt. Because, Royal, you are mine and I can fuck you wherever I want." He groaned as his lips grazed across my neck then nipped at my earlobe which caused me to let out a moan. He moved his left hand in-between my legs, his fingers running up and down my folds. His touch was gentle, hardly touching me but it was affecting me like it had never affected me before.

I dropped my head back as his mouth was on my neck, kissing and trailing his lips down between my breasts before opening a few of the buttons to my shirt. He pulled the front of the shirt open, exposing me as his mouth covered my hardened nipples. He sucked, licked and popped it out of his mouth before he continued his tongue over to my other one, carrying out the same glorious torture. I felt my knickers dampen and saw the smirk on his face.

I lifted myself up, my hungry hands unbuttoning his jeans. He shimmied them down his thighs and stopped just under his knee. I stood up, looking down at him, not breaking my contact for a second as I lifted his shirt up, hooking my fingers in the side of my thong and pulling it down, skimming it over my thighs, bending slightly to take them off my ankles. I stood back up slowly, my thong hanging from my finger as I hovered it over him. I smirked before dropping it into his open hand. I clenched myself as he brought them to his nose, inhaling deeply before his hands were on my bum, pulling me closer towards him. His face was level with my pelvis, and I went to lower myself, but he stopped me, shaking his head. His hand glided up the inside of my thigh slowly, too slowly before he slipped two fingers into me. He pumped them slow and deep, not changing his speed. The ache that was in my stomach was so prominent. I moaned out, his eyes watching me as he continued. He edged me closer to him, his mouth on me, kissing the front of me before his tongue stroked my most intimate part, his tongue flicking across my clit. His hands were holding me firmly in place, gripping the backs of my bare thighs.

"Xavier, stop," I moaned as I fisted his hair, my voice laced with lust.

He broke away for just a moment. "Not a chance, angel," he growled before his mouth was over me again.

I felt the delicious build up bubbling in my stomach, my legs beginning to tremble. I felt his smile on me, pulling away sharply as he pulled me down forcefully on top of him. The feel of his erection underneath me was more than enough to make me come. I moved my hips back and forth, grinding on him, needing the friction. I wrapped my fingers round the front of his boxers, releasing him. I licked my lips, my eyes wide as I took him in my hands. I held him, lining him up underneath me before slowly taking all of him. The delicious feeling of him stretching me was too much. I had to stop myself from coming, he hadn't even moved.

I continued to grind my hips over him slowly, taking my time and enjoying every second of him. He met my movements, his hips rocking up into me, hitting my sweet spot over and over again. He stayed at the same speed, torturously slow but I needed it slow, I wanted it slow.

His breath was ragged, my moans raspy as I felt my walls clamping around him. The sheen of sweat that lay over both of us, the scent of us together was too consuming. I stilled my hips as he rocked himself into me one last time, hitting me deep. I couldn't stop the wave that came crashing over me, my orgasm ripping through me and hitting me at full speed. My legs were shaking, my head falling forwards before I tipped it back as I continued to ride out my sweet release. I heard him grunt as he hit into me once more, finding his own high as he came inside me. He wrapped his arms around me, pulling me closer to him and resting his head on my chest, my heart racing in his ear as I cradled his head, my neck craned as I placed a kiss on the top of his head.

"I love you, Xavier," I muttered into his thick blonde hair.

"I love you too, angel."

Chapter Twenty

We spent the evening snuggled up on the sofa, under a warm blanket whilst watching, *Breakfast at Tiffany's*. I loved this film, the thought that nothing could go wrong at Tiffany's. Holly felt safe, warm and most importantly at home. This is how I felt with Xavier. He was my safe place, my warmth, my home. My eyes were fighting to stay open, I hated sleep. Because in my sleep I felt like we were separated, even though he invaded my dreams, he was just a fantasy, a mirage.

I felt my head nod, my eyes fluttering open for a moment.

"Angel, let's get you to bed. Come," he cooed softly, standing up which made me sit up. I sighed.

"But I don't want to go to sleep," I protested.

"Tough." He winked as he turned the tele off then strolled over to me. I took a moment to appreciate just how handsome he was.

Chiselled, strong jaw. Beautiful eyes, one blue, one brown. His caramel-blonde hair was thick and styled to perfection, pushed back away from his face, his plump lips sitting perfectly in his blonde beard. It wasn't an overly long beard and stopped just past his chin.

"What you looking at?" he asked.

"My life," I muttered, smiling softly as I fell back into the plush sofa.

"Your life?" He shook his head as his eyes narrowed on me, a look of confusion on his face as his brows knitted together.

"Yes." I nodded as I stood up and wrapped my arms around his body, squeezing him as hard as I could. I felt his lips on the top of my head, him inhaling my scent which made me swoon.

"I'm still confused, Red," he muttered into my hair. I rolled my eyes then pulled back from him as I looked up at his beautiful face.

"It's you, Xavi, you're my life," I whispered. I saw his eyes glisten, a flicker of love shooting through them. His hands came up to my face, holding either side of my cheeks before he kissed me softly, tentatively before he pulled away. His head dropped, his eyes closed, his breathing slowed.

"I don't deserve you," he whispered to me, his eyes still closed.

"Of course you do," I argued back against him. I felt lost as he dropped his hands from my face. I stepped back a moment, looking at him. This was the first time he wasn't wearing a suit. He had tight-fitted charcoal tracksuit bottoms on with a fitted white tee that gripped his muscular arms and stomach.

"Royal, please," he pleaded silently, his eyes looked haunted, broken as they flicked up to look at me. My heart started thumping, my blood running cold through my veins. I didn't know what was happening, where he was going with this.

"I have demons, haunting me every single day. I can't rid myself of them. No matter what I do." He sighed as he stepped towards me. "Then I finally got you, the light that I so desperately seeked, the light to my soul." His lips twitched, one side curling into a grin before his lips pressed back into a thin line. "It's been a long time since I've been me. And when you came along, you made me feel things I hadn't felt for a long time, I felt love. Warmth. Compassion. But all it takes is one slip, one moment of darkness to throw me straight back into my own hell."

I took his face in my hands, clasping onto him as I looked deep into his eyes.

"Xavier, you deserve me. You are the most deserving man I have ever met. Okay, sure, things didn't start off great between us, but that's because we were fighting against our souls. Fighting against what was meant to be."

I hadn't realised but I had a tear falling down my cheek. I let out a small laugh. "Has this got to do with a few weeks ago?" I asked. I needed to ask, I just didn't know whether now was the right time to have mentioned it.

He didn't say anything, he just stared at me. His jaw clenched; his breathing harsh through his nose.

"Care to explain?" he snapped.

I was taken aback by his callous tone.

"The other night... Well, a few weeks ago, I woke and you weren't in the bed." I stopped for a moment as I watched him. His eyes hooded, glaring as if he was looking straight through me. He didn't say anything, just balled his fists by his side.

"I heard you talking to someone... I heard you talking to Xander," I rushed out the last bit, my heart was hammering in my chest.

I watched as his jaw twitched, his whole body tensing as he heard the name rip through his soul.

"I didn't mean to eavesdrop, I was just coming to find you... Then I didn't want to interrupt, so I came back to bed." My voice was little as I was trying to explain, not that I needed to explain, he knew exactly what I was talking about. He didn't need to say anything, his body did it all for him.

His breathing became rushed, ragged, his veins popping in his forearms where he was clenching his fists so tight.

"Talk to me, Xavier," I begged. "Please."

"I don't want to talk," he growled at me, his dark eyes penetrating through me.

"But..." I stammered.

"I said I don't want to talk!" he shouted at me, his voice echoing around the room. He stepped towards me, his breath hot, heavy. I flinched, throwing my hands up over my head, panic crashing through me. His face changed; his jaw unclenched. I saw the disappointment in his eyes, but it was too late.

I walked towards the door, not giving him another look when I flinched, the sound of glass shattering making me jump. My face whipped to the side of me, a broken vase lay in pieces on the floor, the roses askew on the carpet. My eyes slowly moved from the vase to him.

His eyes were wide, his fists unclenched, his shoulders sagging.

"Royal..." he stammered.

"Save it, Xavier. I'm done," I said as I walked out the door.

I ran as fast as I could to get to my room, bursting through the door and closing it behind me. I pushed a dining room chair up underneath the door handle, so he couldn't get in and then locked the interconnecting door which led to his room.

I fell to the bed, shock pulsing through me as my hands started to tremble.

I knew he wouldn't have hurt me. I had just never seen him so angry, so disconnected from reality.

The way he tensed completely as soon as I mentioned his name. *Xander.*

It's a name I haven't heard for five years, a name that used to be so prominent in my life, until one day his name became silenced.

Never to be spoken about again.

We weren't close, far from it. But we were acquaintances. He was polite, kind, friendly. A perfect suitor. A suitor I used to wish would have been picked for me. I would have pushed my luck with Christopher, knowing full well it would have been forbidden. I craved the simple life, to marry someone of my choosing. But when you are royalty, you don't get to choose. They get chosen for you. I sighed, shaking my head and letting my hair loose. My head felt hazy, tired, heavy.

I looked down at my outfit, I was still wearing one of Xavier's T-shirts. After the boat incident, we came back to the house to get dried off, he didn't want me out of his sight, so he grabbed the first thing he could for me to wear. It made me smile.

I clenched at the T-shirt, above my heart, feeling it pound against my chest before bringing the material to my nose and inhaling deeply. The scent of him intoxicated me, my soul getting her fix from him. The smell of mint and linen swept through me, making me homesick in an instant. That's the only way I could describe the feeling. I was homesick from not being with him. From not being next to his side like I had been for the last few weeks. And I missed him.

But how can you miss someone you just left? He made me heavy, but I made him lighter in some twisted sort of way.

I fell back onto the bed, my fingers pulling at the hem of the T-shirt, my mind doing overtime. I wanted to know what had happened, what had triggered his reaction.

I slammed my hands down in frustration on the bed covers, annoyed with myself, annoyed with him. I sat up, padding to the bathroom to wash my face and brush my teeth. The tiredness that I felt mere minutes ago had now suddenly vanished. I felt like I still had adrenaline pumping through me.

I walked back into the bedroom, the silence deafening now. I forgot what it was like to be alone, to be a prisoner.

I sat on the bed, knotting my fingers together, my eyes pinned to the door.

I thought he was going to come for me.

I thought he was going to burst through my door.

I thought he was going to beg me to forgive him.

I thought he was going to say sorry.

But he didn't.

I wanted him to come for me.

I wanted him to burst through my door.

I wanted him to beg me for forgiveness.

I wanted him to say sorry.

He didn't come.

But I still sat, I still waited, and he still disappointed me.

Chapter Twenty-One

Xavier

I stood frozen, watching her walk out the door and leave me. I wanted to go after her, chase her, but I couldn't.

My legs were heavy and anchored to the floor.

I should have gone after her.

But I didn't. I let her go.

I couldn't control the feeling of rage that came over me. I was like a volcano waiting to erupt. And I did, as soon as she mentioned his name.

Of course she was going to question me at some point. She knew who he was. How stupid of me to think I would have been able to hide this from her.

I was such a fool.

I was finally able to move, finally able to free myself from my paralysis. I walked slowly over to the broken glass from the vase, dropping to my knees and picking it up. I didn't care if I cut myself, I deserved it. I wanted to feel the pain. I wanted to feel the release from the heaviness that was crushing my chest. I picked up a shard, my eyes narrowing on it, twisting it in my fingers to get a good look at it. Completely clear but full of imperfections. Just like me.

Imperfect.

Ugly.

Callous.

Vicious.

A monster.

A beast.

I hovered the shard over my throat, contemplating just slicing it slowly across, feeling the blood leave me. But as soon as I made contact, flashes of her beautiful face plagued me, making me stop. I shook my head, dropping the piece of glass and standing up and walking to the stairs. Leaving the destruction behind me.

Chapter Twenty-Two

Royal

I sat up in my bed, staring at the wall. It felt like it had been hours, but it hadn't. Time moved so slow without him. I didn't know what to do.

I let out a sigh when my eyes widened, the sound of footsteps approaching outside my room. My heart skipped in my chest; he had come to make things right. I bolted up from the bed, a light knock sounding on the bedroom door. I stood for a moment, trying to collect my thoughts and slow my breathing down. I moved the chair away from the bedroom door. I gripped the handle, pulling it open, my eyes widening, my throat tightening when I saw who was standing on the other side. It wasn't Xavier.

It was Alan.

His slimy, greased-back-hair was saturated in gel.

His weasel-like appearance made my stomach turn in an instant. His yellow teeth were on show as he smiled a wicked grin.

"Missed me, princess?" he asked as he stepped towards me, readjusting his leather jacket.

"Go away," I said boldly, crossing my arms against my chest, trying to guard the door.

"Oh, don't be like that. Were you expecting Xavier?" he snarled. "He isn't coming, sweetheart, don't flatter yourself. I think I saw him go into his office with a couple of pretty blondes."

My heart dropped into my stomach before shattering into a thousand pieces.

No, he wouldn't have.

"You're lying," I stammered over my words as I glared at him.

"Why would I make it up?" He shrugged as he stood directly in front of me.

"Prove it," I chastised him.

"Fine." He winked as he pulled out his phone and showed me a picture of Xavier, walking into his office with said blondes.

My heart obliterated right there, a thousand shards piercing inside of me. My stomach knotted and tightened before my chest crushed.

I felt the tears threatening, but I wouldn't cry. Not in front of him.

"Leave," I whispered, wrapping my arms even tighter around myself, protecting myself.

"Can't do that, *Red*." He used the nickname that Xavier calls me, curling his tongue as the word slipped out.

"Please, Alan, just go," I begged, stepping back inside the door frame and closing the door. Alan pushed his foot in the way, the door stopping on his heavy black boot. I moved behind the door, trying to shield myself from him.

"Told you, I can't do that." He smirked as he pushed the door open, taking me out with it as I fell onto the floor, the door hitting against the wall.

I scurried back on my hands and bum before grabbing the dressing table to pull myself up. But it was no use, he was over me, breathing ragged before he grabbed a clump of my hair and dragged me up. He marched me over to the bed, pushing me down with force. I whimpered out, panic rising through me, bile bubbling away in my stomach. His smell made my stomach turn, he was vile.

"Now, you are going to take it like a fucking big girl. I am going to fuck you until you don't remember who Xavier is. I'll brand you, make you mine." He growled at me as he pushed his knee between my legs and forced them open before he hovered over me, his lips so close to mine. My heart was erratic, fear was coursing through me. I needed to get him off me, I needed to hurt him. My eyes darted around the room, looking for something to hurt him with. But it was no use. Anything that I could use was too far away.

"Do you want to know why Xavier reacted the way he did when you asked about Xander?" he whispered as he started to undress himself. He pulled out a pair of handcuffs from the back of his black jeans, leaning over me again and grabbing my arms as he pulled them above my head. He cuffed one of my wrists tightly then dragged me up the bed, so he could wrap it around the small spindles that were in my headboard. He pushed my other hand through the other cuff, closing it shut tightly. The cuffs nipped at my skin. I cried out; without my hands I was useless.

"He killed him. Killed him because he couldn't bear the thought of you being with Xander and not him. He always wanted you, but when he saw you were possibly being suited with his brother, he had to act. So that night when you last saw Xander at the ball, he took him out to the forest, shot him through the temple, blowing his brains to smithereens."

I gasped, a shiver running down my spine. No, he wouldn't have. He couldn't have.

"Bullshit," I said through gritted teeth.

"Oh, baby, no. Not bullshit. He is a fixer, remember? He *fixes* things. He has people who work for him, who can make people disappear. He made it look like a suicide. No questions asked." Alan grinned down at me, he was now completely naked, kneeling on my bed. I couldn't even look at him.

"Alan, please don't do this," I cried out, pleading with him. My eyes closed shut.

"Oh, but I want to." He laughed as his voice got closer. His hand was on my bare thigh, pushing Xavier's T-shirt up to reveal everything. I wasn't wearing any underwear due to getting changed after the boat. He reached behind him, pulling out a gag ball. He pushed the ball into my mouth and I shook my head, trying to stop him, but I couldn't. He grabbed my chin tightly and held me in place as he pushed the ball into my mouth, making me gag before doing the strap up behind my head.

"Perfect," he snarled.

I tensed, completely clammed up. I closed my legs, squeezing them together as tight as I could when I heard him growl, both of his hands now on my knees as he forced my legs open, laying himself in-between them.

I was covered in a cold sweat, silent tears escaping my eyes as his hand wrapped around my throat.

"I am going to fuck you, then I'm going to strangle you," he threatened as a sickening grin spread across his face.

I don't know what made me open my eyes, but I did, and there, in the doorway, was Xavier.

His eyes narrowed on Alan, his jaw clenched tightly,

his hands fisted by his sides. His eyes moved to mine, and I could see the sheer pain in them as he brought his finger to his lips for me to be quiet. My eyes widened when I felt Alan's hand down there, grabbing me as his mouth came next to my ear. "Such a tight little pussy, obviously Xavier doesn't know how to fuck you properly. I am going to ruin you," he said as he started laughing like a menace. He crawled back, looking down at himself as he started fisting up and down, reared up and ready to take me, when Xavier sprinted from the door, grabbing Alan round the back of the throat and throwing him on the floor like he was a ragdoll. Xavier was on top of him, punching him, blow after blow.

I watched in horror as Alan's nose exploded, blood covering his face, but all he did was smile at Xavier, which only spurred him on more.

I screamed through the gag, writhing on top of the covers, hoping it would loosen the cuffs around my wrists, but it didn't, it only made them worse.

"I'm going to kill you," Xavier said through gritted teeth as he wrapped his hands around Alan's neck.

"What, like you killed Xander?" Alan spat back at him. I saw Xavier freeze, his hands tightening round Alan's neck... I thought he was going to snap it in two.

I screamed out again, hoping to get Xavier to look at me and snap out of it.

He stopped, his grip loosening on Alan's throat as he

sat back, his head turning slowly to face me. I saw the shock and horror that consumed him, and most of all, guilt. He dropped his head, which is when Alan took his opportunity. His hand flew up around Xavier's throat as he pushed him back off of him. He pinned him to the floor. His arm swung back behind him as he threw his fist forward, connecting with Xavier's jaw. I screamed; tears were streaming down my face as Alan hit him again. It was like Xavier had given up, and just when I thought he was just taking it, his hand came up, grabbing Alan's balled fist, twisting it back which caused Alan to cry out. Xavier pushed him off of him, standing and dragging Alan up to his feet, pulling him closer to him as he headbutted Alan. I watched as he fell to the ground like a sack of potatoes, landing in a crumpled heap, out cold. I felt relief sweep over me. Xavier stood over him, spitting blood from his mouth onto him. His chest was heaving up and down fast as he took a moment to catch his breath, his eyes moving to mine. It was as if he forgot I was here for a moment.

"Red." He gasped as he ran over to me, pushing my tee down to cover me, pulling me forwards and undoing the gag from the back of my head, pulling it off of me. I coughed and gasped.

"Are you okay?" I asked crying, I couldn't stop.

"Baby, I'm fine. It's you I am worried about. Are you okay?" he asked as he cupped my face, rubbing the tears away with the pad of his thumb.

I didn't answer, just nibbled on my bottom lip before shaking my head. I wasn't alright. Not one bit.

"Let me find the keys," he said exasperated as he looked at the cuffs. He pushed himself off of the bed and dropped to his knees as he went through Alan's clothes. I heard the small clink of the keys and let out a sigh of relief as he walked back over to me, undoing the cuffs. He held my arms gently as he held onto them and slipped the cuffs off. His brows furrowed at the cuff marks on my delicate wrists. He brought my hands to his lips, kissing both wrists, his eyes flicking up to mine. My heart broke even more, the look on his face was heart-breaking. I could see the sadness consuming him, the guilt eating him alive.

"Let me deal with this piece of shit, then I'll be back, okay, angel?"

I nodded. I couldn't speak. I was trying to process everything that had happened.

But most of all, I needed to come to terms that Xavier murdered his own brother.

Chapter Twenty-Three

We sat on the sofa, I was snuggled under a large blanket, cradling a hot cup of tea. My hands had finally stopped shaking, the shock starting to subside.

We hadn't spoken, Xavier was just stroking my arm. I knew we had to speak, but I just couldn't muster the words.

As if he could read my mind, he spoke, his voice quiet and soft. "Ask me."

I fluttered my lashes down, trying to focus on my short breaths, I needed to calm myself down before we spoke. I flicked my lashes up, my eyes on him as I stared at him. I swallowed, then took a mouthful of my tea to try and rid myself of the dryness in my throat. I placed the cup back in my lap, stumbling over the words when they just ricocheted out.

"What happened?" I asked quietly. I didn't want to

ask what happened, I wanted to ask, *"Why did you murder your twin brother?"* But I just couldn't. I wanted to give him the benefit of the doubt and the chance to explain his side of things.

"With Xander?" he said after a while of silence, letting out a deep breath.

I nodded.

"We never got along like you would expect twin brothers to…" His voice trailed off for a moment as he took a mouthful of his drink.

"I always watched you from a distance, we both did. He was the good, I was the bad. He was the light; I was the dark. He was the hero; I was the beast." He sighed. "I am trying to explain the best I can without ripping your heart out, angel."

I didn't say anything, just kept my eyes on him.

"I knew you were friends, but you weren't meant for each other. You were meant for me. I knew from the moment I saw you all those years ago, you were always meant to be mine. Xander kept telling me that he had heard that he was going to be picked as your suitor. That made me angry, because I knew that he would have been the right choice for you. But I couldn't let it go. We both got drunk one night, I confessed and told him that I had always liked you, that my soul yearned for you. That we were connected. You know you feel it too, Red." He squeezed my hand, giving me a little smile. I wanted to tell him that I felt it, so strongly. But I couldn't. I just listened.

"Anyway... We got drunk together the night before the ball on your sixteenth birthday, Xander was riling me up, telling me everything he couldn't wait to do with you. To finally be chosen to be your husband. But he didn't stop, he just kept on and on and on." I watched him drop his head, shaking it. "I'm truly disgusted with myself," he mumbled, his thoughts speaking out loud. A moment of silence passed, then he continued. "We got into a brawl, we threw a few fists at each other, and that's it. Well, so I thought. He had a shard of glass in his hand, he threw another punch but this time he sliced my face, hence the scar." I saw his shoulders sag, I could hear the pain in his voice, his eyes brimming with unshed tears.

"I told him to get out, I told him we were done, we were through. He stumbled out drunk, rambling on about how much of a fuck-up I was and how no one could ever love a beast like me. That I was savage, cruel." At that moment I took his hand in mine, it was my turn to squeeze his hand.

"Xavi," I whispered.

"Let me finish, please," he pleaded, his voice so terribly pained and tortured that he was ripping my heart out.

I nodded.

"Typically, Alan came through at that moment, asking what had happened. I still hadn't registered that I was bleeding that bad, I was just so angry and disheartened by what had happened. Once Alan had cleaned me up and stitched me, he got me a bottle of whiskey, wanting to know the ins and outs of a duck's arse." He let out a small laugh, I think the nerves were starting to hit him. "I was really drunk by this point, telling Alan how much easier my life would be without Xander in it, and that I would stand more of a chance with you if he was dead and out of my life for good. I said that if I was really as savage and cruel as people thought, I would have gone after him and ended his life." He sniffed, rubbing his eye of a stray tear. My heart was breaking, but at the same time, I was terrified.

"I don't remember much after that moment, just woke up with blood all over me. I was in my bed. I shot up to find Alan, who told me that I took Xander to the woods and shot him." I saw his face change, his eyes darting back and forth as if his eyes were trying to connect the pieces. The confusion was evident on his beautiful face. "But I made it seem like a suicide. But I knew he was lying, I knew I wouldn't have killed him, I *know* I didn't kill him. I don't know if it's a twin thing, but I felt so connected to him that I would never have been able to do it. I wouldn't have been able to pull the trigger. The grief and the heartbreak took over, and I vowed to never let my heart love again. I wasn't deserving of love; I didn't deserve someone to love me." He shook his head; his eyes were looking to his lap. "The days were all rolling into one, and I had no recollection of that evening. I started looking through the security camera's, when I found something. The night of Xander's murder, I was otherwise occupied." His eyes came to mine, and I could see the fear imbedded in them. "I was taking two blonde girls into my office, to try and calm down after my argument with Xander. I never left the house that night, I didn't kill him. I don't know why I was covered in blood, I just assumed it was from my cut on my face." He shrugged. "I live with the guilt every day, knowing it was me that made him end his life. This is why I don't like telling anyone. Honestly, if it wasn't for you, I would have taken my life as well. He should be here, not me. He should be loving you; you should be loving him. That's the way it was meant to be, like the fairy tales. The princesses always end up with the prince. The light ones. The princess doesn't fall for the beast. But you, you did. You fell for the beast, the monster." His voice was quiet now. He fell silent, his eyes searching back and forth from mine, waiting for me to speak.

"I'm sorry," was all I could manage. My throat was tight, constricted. My chest felt like an elastic band was around it, crushing it little by little.

"It's okay," he cooed. "I feel better telling you."

"Would you have told me if I hadn't heard you talking out loud to him?" I asked.

He sat silent for a moment, his eyes never leaving mine as he pondered his answer. "Yes."

"Really?" I asked hesitantly.

"Yes, Royal. Maybe not yet, but I would have in the near future." He brought my hand to his lips and placed a soft kiss on the back of it.

I was trying my best to get my head around everything he had just offloaded to me, but I couldn't help but feel angry, confused and sad. But I didn't know why.

I felt a wedge being pushed between us.

"Xavier..." I mumbled as I pulled my hand from his then stood. I knew I was going to destroy him, but I needed to do what was right for me. I needed to take a step back. I needed to leave.

His eyes were on me, his brows pulled together, little creases appearing on his forehead. My heart was breaking.

"I can't stay here anymore, I need to go, I need some time..." Before I could even finish my sentence, he was in front of me, his forehead pressed against mine.

"Angel, please. Don't leave me," he begged.

"I have to," I whispered, fighting back my own tears, the lump so big in my throat as I stepped away from him.

"No," he shouted out as he grabbed my arm and pulled me back to him. "I will fight... I'm sorry. I am so sorry. I am sorry for treating you the way I did. I'm sorry for making you unhappy and scared. Just, please, Royal...

Just please don't leave me. You said you wouldn't run, you promised me, you said you wouldn't leave me. You said you would grow old with me."

As soon as the last part of that sentence left his lips, my mind flashed back to the moment after the boathouse, this afternoon. So much had happened today, it felt nearly impossible that this was happening.

"I love you, Xavier, with everything I have," I told him.

"Not as much as I love you, angel." He smiled.

"I can't wait to watch our life, to watch our love story unfold, to grow old with you and remember all of this..."

The pain seared through me; I was obliterating him... I was obliterating myself.

"I know I did, but... I... I just can't do this, Xavier," I stuttered over the words. I pulled his hand off of my arm, trying to break him away from me. I started walking back, watching as he fell to his knees, his head tipping back. I stopped for a moment. I had torn him apart, like he was nothing more than a sheet of paper. His head snapped forward as he lunged himself towards me, his hands going around the top of my legs, clinging onto me tightly.

"Xavier, please," I cried out.

"Don't, no, Red. You can't." His voice was barely a whisper, his face broken, his eyes glistening. I had never seen him look so hurt and distraught. So broken.

"I can, and I am, Xavier." I gripped onto his hands around the back of my legs as I prised him off of me. It took all my might and strength to get him to let go, and he did. He fell onto all fours, tipping back onto his knees, completely broken and defeated. His head dropped forward, not looking at me again. I turned on my heel and walked out of the room, feeling completely empty. It took everything in me not to turn around and run back into his arms, to scoop him up and tell him I was not going to leave, when I heard his cry. It ripped through me like a thousand knives.

I had never heard pain in someone's voice until I heard his cry.

I had broken him.

Chapter Twenty-Four

Xavier

The pain seared through me.

She ran.

She left.

She promised.

I wasn't enough.

She was my light, my saviour, my everything.

Chapter
Twenty-Five

Royal

I ran as fast as I could to my room, pulling out my bags from under the bed and throwing as much as I could into the holdall. I don't know why I was rushing, he wasn't coming after me.

I had left him a broken man. Completely destroyed.

I zipped my bag up, grabbing my keys from the bedside unit as well as all of his handwritten notes before opening the door and fleeing down the stairs, opening the front door and unlocking my car.

I threw my bag into the boot before slamming it shut and sliding into the driver's side. I pushed the clutch down before turning the stalk, hearing the engine roar under me. I slipped it into first and sped off, not looking back. Each minute I was getting further, my heart was breaking that little bit more. All I could hear was his cry, it was echoing around my head, haunting me. I didn't want to think about it anymore, but I couldn't drown it out. I blasted music so loud until it felt like my ears were going to bleed, but it was no use.

I just wanted to get home.

I felt nervous as I pulled into the grounds of my parent's castle, parking the car outside the entrance. I was greeted by the two doormen, holding their hands out for my keys.

"I need to get my stuff," I said before they could talk.

"We will do it for you, your highness," one of them offered as they walked towards the boot.

"No, it's fine, thank you." I smiled softly as I opened the boot and grabbed my bag. I ran towards the stairs, my head snapping round when I heard the engine purr, my heart crushing, thoughts of Xavier plaguing me again.

I pushed them to the back of my mind as I opened the front door, dropping my holdall on the marbled floor. It took me a moment to register where I was. It didn't feel like home anymore; my home was with Xavi.

I looked up towards the stairs and saw Betty standing there, shock all over her face as she came running towards me, embracing me in a tight, motherly hug.

"What are you doing home? How did you get free?" she asked, clearly confused.

"He let me go, I told him I needed to go," I said

quietly, trying not to get upset.

"He let you go?" She shook her head a little.

"Yeah, he isn't a monster," I said defensively.

"But––"

"But nothing, Betty, don't assume." I scowled as I raised my eyebrows at her.

"Sorry, Royal." She dropped her head. "I'll take your bag to your room. Your parents are in the lounge," she said as she walked towards the stairs.

"Thank you." I smiled a fake smile as I started walking towards the lounge. I felt so anxious, I felt lost without Xavier, but I needed to put some distance between us. I needed to just think, and not get clouded by him.

I stopped outside the double white doors, taking a deep breath before I reached forward and slid the doors open, both my parents turning to look at me.

"Oh my God, Royal," my mum exclaimed as she stood from the sofa and ran over to me. "You're home," she said as she squeezed me tightly.

"I am," I said as I hugged her back.

"Are you home for good?"

"No." I smiled at her. "Just a few nights, I think. Is that okay?"

"Okay?" I heard my dad bellow as he came to stand next to me, and I couldn't help but notice how gaunt he looked, his eyes tired, his skin grey.

"Of course it is okay, Royal, darling, this is your home. This will *always* be your home," my dad said as he hugged me, my mum stepping to the side.

"Why are you home? Did that monster hurt you?" my dad snapped as he pulled away, both hands still firmly on the top of my arms as he looked me up and down.

"No, he didn't. And he isn't a monster," I snapped, my voice betraying me slightly as it began to shake. I couldn't stand people branding him a monster. He wasn't a monster. He was so much more; he was everything to me. I loved him.

"Then why?" my mother asked, her tone soft.

"I wanted to. I needed some time to myself." I nodded as I took a seat on the sofa, one of the servers handing me a cup of tea. "Thank you," I muttered to him as I brought the china tea cup to my lips, sipping and letting out a little moan in appreciation.

"Everything okay?" my mum asked, sipping her own tea and raising her eyebrows.

"Everything is fine," I reassured her. "Dad, are you okay?" I asked, I was more concerned about him than myself at the moment.

I saw my mum shoot my dad a worrying glare before she moved her eyes back to mine. "We are waiting on some tests; your father hasn't been feeling great lately." She sighed. "But we are just trying to keep positive, aren't we, darling?" she said as she looked at my father with adoration in her eyes.

"Yes, keeping positive," my dad repeated, his voice quiet, his expression vacant. His mind was clearly somewhere else.

"When will you hear back?" I asked as I placed my cup down on the side table next to me.

"Next couple of days I should hope," he grunted as he flicked the tele over to another channel.

"Okay, well, I will stay until you get your results, Dad," I said confidently before standing up.

"You don't need to do that, darling," my dad said in a hushed voice as he looked over at me.

"I know I don't, but I want to." I smiled at him as I walked towards my parents, giving them both a kiss on the cheek. "I am going up to bed, it's been a long night," I said as cheerfully as I could, even though on the inside I was completely and utterly broken into a thousand pieces.

As I wandered down the corridors to my bedroom, I couldn't help but feel homesick and empty. I missed Xavier so much. But I needed this, he needed this. It was a lot to take in, I just needed some time to digest it. It didn't help thinking that Xavier killed him because of what happened the night of their argument. I knew he hadn't killed him; he knew he didn't kill him but the doubt was still there, apparent in his conscious.

Once I was in my room, I closed the door and flopped down on my bed. My mind started replaying his conversation over and over again. Then it clicked. Xavier said that he was in his office with two girls. I shuddered at the thought of him being with anyone other than me. That was most likely the same image Alan showed me earlier this evening. He was playing me, playing Xavier. I started to worry, my skin prickling, but I knew everything was okay because Alan was taken care of.

It broke my heart knowing that he thought, if only a little bit, that he may have killed his brother. I knew I was doing the right thing by leaving him tonight, we both just needed some alone time. Everything was crushing down on me, an unbearable weight on my shoulders. I couldn't imagine what Xavier was feeling. I shook my head; I couldn't think about that now. I needed to sleep, I needed to try and quiet my mind.

I stripped off and washed the evening off of me under the flowing shower. I dried myself and towel-dried my hair before padding back into my room and grabbing shorts and a tee before diving under my covers. It wasn't until I was in bed that it hit me. The sobs left me, the pain that was piercing through my chest was unbearable. I had not only broken his heart in doing so, I had broken mine too.

***

I didn't know what time I fell asleep, but it must have been late as when my eyes opened, I felt like I had been asleep for barely a minute. I rubbed the sleep out of my eyes and threw the duvet back. The heaviness crashed down on top of me, the substantial weight in my chest was so present and thick, I wanted it to leave, but I knew the only way it would leave was to be back in Xavier's arms. But not yet. We needed to put the space between us, needed to focus and learn to live alone for a few days. He needed the time out; I needed the time out. We had become so self-absorbed in each other, living in one another's pockets that we had forgotten how to be apart, how to be alone. I freshened up, brushing my teeth and pulling my long red hair into a messy ponytail. I rummaged through my wardrobe, smiling at all my clothes in my wardrobe before grabbing a pair of jeans and a long-sleeved top. Once dressed, I made my way downstairs to be greeted by my parents who were sitting at the table, breakfast in front of them.

"You don't know just how much we have missed having breakfast with you." My mum smiled at me as I took my seat in-between them. "It's been so quiet and lonely without you." She sighed as she started tucking into her eggs, muffins and hollandaise sauce. My stomach grumbled, the last thing I had eaten was the picnic yesterday lunchtime, but it felt like it had been days.

I picked my knife and fork up and started dissecting my food, pushing most of it around the plate. I was hungry, I wanted food. But I felt too goddamn sick to eat it.

"What's wrong, Royal?" my father asked, his brows raising as he looked over at my full plate.

"I just feel off, it's just weird being back home." Even saying the word "home" left a bitter and sour taste in my mouth. I screwed my nose up, twisting my mouth as a wave of sweat came over me. "Can I have a glass of water, please?" I asked the young man standing against the wall.

"Certainly." He bowed his head slightly as he stepped forward and reached for the water on the table, pouring me a glass. I wanted to pour it myself, but I know I'm not allowed. Here, you are waited on hand and foot. I came to realise, I didn't like it anymore.

He handed me the glass of iced water, and I took a big mouthful, instantly feeling better. The man stepped back to his station by the wall as we continued to sit in silence.

Once breakfast was finished, I excused myself from the table and walked towards the back door. I wanted to feel the brisk autumn breeze on my skin. I wanted to feel the goose-bumps like I did whenever I was with Xavier and this was the only way I was going to get my fix. I strolled slowly towards the stables, the one thing I truly had missed about being here was the horses. I beamed as I walked towards my stunning white Andalusian horse. I called him Prince and snorted when I thought back. I named him that because I knew I could always choose him, and I would always have him.

"Hey, you," I cooed as I stood in front of his stable, rubbing my hand down his nose. "I missed you," I muttered as I kissed his nose.

He looked amazing. His long white mane was getting too long, I needed to trim it. I tacked him up before stepping into the stirrups and pulled myself up. I felt instantly relaxed as soon as I was sat in the saddle. I needed this, my mind needed this and so did my soul. I felt like I needed to cleanse myself completely before going home to Xavier.

I kicked my boots into his sides to get him to walk out of the stables, the air filling my lungs as we walked onto the rolling green grass. I couldn't help the smile that graced my face as I tightened my grip on the reins, nudging him with my boot again and going straight into a canter. This is what I needed.

I needed to feel free.

Chapter Twenty-Six

Xavier

She hadn't even been gone twenty-four hours, yet it felt like a lifetime. I was plunging back into darkness, back into hell. This was torture, the ache in my chest, the agony in my stomach was overwhelming. I couldn't eat, I couldn't sleep. I couldn't even cry anymore. I had nothing left to give. All I could do was drink myself into oblivion, to help numb the excruciating pain that was shredding through me. My heart ruptured in my chest, no longer full of love and hope. It was just dust now, sifting through my body, looking for an escape.

The same as me.

I just wanted to escape.

To leave this earth and no longer hurt.

Maybe that way, we would be back together again. Our souls finding one another again and interlinking with each other, never being able to break again for they loved each other, way before we did.

I took another swig, my eyes like slits, my vision blurred as I looked around the room at the mess. The room completely trashed, but I didn't just stop there. I tore every room apart we had ever been in together; I couldn't bear to be in there without her. I couldn't bear to be here, living, without her.

Chapter Twenty-Seven

Royal

The next few days passed surprisingly quick. We had just eaten lunch and I was due to go back out on Prince; it became my favourite thing to do. There wasn't a moment that went by without Xavier being on my mind, he was always on my mind. Completely imprinted on me.

I was brought back from my thoughts when Betty walked into the dining room with a grimace on her face.

"It's the doctor, your highness." Her voice was timid as she wheeled the phone next to my father. I felt anxious, my heart in my throat. I looked over at my mum, her hands were gripping the table napkin, her eyes on my dad the whole time. I volleyed my eyes back and forth between them, trying to read their faces. I could feel the tension in the room, it was so thick it was making me uncomfortable.

"I see," I heard my father's voice, low, deadpan. His

eyes flicked to my mum's, a flat line smile at her. He looked broken.

"Thank you, doctor," he muttered before placing the phone back down, Betty hovering round, waiting for him to speak. My father placed his hand on the table, his head was bowed. His other hand moved to his face as he pinched the bridge of his nose, exhaling loudly. He dropped his hand, his head tipping back before he looked deep into my mother's eyes. Betty stood by my side, her hand on my shoulder gripping tightly.

"It's not good," he stammered, tripping over his words.

"Patrick..." My mother's voice was hushed. She reached over, placing her hand over his.

"I have bowel cancer. It has spread to my lymph nodes and is in my bone's, darling, it'll be a matter of weeks," he rushed out. I could see the worry plastered all over his face. His frown lines were deep, his eyes glassy and wide as he stared at my mum with the most admiration and love I think I have ever seen. My mum was quietly sobbing, my father standing from his chair and wrapping his arms around her, comforting her in the best way he could. I sat frozen, my already battered and broken heart dropping into the pit of my stomach, nausea creeping up. I threw my hand to my mouth, trying to stop myself from being sick. It was no use, I pushed away from the table and ran towards the bathroom, falling to my knees and throwing up my lunch. Once my stomach was completely empty and the dry heaves stopped, I rolled back onto my knees before sitting against the wall. I was clammy and hot. I threw my head in my hands, the hot tears escaping my eyes and running down my cheeks before my hands absorbed them. My father was terminally ill. He wasn't going to recover from this. We had the best doctors money could buy, and still they couldn't save him.

How could I leave now? How could I abdicate the throne? This was my duty, as the king's daughter. My job and role were to become queen.

And that's exactly what I would do.

I would do justice to my father and make him proud.

***

That evening my father called for me to join him in the lounge. He was sitting in his favourite chair. It was highbacked and winged, covered in a mahogany leather. It was where he always told me about fairy tales and stories from his childhood. I used to sit and listen in awe, mesmerized by everything he told me. I felt the tears threatening, but I couldn't cry. Not in front of my father. But it was no use, as soon as I heard him call me, I couldn't hold them back.

"Royal, baby." He smiled as he held his arms out.

"Daddy." I sighed as I reached him, a single tear rolling down my cheek.

"Oh, my darling, please don't cry. Nothing is worth your tears, especially not me." He chuckled softly.

"Dad," I choked. "Don't," I said, sniffling before holding his hands.

"I want to talk to you, sit." His hand let go of mine as he ushered for me to sit next to him. I did, taking a glass of whiskey from him. I didn't even like whiskey, but I wasn't going to turn it down.

He then poured his own, placing his crystal decanter down on the table next to him, he brought his glass to his lips as he took a mouthful. I copied, my hand trembling. The whiskey burned my taste buds, then they exploded from the rich taste as it ran down my throat like pure silk.

"I have a matter of weeks left, if I'm lucky." His lips twisted one side as he smiled. "First of all, before I get into the nitty gritty of it all, I'm sorry." His head dipped, his eyes watching the swirling amber liquid in his glass.

"Sorry for what?" I asked confused as I tapped my finger on the side of my glass.

"For gambling you away," he said deadpan, no emotion in his voice whatsoever.

"It's fine," I mumbled.

"No, Royal, it's not fine. I'm nothing but a coward, I gave in. I couldn't stop, and I lost the most important thing to me. I lost you, I handed you over to that monster, that *beast*." My dad's face was a crimson red, his temper raging.

"Dad, calm down," I said softly, leaning forward and touching his hand. I felt the rage growing inside me at the words he used for Xavier, but this wasn't the right time to voice it. "Please, forgive yourself... I forgive you." I smiled sweetly, my head tipping to the side slightly as I gazed at him. "Plus, Xavier has been wonderful, Dad. It took us some time, we are both head strong and fiery, but we work." I sighed, blissfully happy. "I love him," I muttered, watching my dad's jaw drop open, his eyes wide.

"Love?" he snarled, narrowing his eyes and pulling his head back, looking at me with pure confusion.

"Yes, Dad. Love."

"Why did you come home if you love him?" he asked, sliding his hand out from under mine.

"Because I needed some time out, I wanted to come to see you and Mum," I admitted, shrugging.

I could see the disappointment on his face, and I would be lying to say I wasn't upset. But I pushed the feeling down, the sicky feeling rising again. We sat awkwardly for a little while, his eyes looking me up and down as he continued to drink his whiskey. I mirrored him. I huffed, putting my glass on the floor as I went to stand up and he shuffled forward in his chair, grabbing my wrist and sitting me back down.

"I'm not finished," he growled.

I sat in my chair, waiting for him to continue.

"I don't want you to be queen, Royal," he said

deadpan.

I sat shocked, my hands started to tremble. "Dad…" I said, gasping in a whisper.

He held his hand up, stopping me. "I don't want to burden you with this, I want you to live your life how you wish to live it. This wasn't meant for me; I was thrown into this because my brother abdicated. This is no life, Royal, and I don't want this for you."

I felt torn.

"I want to do this for you." My voice was constricted, quiet.

"But I don't want you to do this, I want you free, my darling, free from any burden," he said with authority in his tone. I just nodded, biting hard on the inside of my lip to stop myself from talking anymore.

"Just be happy, my darling girl, I just want your happiness. I will die a happy man knowing that you are happy, loved and free." He sighed, wiping his eyes. "Can you do that for me? See it as my last dying wish." He winked at me, smiling a heart-breaking smile.

"I can, Daddy, I promise."

Xavier

It had been five days.

Five days since she walked out of my life.

I don't blame her, I mean, why did I ever think she could love me?

I looked at myself in the mirror, my eyes dull, my skin washed-out. I was a shadow of myself. Half of me left five days ago. I thought she may have come back, thought she may have had enough time by now, but no, she still hadn't return.

I cradled the bottle of whiskey; I couldn't be bothered with the glass anymore. I only threw them at the wall to try and relieve some of my hurt and anger, but it didn't help. How silly was I to think she would want me? Was it all a show? Did she pity me? Did I force her to love me because I kept her a prisoner, like Stockholm syndrome? I rubbed my tired eyes; I couldn't remember the last time I slept for more than an hour. Every time my eyes closed my dreams were plagued by her. She invaded them.

I looked at the grandfather clock to see it was seven p.m. The night was already dark, deadly silent. Nothing but me and my thoughts to see me through another never-ending evening.

I took a swig of the poison in my hand when I heard the doorbell chime, the noise splitting straight through me. I winced, waiting for someone to answer it for me. But then I remembered that I let them all go. There was no use for them now.

Again the doorbell rang, and I growled as I stomped

out of the library and down the hallway towards the door. I swung it open, anger boiling inside of me. I didn't know who I was expecting, but it definitely was not Red's little wench, Betty.

"Xavier," she said curtly.

I threw my hand over the door, gripping onto the door frame to barricade her from coming in. But that didn't stop her. The little sneak ducked under my arm and was now standing behind me. I spun on my heels, facing her.

I watched as she undid her little clear rain hood, folding it and placing it into her small handbag that hung on her arm. She looked worn out, the creases in her face more defined than they were the last time I saw her.

I sighed before narrowing my eyes on her, glaring down at her, trying to intimidate her.

"You don't scare me, you know." She shrugged nonchalantly. Her head shook as she looked around the hallway.

"Don't you have any manners?" She scowled at me.

"What do you want, Betty?" I said through gritted teeth, the door still wide open.

"I would love a cup of tea, anywhere for me to sit?" Her mouth twisted into a pout, the corners slowly turning into a smile.

I didn't say anything to her, I stormed past her and walked into the library. The only room I hadn't trashed. It was Royal's favourite. My heart hurt as it twisted and knotted in my chest.

"I don't have tea, only whiskey. Care for some?" I asked her, my voice flat.

"I suppose that'll have to do." She rolled her eyes as she took a seat in the high-backed chair overlooking the grounds. I left her there whilst I walked out of the room to get her a glass. Once in the kitchen, I grabbed the first one I saw that wasn't broken. I huffed, padding my bare feet back into the library where the wench was waiting for me. I handed her the dirty glass, her eyebrows raised, but not one sign that she was disgusted. She merely reached into her bag, pulling out a handkerchief and rubbing the smears off of it. Her eyes peered at me through her short lashes, her glass held out in her stretched-out arm. I rolled my eyes, stepping closer to where she was sitting and poured the contents of my bottle into her glass.

"I hope you haven't spat in this." She tutted before taking a mouthful. She didn't even wince.

"What do I owe this pleasure, Betty?" I asked deadpan, my heart racing in my chest but I didn't want her to see how anxious I was. How affected I was by all of this.

"I just wanted to let you know that Royal won't be back for a while." I heard the air whoosh out of her lungs as if she was trying to prepare herself.

I felt like I had just had a baseball bat swung and

smashed into my back, I felt the air choke out of me. My grip tightened around the neck of the bottle, and I felt it soften under my touch which made me stop. I needed this drink; I couldn't let it go to waste.

"King Patrick has been taken ill; he has weeks to live." Her voice rushed out, pained. "As you can imagine, Queen Mya and Royal are devastated. We all are." I could hear the tightness in her voice, the lump apparent in her throat. I actually felt sorry for her, for all of them. But my heart ached for Royal.

"Royal wants to be by her father's side until his last dying breath, as I'm sure you can understand." I watched as she stood from the seat, bringing the glass up to her thin lips and knocking the whole drink back. She stepped towards me, handing the glass to me before wrapping her hands around mine. "I just wanted to let you know." Her voice was hushed, the warmth of the whiskey thick on her breath.

She walked past me, gripping onto my arm as she did.

I stilled for a moment, my head dropping, my eyes closed.

"Does she miss me, Betty?" I asked, my heart clinging onto this thin line of hope.

I heard her take a sharp intake of breath before sighing. "She hasn't mentioned you."

Her words sliced right through me, my heart falling

from its dangling thread.

I didn't see Betty out, and as soon as the door was shut, I roared as loud as I could, throwing the bottle of whiskey and watching it obliterate. Just like my heart.

***

Royal

The weeks had all rolled into one. I didn't plan to be away this long, I didn't want to be away this long but what with my father's illness, I didn't have a choice. I knew Betty had gone to Xavier's to tell him I wouldn't be back for a while, but that's all she did say. I untacked Prince before leading him to his stable, topping up his water and hay. I strolled back to the house, the evenings drawing nearer as we approached winter. As I walked along the grass towards the palace, my heart dropped. The doctor's car was pulled outside, and next to it was an ambulance.

My father had deteriorated quickly, we knew he only had days left. But it couldn't be today. He was bright and cheery this morning, sitting in his bed as he watched the tele with my mother by his side. They were taking a little trip down memory lane, my mother's eyes always glistened when he spoke, the sign of her pent-up tears. She always waited until she was alone to cry, she never wanted to cry in front of him. I burst through the door to his room, which was now situated downstairs. I was panting and breathless from running. My dad was barely awake, my mother sitting in the chair next to him, her top half thrown over his body as her silent tears soaked into his gown.

"Royal, darling, is that you?" he asked, his eyes like slits.

"I'm here, Daddy," I wailed as I stepped towards him, scooping his hand in mine and bringing it to my lips. "I'm here," I whispered.

"My two favourite girls." He beamed, a beautiful smile spreading on his face instantly glowing his skin, his eyes moving to my mother. "Mya, angel, please don't cry over me, we knew this was coming. It's just a little sooner than we both wanted," he managed to get out after stammering.

"I love you, Patrick," my mum said hushed, her tear-stained face focusing solely on him.

"I love you, love," he whispered as he focused his breathless voice towards me.

"I love you too, Daddy, always," I chimed as I kissed the back of his hand.

"It's time. I'll be waiting for you, Mya, it's just not your time yet. I love you both, forever and always." His voice was strained and quiet as his eyes slipped shut, the last draw of breath leaving his lungs as the monitor showed a flat line where his heart had stopped. I gripped onto his hand, not wanting to let go. I looked at my mother, the screams leaving her were too much. I blurred everything out around me, just looking at his peaceful face. Away from the pain, away from us. Forever.

***

I laid on my bed, wide awake, not able to shut off. This morning was perfect. We all had breakfast together in Daddy's room, the room was full of so much love and happiness, and now it was broken. Never to be fixed. I felt lost without Xavier, and he is still here, on this earth with me. Yet my mother had just lost her entire world in an instant, her husband, the love of her life and her soulmate. She would never see his face again, hear his voice or kiss his lips. I knew it was the wrong time to run, but I needed to go back to Xavier.

If these last few weeks have shown me anything, it's that life is short.

Xavier is my life and I didn't want to lose another minute with him.

Chapter Twenty-Eight

Royal

I told my mum that I was leaving the next morning and I wanted her to come with me. She refused, telling me she wouldn't leave, and she would be fine. She agreed that I shouldn't waste another minute without him if I loved him as fiercely as I said, that I should go, and she wouldn't stop me.

I had to sit down in front of the court to abdicate my title, like my father wished. I didn't want to do it, I wanted to be queen, to run the country and step into my father's shoes. To be honest, they would be pretty big shoes to fill and I would fail miserably because he was a great king, adored by many.

I sat in with the court, nerves crashing through me as I stood up, agreeing and showing my father's last testimony in his will that he wanted me to abdicate the throne. After a few hours, it was done. My title stripped from me in an instant.

I felt empty losing my title as queen. I felt purposeless, hollow, worthless.

My mum sensed my shift in mood, her hand holding my hands.

"Darling, what's wrong?" She sighed.

"I didn't want to abdicate, but I couldn't go against father's wish. We haven't had a chance to mourn, to grieve and as soon as he is gone, it's back to business." I shook my head, my head dropped as I looked into my lap, my vision blurred as my eyes filled with tears.

"Sweetie." She smiled softly at me as she turned to face me. "This is why he didn't want you having this life. When your father lost his father, he was pulled from the room, the wheels set into motion for his coronation. He never grieved, his feet hardly touched the ground, he didn't want this life for you. This is no life, my darling."

"What will happen to you?"

"Not a lot." She let out a soft chuckle, but the pain was so clear in her eyes. "I will still carry the title of queen, and I'll be known as Queen Mya, then your uncle Tristan will take the throne, us losing our royal status in an instant." I watched her expression, it was like relief washed over her, her chains being cut. She was finally free.

Once we were home, we both freshened up and

dressed in black dresses ready for our mourning. My mum wore a black veil covering her face. Our kingdoms flag was dropped to half mast, the Juliette balcony doors were swung open as we walked hand-in-hand out in front of our kingdom. As soon as we were in sight, every single person bowed their heads, complete silence swept over the courtyard. It was heart-breaking. I squeezed my Mum's hand, my head turning towards her as I saw the tears streaming down her face, her own head bowed. After a few minutes of silence, the noise elevated as the crowds stood tall, their voices booming around the courtyard as they sang to honour my father. The best king they ever had. My voice cracked, I wanted to sing with them, I wanted my father to be able to hear us, wherever he was. We would always honour him; we would always love him and we would always miss him.

I was emotionally exhausted by the time we were back inside, my mum sat in my father's favourite chair, still wearing her black dress. My uncle was due to arrive tomorrow morning, my mother would move to the west wing of the palace, merging with their family and I would go back home to Xavier. I couldn't settle the butterflies that were swarming in my stomach. I wanted to stay with my mother, but I needed to sleep... Well, try to. I hardly slept last night, grief consuming me.

I stepped over to my mum, leaning across her and kissing her on the cheek, wishing her goodnight. As I stood, she wrapped her hands around my waist, pulling me to her, breaking down into a sob. I cradled her, for as long as she needed me. I wasn't going to leave her when she needed me.

"I will always love you, Royal," she choked out in a whisper, it breezing through my ear. "Always."

*** *** ***

I woke in the morning, the room still dark from the cold winter mornings, my mum laying on her side with her knees pulled up to her chest. She was still in her black dress, her beautiful face stained and streaked with mascara. I didn't know when she crept in, but I was glad she did. I tiptoed out the bed quietly, pulling my duvet over her and tucking her in. I wanted her to sleep, she needed to sleep.

I stepped under the shower, then slipped into a gown with the help of Betty. I had to wear our Royal colours of ice-blue and gold as my uncle was due to arrive. As soon as we had done the necessities, I was getting straight into jeans and a jumper. My heart thumped against my chest as I slipped the ice-blue gown up my body, Betty doing me up from the back.

"Everything okay, Royal?" she asked, her eyes looking round from behind me and into the mirror, so I could see her.

"I think so, it's just the last time I wore this was the night Xavier took me." I sighed. "Bittersweet memories."

I nibbled the inside of my lip, shaking my head as I tried to forget for a moment.

I stepped off of the raised pedestal that I was standing on while I was dressed, reaching for my delicate crown and slipping it into place.

"Stunning," Betty muttered as she started clearing things away.

"Is mother awake yet?" I asked as I walked towards the door of the dressing room.

"No, not yet. I am going to start breakfast and put a pot of tea on before your uncle gets here. I don't want her stressing and thinking she has to do anything. She is still our queen, she is not to lift a finger around here and I will make sure of it," Betty said with assertiveness, nodding her head at her aloud thoughts.

I didn't say anything, just sighed as I walked down the stairs, the heavy burden apparent in my chest. I just wanted to go home, but I had to get through the next few hours and then I'd be reunited with Xavier. My love, my life.

I just hoped he understood why I had to do this, why I did this.

I shook away the thoughts as I strolled into the dining room, sitting at the table and waiting for my mother to join me.

An hour passed, but she didn't come.

The breakfast sat there cold, untouched. I pushed

myself away from the table as I rushed quickly to my room, pushing the door open and standing at the side of the bed where she was laying. The air was robbed from my lungs. I gasped, clutching my chest. I was trying to do everything to not let it leave, my heart plummeting to the bottom of my stomach, knotting and twisting as the feelings overtook. I felt my legs buckle, my knees trembling as they gave out under me as I fell to my knees, screaming for someone, anyone to come and help.

They came, they tried, they failed. I sat in the spot I collapsed in as I watched them try and bring my mother back. But it was too late. Her beautiful soul had already left.

My mother had taken her life. She fell asleep next to me, knowing that this was our last night together. The pain too much for her to continue this life without my father.

I was alone.

I was broken even more so than I was this morning. The heavy weight slowly crushing my chest.

It's just me.

Alone.

I dashed into my room, grabbing as much as I could off the rails and throwing it into the bag. Betty was at my door, grief etched onto her tired face, her eyes dull and lifeless.

"Royal..." she breathed out, and I knew exactly what

she was thinking. She didn't want me to leave, she wanted me to stay.

"I can't, Betty, I need out. I need to get home. I can't breathe." I gasped as I stepped back, the bed frame hitting my knees, making me fall. I sat on the bed, taking deep breaths in and breathing out slowly. I kept my eyes closed. My world had fallen down around me, I just couldn't stay here any longer. She sat down next to me, taking my hands in hers as she rubbed her thumbs across my numb skin. "You've always got me," Betty said quietly, a motherly glow beaming from her.

"I know," I whispered, looking at her and smiling. "But I need to go home, I can't stay here." I nodded as I sniffed.

"I know, darling." Her hands wiped my tears off my cheeks.

"Come with me," I pleaded with her as I pulled my hands out of hers, my fingers playing with the tulle skirt of my dress.

"I will, but not yet. I need to get things settled here with your uncle and his family. Give me a couple of weeks." She smiled as she stood up. "Now, let's get you packed. I'll contact you and let you know when your parents are being laid to rest."

After the small conversation with my uncle as I was running out the door and him offering his deep condolences, I bid him farewell and made the way to my

Porsche. I was in such a rush that I didn't even want to get changed out of my gown. I threw the bag in the boot and hitched my dress up as I slid into the driver's side. I started the engine, the roar vibrating through to my bones. I took one look behind me at my family home, nothing but sadness surrounding it now, my heart splintering in my chest as I pushed my foot on the accelerator and drove away.

Chapter Twenty–Nine

The drive back to Xavier's was just a little over an hour, the heating was on full blast as I tried to warm up. But it was no use. I was completely numb. It had just gone four p.m.; the night was starting to draw in already. I tried to keep my mind busy, trying not to think about the loss in these last twenty-four hours. My mind wandered to Xavier, and I wondered how he had been. Betty didn't say much when she came home, just that she had told him that I would be away for a while. I couldn't wait to kiss his lips and have his hands holding my face, the scratch of his beard moving over my sensitive skin. I felt my breath hitch, thinking back to when we were intimate, a day before everything turned into an utter shit show.

It was the day before the boathouse, we had spent a lovely day together. We decided to spend the evening in the lounge, we both sat for a moment, complete silence around us as I stared into his soul. I felt the heat creeping over me, the delicious ache in my stomach growing. I knew he felt it too. I could never have enough of him. I hopped off the sofa, pulling my tee down just under my bum and falling to my knees in front of him. His eyes were wide, his bottom lip pulled in-between his teeth as he let out a low hum. He was wearing tight grey jogging bottoms. I could see how hard he was through the constricting material. I ran both of my hands slowly up his thighs, taking my time but keeping my eyes on his. I palmed him through his trousers, teasing him. He let out a low groan, his eyes hazed over. That was my favourite look, when he was so intoxicated by me.

I perched myself on my knees, reaching up and grabbing the waistband of his trousers and pulling them down, exposing him. His thick, hard cock sprung free. Pre-cum beaded on the tip of him. I placed one hand back on his thigh, the other I wrapped round the base of him, my hand moving slowly as I started to pump him. The delicious moan that left his lips spurred me on, I loved making him feel like this. I dropped my eyes from his, pressing my lips on the tip of his cock before my tongue flicked out, licking the beading of cum away, then my lips pushed around him, sucking him softly as I pulled him back out and rested him between my lips. His hips thrusted up slightly, his hand in my hair. I popped him out, running my tongue from the base all the way to his tip, my tongue swirling around the head of him. I pushed my lips down over him, taking every inch of him deep into my mouth. A low, pleasured growl hummed from his throat as I bobbed my head up and down. I did the same each time, pulling him out to his tip, him resting between my lips before I took him deep, my hand pumping at the same time. His fingers tightened around my hair, his breathing fast and ragged as I brought him to his release.

"Fuck, angel." He groaned, his balls spasming as he was getting close to his release. "I'm going to come," he cried out. I drank every bit of him, cleaning him and licking the tip, making sure I hadn't missed a drop. I used my ring finger to wipe the corner of my mouth, then sucked on it to make sure I had every last drop of him.

"You're something else," he sung, still coming down from his high.

"You make me that way," I teased as I stood slowly, looking down at him.

He grabbed my hips, pulling me forward and down onto his lap. I hovered over him, my hands round his face as I pushed my lips against his, my tongue slowly invading his mouth. Our tongues danced with each other, swirling and tasting.

I could feel him growing underneath me, excitement pulsed through me. He pushed me to the side, so I was laying on the sofa, legs apart as he laid between them. His fingers glided down my centre, a gasp of breath leaving me.

"So wet," he mumbled as his finger twirled at my opening. His finger slowly pushed into me, his thumb pad sweeping over my clit. I moaned, the feeling of heaven coursing through me. I could never get enough of him and the way he made me feel.

"I'm going to fuck you so hard, baby, I want you sore. I want you to remember this evening when you wake in the morning."

I clenched my muscles, his words ripping through me.

"Fuck me, Xavier," I begged as he continued to pump his finger into me. "Please, I need to feel you."

He slipped his fingers out of me, and I whimpered at the loss of contact. He lined himself up at my opening, then rocked his hips slowly into me. My eyes rolled in the back of my head, the feeling of him filling me was like pure ecstasy.

Once my body had adjusted to him, his hips pulled out of me slowly, then thrust into me hard. One of his hands was on my hip, his eyes watching himself push and pull out of me, his other hand wandering up my body, bunching my tee up round my neck so I was completely naked under him.

"Perfect," he growled through gritted teeth as he

sped his hips into me, the feeling overwhelming. I could feel my muscles starting to tighten, the delicious burn in my stomach spreading as I started my climb to my orgasm. He stopped suddenly, whipping out of me and spinning me over onto my front. I knelt on all fours; his body close to mine. He pushed into me hard this time and didn't stop his harsh poundings. And I didn't want him to. His cock was so deep, stroking my spot again and again. His hand was in my hair, pulling my head back so my back was arched. I couldn't hold off much longer, my walls clamping down around him.

"I'm so close," I moaned out, panting.

"Come for me, baby, I want you to come all over my cock." His dirty mouth turned me on, spurring my orgasm to explode around him. I cried out, calling his name, begging him to keep going so I could get the most out of this orgasm, riding it out.

"That's it, baby, I can feel you. So fucking tight. And all mine." He grunted as he throbbed and pulsed inside of me as he came. A loud roar ripped through me as he found his release, his hand still gripped round my hair.

We spent the rest of the evening enjoying each other, him slipping in and out of me until the early morning.

I felt my heart seize, I missed feeling that close to him. I missed the feel of him all over me. The drive seemed to drag; the roads so dark I had to slow down so I could pay attention. My heart started jack-hammering in my chest as I pulled up to his gates. They were wide open. He never left them open. I felt a chill creep over me as I pulled into the driveway, the silence of the night was deafening. All I could hear was the wheels on the gravelled driveway.

I stopped the car outside the front door, a familiar fear ripping through me. I turned the engine off, gripping the keys before running up the stairs and opening the door.

"Xavi," I called out, breathless. I didn't hear anything.

I walked through the older part of the house, hoping to see Mabel or Christopher, but there was no one. The house seemed empty.

Panic started climbing up my throat, crippling me. I ran through the kitchen and into the conservatory before I got to the lounge. My hand came to my mouth, a gasp leaving me. The whole room was trashed. The sofas were upside down, ripped and falling apart. Every bit of glass was shattered, the vase that he threw still on the floor. I rushed through to the hallway and into his office to see the same thing. The whole room trashed and upside down. My body hummed with anxiety and fear.

Something felt off.

I rummaged through his desk drawers, knowing he kept a gun in there. Not that I knew how to shoot a gun, but it was better to be prepared than walk into a situation blind.

I walked to the next door which was the library. I twisted the door knob, slowly pushing the door open and putting my head round first. I scanned the room, this room was immaculate, apart from the smashed whiskey bottle on the floor and the one glass that sat on the side table. I walked cautiously, my heart thumping in my chest, the blood pumping in my ears. I noticed the bookcase was slightly out of line, the bit that opened up and took you to the basement. Where I first saw the pictures of Xander.

I moved as quickly as I could, cursing myself for not getting out of my gown. I pulled on the bookcase, swinging it open as I ran down the steps. "Xavier?" I called out. Then I saw. I stopped, frozen on the spot, completely paralyzed.

On his knees was Xavier, cuffed and bound with his hands behind his back. His head bleeding, blood trickling down his face. His eyes covered in black and blue bruises; his nose busted. Next to him was Alan, holding a gun to his head, his eyes on me. I held my hands up, showing I wielded no weapon.

"Look who finally decided to come back," Alan's voice ripped through me. Nausea swam in my stomach and I swallowed down, praying that I wasn't sick.

"Red," Xavier gasped. I studied him, his hair shaggy,

his beard longer than usual, his eyes hollow as he gazed at me. It was as if his soul had left him.

I didn't move a muscle; I was too scared. Not for what would happen to me, but for what would happen to Xavier.

"Isn't this wonderful?" Alan sniggered. "All reunited," he chimed.

"You came back," I heard Xavier's voice crash through me, his words splitting through my heart.

"Of course I came back. I was always coming back," I said hushed, my eyes volleying between Xavier and Alan.

I wanted to run at him, throw myself over him and act as a shield taking the bullets that Alan was threatening to fire.

"Shut up," Alan sniped as he hit the gun round the back of Xavier's head, Xavier winced and dropped his head, going limp.

I shouted out. "No! Please, what do you want? I'll do anything, just don't hurt him." Panic rose in my throat, my voice showing just how vulnerable I felt.

"What do I want?" he asked, a sleazy smile creeping onto his weasel face. "I want to fuck you, in front of your beau here. Then, once he has watched and has the image of you moaning and crying out my name, the sound imprinted on his brain, I want to blow them out just like I did to his brother's."

The blood in my veins ran cold.

I heard Xavier grunt, his head rolling round and up. "You fucking arsehole," I heard him growl from the floor. Alan grabbed him up, so he was back on his knees as he pressed the silver revolver to Xavier's temple.

"Don't test me, beast, I will fucking splatter your brains all over the wall," Alan threatened.

I stepped towards Alan, slowly, carefully. I ran my hands round the back of my dress, trying to stop the sweat from puddling on them.

He turned the gun towards me, kicking Xavier in the chest so he fell on his side. My eyes were wide as I looked at Xavier, I wanted to try and reassure him that this would be okay. I had him. I had this.

I held my hands out. "Alan, put the gun down. I don't have anything, I'm coming to give you what you so desperately crave, what I have always so desperately craved." I felt the bile rising up my throat as I stepped closer to him. He was heaving, panting, his eyes devouring me as I stopped in front of him, his tongue darting out and running across his bottom lip. He reached out for me, grabbing me and pulling me into him. The smell that left him made my stomach flip and turn. I had to stop myself from gagging, his breath stale and like an ash tray. He ran the barrel of the gun under my chin, pressing it into me so my head was tipped up. My eyes strayed over to Xavier; his eyes filled with panic. I had never seen anyone look so scared and lost. And at this moment in time, there was nothing I could do about it.

"Before I fuck you, how about a little story time about Xander? Neither of you will be getting out of here alive, so I may as well fill you in. Tell you his last words, explain how I watched the last breath leave his body, his soul screaming…" His voice trailed off from its sickly tone. I felt my skin go clammy, the goose-bumps prickling all over my body. The gun-sight was pressing under my chin even harder, his finger firmly on the trigger.

"After Xavier and Xander had their little spat…" He sniggered, the gun being pressed further into the bottom of my head. I was struggling to swallow, it hurt.

"Xander needed to cool down, he was angry. I offered to take him for a drive, time for him to clear his head. He didn't talk in the car, which did me a favour because I didn't want to sit and listen to him whining and moaning about his brother issues." He rolled his eyes. Xavier rolled onto his back, and I saw the panic in Alan. He knew if Xavier got up, he would kill him. He stepped to the side, pressing his foot into Xavier's chest to hold him in place. I heard a wheeze leave Xavier's lungs. "Think about moving, I'll crush your fucking ribcage," he snarled at Xavier before he looked back at me, smiling.

"Once we got to the woods, I told him to get out. The fresh night air would do him the world of good. And like the stupid prick he was, he listened. He was muttering away about how he should apologise, that you and him always fought. You were twins, that's what siblings do. They fight, they make up. No big deal. Then he started speaking about you, *princess*. How much he liked you, but he wouldn't go to the ball to be suited to you. That his brother could step in, fill his shoes for the evening. It made me sick, listening to him being such a pussy. I slowed behind him, taking a few steps back before I kicked him in the back of the knees, watching him fall at my feet. He rolled over, anger all over his face. He went to stand up, but I didn't give him the chance. I pulled my gun out..." He trailed his voice off, pushing my head up further, his head cocking to the side as he admired the gun. "It was this gun actually, this gun that I pulled out, pushing myself onto him. I straddled him, so he couldn't go anywhere. One hand round his throat, softly squeezing, the other pressing the gun to his temple. I didn't give him a chance to speak, but if I could show you the fear in his eyes, the little tears that escaped his eyes as I did it, I would. It was fucking perfect. Having him scared and completely in my hands to play with. I didn't give it another thought, I pulled the trigger, hearing his last gasp of air leaving his lungs, I smiled while watching his lifeless body bleeding out in the leaves. I cleaned the gun, placed it in his left hand then removed my gloves." He shuddered, his sickening grin spreading further across his face.

"And now it's time for you to join him. Both of you,

together." He laughed. "This is perfect." He grunted as he pushed harder onto Xavier's chest. "It'll be like a modern-day Romeo and Juliet. A tragic love scene, but in this version, you both die. Not just one of you." I watched as he turned the gun on Xavier, hovering it between his eyes. "Now, which one shall I do first?" he asked himself. This was my moment; it was now or never. I dropped to the floor, hitching my dress up slightly and pulling the revolver out of my sock. I snapped up, holding the gun at Alan.

"Oh, princess, stop trying to be the hero, the only hero in this story is me." He threw his head back laughing as I saw his finger tighten on the trigger, but as he did it, the gun spun round to face me. I pulled the trigger as quick as I could, not looking where I was aiming.

I watched as he fell to the floor, my heart racing when all of a sudden, I felt a burning sensation, a pain so sickening searing through me. Before I could look down, I fell to the floor, the room going black. All I heard before I blacked out completely was Xavier's scream.

***

I tried to fight the darkness, but I couldn't. I felt like I was floating. When I looked around, I was sitting on the boat, in the lake by the boathouse. One side of me was Xavier, the next, the bright light. I heard my mum's voice calling me, soothing me. I started rowing towards her voice, the bright light getting bigger. Then my head snapped round, the sound of Xavier. His voice was strained, begging and calling my name. My heart thumped; it only beat for him. It was always him.

I started rowing the other way, away from the light. But before I reached him, the noise got too much, the sound of chattering was so loud.

All I could hear were loads of voices consuming my thoughts before it all went black again.

Chapter
Thirty

Xavier

I sat in the hospital chair, rocking slowly back and forth. We had only just got here, blue-lighted all the way. Whilst sitting quietly, my mind was far from quiet. It replayed what happened over and over again. The event was on a constant roll, not stopping for a moment.

I watched Alan go down like a sack of shit as the bullet hit him straight between the fucking eyes. But in her pulling the trigger, Alan pulled his too. I watched the bullet as it penetrated through her. Her face, so proud that she had saved me, saved herself. But that proudness soon faded to anguish, her eyes dropping to her chest where blood was oozing from. Her eyes flicked to mine, her mouth parted before she fell down in front of me, her head smashing on the hard floor. The sound of her skull hitting the concrete haunted me, I heard the crack echo round the room.

I screamed, fuck did I scream. But no one was here. No one could hear me.

I sat up, shuffling over to her. I couldn't do anything as my hands were still tied behind my back. My throat burned from screaming, my eyes sore after I cried a thousand tears. I had to accept that she was gone.

That my happily ever after was over.

Just as I was about to give into the darkness, I saw her. Fucking Betty walking through the door, like a wench in shining armour. And fuck, I had never been so happy to see her.

"Betty," I shouted out, my throat tight.

"It's okay, I'm here," she hushed, wrapping her arms round my head and pulling me into a motherly embrace.

"She's dead, I think she's left me," I choked.

"She wouldn't give up that easily." She gave me a small smile before untying my hands. I rushed over to her, crawling on my hands and knees. My fingers were on her neck, her pulse was still beating, but barely.

"Betty, call for an ambulance," I shouted as Betty fumbled with her phone.

"Angel, it's me, can you hear me?" I whispered in her ear as I cradled her, her beautiful blue gown saturating in blood. Her fiery-red hair stained from the

blood coming from her head.

"You're going to be fine. Our love is too strong for us to lose each other now," I muttered, hoping she could hear me.

Within minutes, the ambulance was here. And now, I'm sitting and waiting while she is in surgery. The bullet is lodged in her chest, just next to her heart.

I saw Betty walk in, sitting down next to me and looking utterly exhausted.

"How you doing?" she asked as she placed her hand on my thigh, giving it a gentle squeeze. Her eyes were burning into me.

"Awful," I admitted, sighing as I shook my head. "It should have been me, he came to shoot me, not Royal. Not my angel." My voice was strained. I coughed, clearing my throat, trying to distract myself from the fact the tears were brimming in my eyes. "Erm, the nurse came in asking for Red, I mean Royal's next of kin details, so I gave them Patrick and Mya's details. So hopefully they are on their way," I muttered, my eyes rising and peering at Betty. Her whole body tensed; her eyes weepy as she started speaking. "She didn't tell you?" Betty asked confused.

"Tell me what?" My eyes were now pinned to hers.

"Patrick and Mya, they... They..." she stuttered before pushing the tears away. I just sat, waiting, but nothing could prepare me for the words that came out of her mouth after that.

"Patrick died yesterday afternoon; Mya was found dead this morning. She fell asleep in Royal's bed and never woke. We think she took her own life." Betty sobbed.

My poor Red.

And after all that grief, she still came home to me, to save me.

***

After four hours, the doctor walked into the waiting room.

"Mr Archibald, Betty." The doctor nodded his head curtly.

"Doc, tell me she is okay, please," I begged as I stood, grasping the doctor's hand.

"The surgery went well. There are some bullet fragments that have been left behind, but they will eventually disintegrate. The nurse will take you to see her shortly." His face had a soft smile, and he stepped back away from me. I couldn't even describe how relieved and happy I was. Betty cried quietly next to me, relief sweeping over her.

"Oh, Mr Archibald," the doctor said as he turned around to face me. "The baby is fine." His smile grew on his face. My heart raced, my jaw laxed and my eyes bulged as I gazed at the doctor, a blank expression on my face.

"She's pregnant?" The words left me in a whisper, I was shocked. But so happy.

"Yes." The doctor looked at me confused. "You didn't know?"

I shook my head, my eyes wandering to Betty. "Did you?"

"No." She shook her head. "And neither did she, and if she did, she didn't mention it which is unlike Royal. She would have told me." She shrugged, her head shaking side to side softly

"We think she is about seven to eight weeks pregnant. We will be telling her once she is awake. She is in a medically induced coma due to a slight swell on the brain from her fall."

I could hear the distant chatter, the doctors voice humming through me. But I didn't hear what else he had to say.

I was in a daze.

Royal was pregnant with my baby. I'm going to be a father.

***

After an hour, a young nurse came and collected me and Betty. She walked us through the long corridors. My heart was hammering in my chest, I was anxious but excited to see her. I just wanted to see she was okay with my own eyes. I saw her name on the door, and I touched the nurse's elbow, stopping her outside the door.

"Everything okay?" she asked as she turned her head to face me.

"Yeah." I swallowed down the lump in my throat. "But I would like it if I... We..." My eyes looked at Betty. "Could tell her about the baby?"

The nurse smiled at me. "Of course." She nodded softly, stepping towards the door and opening it.

The lump that I swallowed down was slowly creeping up my throat again as I saw her laying there, completely helpless, tubes in her veins, coming out of hands and arms. She had wires attached to her chest and an oxygen tube in her nose. She looked so peaceful, her fiery-red hair fanned out behind her, her creamy skin smooth, her cheeks slightly flushed from the heating. Her cherry lips parted, I wanted nothing more than to kiss her, to let her know I was here. I choked, my eyes stinging. I didn't want to blink, because if I blinked, I was letting the tears fall.

I sat in the chair next to her, pulling it closer as I grabbed her hand, holding it and not letting go. I wasn't going to leave, not until her eyes opened. I wanted to be the first thing she saw when she woke up.

Betty came and stood behind me, her hand on my shoulder as she gave me a gentle squeeze.

"Do you want anything to eat? Drink?" she asked in a soft, soothing voice.

"No thank you," I muttered, my eyes not leaving Royal.

"Okay, I'm going to go and get some clothes, I'll get some for you as well, if that's okay? Where are your housekeepers?" Betty asked as she stood next to me.

"I let them go," I mumbled, my voice barely recognisable, hurt lacing it.

"Why?"

"I had no use for them, I was getting ready to take my own life. It wasn't worth living without her." I sighed, closing my eyes for a moment.

"Xavier," she said breathlessly, her hand on my arm. "She was always going to come back." She smiled at me.

"I didn't know that though. I broke her, I upset her. Why would she want to come back to me?" I shook my head from side to side gently.

"Because she loves you." Her hand squeezed my arm. "I'll get you some clothes, unless you don't want me rooting through your things?" Her voice was still soft as she walked towards the door.

"It's fine. My room is in the second part of the house, third door on the left once you get up the stairs." I turned my head to face her, giving her the faintest of smiles. "Thank you." I bowed my head for a moment before I whipped it back around and focussed all of my attention on Royal.

She didn't say anything else, she just slipped out the door quietly.

I don't know how long I sat there for before she came

back, shoving a hot cup of coffee in front of my nose. As much as I didn't want it, the smell swam through my nostrils, awakening my tired and grouchy soul.

I took it off of her, bringing it straight to my lips and taking a mouthful, letting out a little groan in appreciation.

"Go and stretch your legs, you have been sitting here for a while," Betty said as she stood at my side.

"But I don't want to leave her..." I trailed my voice off before sighing, looking down at her beautiful face.

"I know you don't, but nothing is going to change at the moment. And if it does, then I'll find you. I promise." She smiled. I debated arguing back, but I could do with a wander, just to stretch.

"Okay," I said slightly hesitant.

"Go." Her voice was stern but warm. Motherly. It made me feel warm and fuzzy inside, I missed my mother terribly, and having that little bit from Betty made me miss her so much right now.

I huffed, pushing myself up in the chair, reaching for the ceiling. It felt good to stretch.

I looked down at my clothes, I was still in the clothes from last night, sweaty, clammy and covered in mine and her blood.

"Betty, did you get me some fresh clothes?" I asked as I stepped away from the bed, my heart instantly hurting.

"Yes, darling, in the holdall by the window." She smiled as she sat in my spot. I instantly felt anger brewing, jealousy ripping through me. I forced my eyes shut, taking a breather for a moment. *She is a saint,* I reminded myself.

The thought swirled around in my mind before I opened my eyes.

"I packed you a few outfits, toothbrush, toothpaste." She looked at me. "I knew you wouldn't be leaving; I can go back in a couple of days and get you some more." She turned her head to Royal, and I watched as Betty took her hand in hers. Her thumb rubbed across the back of it. I clenched my jaw. I didn't like anyone touching her bar me. *She was mine.*

I looked down at my fists balled tightly by my side.

I shook them out, relaxing suddenly. I stalked over to the bag, grabbing the handles and walking out the room. I didn't look back, because if I did then I wouldn't leave.

***

I splashed my face with cold water, my hands tightening round the edge of the sink in the toilet. I lifted my head slowly, looking at myself in the mirror. I didn't recognise the man looking back at me. I was broken, haunted and racked with grief.

I grieved for Xander. I grieved for Royal. I even grieved for Patrick and Mya. *After all of that, she still came back to me.* I felt dumbfounded.

I pushed my wet hand through my hair in frustration. I pulled my toothbrush out, running it under the cold tap and squirting toothpaste along the bristles.

Once brushed, I ran my tongue over my teeth. I felt slightly better.

I just needed a beard trim, but that could wait. It wasn't important.

I dropped my toothbrush and toothpaste into the holdall, my dirty clothes in a linen bag that Betty had put in there. I smiled slightly, letting out a scoff.

Damn Betty.

I strolled back towards the hospital room, my heart dropping that she hadn't moved, Betty still cradling her hand.

"No change?" I asked deadpan, my lips pressing into a thin line.

"No." Betty shook her head. "But the doctor is coming round shortly."

I watched as her eyes trailed up and down my body. I furrowed my brows at her, slightly confused by her glare.

"You look nice." She beamed.

"Erm, thanks?" I laughed softly.

"I know I am old enough to be your mother, maybe... But still... Nothing wrong with a bit of eye candy." Her laugh filled the room. I felt instantly lighter, it was nice to hear some laughter. I laughed with her, and man, it felt good to laugh.

Even if it was for a minute before I was plunged back into darkness.

Chapter Thirty-One

Xavier

It had been ten days. Ten days and still no movement. I couldn't help but worry. I had stayed here every day, and every night. The only time I got up was when Betty was practically shoving me out of the chair to take some time away.

Betty had honestly been a God send; I really don't think I could have got through this without her.

Physically I would have, but not mentally.

I spoke to the baby daily, along with Royal. The doctors checked the baby every day, things were going well. I was just sorry that Royal was missing out on this.

I shuffled in my seat, still holding onto her hand and moving myself forward slightly so I could get closer to her.

"I miss you, baby," I said softly, bringing her hand to my lips and kissing the back of it.

"You saved my life, not just ten days ago, but from the moment I brought you into my life, you saved me, Red." I couldn't even explain how much I loved her.

It should have been me saving her, protecting her.

But I failed her.

It was her who came in and saved me.

I gripped her hand tightly, my lips brushing along the back of her perfect hand.

I felt my eyes sting, brimming with tears.

"Baby, please come back to me, I need you. Our baby needs you," I whispered. "Our lives have only just begun, I'm not ready to lose you yet. You're mine, Royal, always mine. Wherever you go, I'll go." My lip trembled; my voice hoarse. My throat was burning, the lump so thick in my throat that I was struggling to swallow it back down. I felt the tears roll down my cheeks, but I didn't want to wipe them away, because that would mean I would have to drop her hand, and I didn't want to let her go. Not even for a moment.

I heard the door go, the noise of the handle clicking making me jump.

"Sorry, Mr Archibald, only me," the doctor reassured me. I internally cursed, but he was looking after my girl, so I couldn't be too mad.

"Hey, doc." I groaned as I sat back slightly, still gripping her hand.

"How are you doing?" he asked as he grabbed Royal's

chart, flicking the pages.

"How is she doing?" I asked, ignoring his question.

"She's getting there. We will be taking her for a scan shortly to check the brain swelling." His voice was flat, his brows furrowing as he looked at her chart.

"What's wrong?" The panic was clear in my voice, a cold shiver spreading across my skin.

"Nothing." He smiled at me before diverting his eyes back to the chart.

My jaw ticked. I felt my teeth grind slightly.

"Can you tell me?" I said through gritted teeth. "Please?"

The doctor flicked the pages back over, the clipboard going back on the end of the bed as he walked closer to Royal.

"It's nothing, please, I am sorry I worried you. I just expected her to have shown some signs of wanting to wake up." He watched her machine; the soft beeps had become a thing of comfort these days.

"But sometimes patients just need a little help to wake." He smiled at me. "I'm going to see if I can take her for her scan now, get her pushed up the list." His voice was muffled, his torch shining in her eyes. He turned it off, slipping it in the pocket of his white coat.

"I'll be back in a moment, I'm going to see what I can do about the scan."

I didn't move, I just waited for the sounds of his

footsteps to disappear and the door shutting. I let out my breath, my nerves crashing through me. *What if something is wrong? Was there something wrong with the baby? Was she going to wake up?*

The questions were swirling around in my head. I needed answers, I needed to know she was okay.

"It's going to be fine, angel, you're just having a little more rest than needed. You'll be awake soon enough, and once you are, I am never letting you go," I muttered to her.

I heard the door go, the doctor walking back in with two nurses.

"Mr Archibald, we have a space. We are taking Ms. Sorrell down now. We won't be long." His face turned into a smile as they put the sides of her bed up.

"Sir, I need you to let go," one of the nurses said.

"I don't want to," I whispered.

"I know, but the quicker you let go, the quicker I can get her back to you." She smiled.

Reluctantly, I let go, instantly missing the connection.

I stood, watching them wheel her out, the beeping from her machine fading into the distance.

I was left with complete silence and my thoughts.

The worse thing I could've been left with.

***

Betty walked through the door twenty minutes later, her eyes wide as she looked round the room.

"Where is she?" Her voice was panicked.

"They're scanning her, wanting to see if the swelling has gone down." I sighed.

"Is everything okay?" she asked as she sat in the chair in the corner.

"I don't know, I really don't." My voice was a whisper.

"What did the doctor say?"

"Not a lot, just that he would have thought she would have showed signs of waking up by now." I couldn't help but shrug my shoulders. "I'm not panicking until they're back." I nodded.

On the outside, I looked like I was handling it.

But on the inside, I was falling apart. Each time she was away from me, I lost a little more faith, a little more of her. I felt like she was slipping through my fingers.

I shook away the thoughts. This is what happens when you're left alone with your thoughts.

I growled, throwing my head back then pushing my hands into my blonde hair, gripping at it and tugging. I needed to feel something other than what I was feeling now.

I felt useless.

Forty minutes had passed, and Royal was wheeled back into the room. My heart skipped with relief, my thoughts silencing as soon as she was near me again. I grabbed onto her hand as soon as she was through the doors, walking at the side of the bed. The nurses smiled at me, a look of adoration in their eyes.

"She's a lucky girl to have you," the dark-haired nurse cooed.

"No, I'm lucky to have her. Trust me," I muttered, my eyes on Royal the whole time.

The nurses made sure she was comfortable before walking out of the room, the doctor returning just after they left.

"How did it go?" I asked anxiously, literally jumping down his throat.

"It was fine, the swelling has gone down considerably. We will start waking her tonight, but, Mr Archibald, it won't be instant. It can take some time for a person to come around when they're forced out of a coma," he said as he marked something down on her chart. "Also, you need to be ready in case she has any long-term brain trauma." His face was dull, his lips in a thin line.

"Brain trauma?" I shook my head.

"From the head injury. We won't know until she is awake and conscious, but from what I can see on the scans, I'm not concerned." He walked towards me as he placed his hand on my shoulder. "But we can't assume. We will know soon, try not to worry. I'll be back in a few hours." His face showed a grimace, but he still smiled as he strolled towards the door, closing it behind him.

Of course I was going to worry.

I just wanted her awake now.

I wanted her to be reunited with me.

Forever.

Chapter Thirty-Two

Royal

I felt the darkness lifting, but I couldn't open my eyes. They were heavy, I could hear muttering, but I couldn't decipher who it was. I tried so hard to open my eyes, I really tried. I put all my energy into moving my fingers, to let them know I was here, I was waking.

I felt exhausted and I wasn't even awake yet.

My mind was hazy.

"Royal, baby?" I heard his voice. "Betty! Get the nurse! Get the doctor!" His voice was getting louder.

My eyelashes fluttered before I slowly opened them, the bright lights hurting my eyes. I rushed to close them again.

"Angel, can you hear me?" His voice echoed around me.

"Doc, she's waking up!" I heard the relief in his voice.

I'm here, baby. I'm trying. Keep talking, your voice is helping.

I was screaming the words, but nothing was coming out.

"Royal, can you hear me?" I heard a voice I didn't know, and it unnerved me, making me anxious.

I tried again to open my eyes, I needed to get past the brightness. They fluttered open, and this time I fought the urge to close them again. I blinked a few times, my eyes squinting as they adjusted to the room.

"Royal," I heard the voice again.

I was trying to search the room, for him. My love. But I couldn't see him.

My heart was thumping.

I had nurses around me, a doctor leaning over me as he checked me.

One of the nurses sat me up slowly, the other putting a plastic cup of water to my lips.

"Small mouthfuls, small mouthfuls," she muttered.

I felt claustrophobic.

I felt smothered.

I wanted to scream, I wanted to shout but I couldn't.

"Can we give her some space? Fuck!" I heard his voice. My heart fluttered, the warmth smothering my cheeks.

Then there he was.

My king.

"Angel, fuck... Red." He gasped as he cradled my face with his large hands, his forehead pressing on mine. "Baby, I missed you." His voice was quiet.

"I missed you too." My voice was barely audible.

But from the look on his face, he heard me.

He pressed his lips onto mine, my heart exploding in my chest from his touch.

I panicked when he stepped away from me. "Don't leave me."

"I'm not leaving, I just need to let the doc finish your check over." He smiled at me, sitting down in the chair next to me.

"How you feeling, Royal? Any pain?" the doctor asked, his voice smooth.

I shook my head. "Nothing too bad, my head feels tight, my chest is sore but I'm managing." My smile was small.

"Is your head aching?" he asked.

"A little." I nodded.

"I'll get some more pain killers for you. I'll let you have some time, and I'll be back in an hour." The doctor smiled at me before he walked out the room.

My eyes scanned the room, my heart racing when I saw Betty. All of a sudden, a crushing pain seared through my heart. The flashbacks of my parents haunting me. Then I saw Xavier, on his knees, gun to his head, my whole world going black around me.

My last thought was that I wasn't ready to lose him. I wasn't ready to be without him. Never. I would never be ready.

My face fell, my eyes glistening as I looked at him. My beau.

"Baby..." Xavier's hand covered both of mine. "What's wrong?"

"It all just hit me. The flashbacks." My hands started to tremble, my throat tightening. I felt like my skin was crawling.

"Of what, angel?"

"Everything. My parents, you, Alan." I choked.

"It's okay, Red, I'm here. I'm here," he said hushed as he leant over me, hugging me tightly.

I winced, the pain from my chest burning

"Shit, Red, I'm sorry." His eyes were wide, his lips pulled down at the sides, his brows furrowed.

"It's okay, it's okay." I nodded as I clung to his arms, not wanting him to let me go.

"Don't let me go." I shook my head, the panic ripping through me.

"I won't. I'm not going anywhere." His eyes were warm as he stared at me.

I pulled my eyes from him; Betty was by my side.

"Darling, you okay?" she asked as she sat on the edge of my bed. Xavier still had my hands, and I was glad.

"I am." I nodded. "I feel empty, but not in a bad way."

I pinched my brows together. I knew it didn't make sense as such. I was empty without my parents, a part of me missing, but Xavier made me feel so full.

"What are you thinking?" Betty asked me, her face full of concern.

"Just about my parents." I sighed, my eyes looking down at my hands that were cocooned by his.

"I miss them too." She wiped her eyes, but her face was graced with a smile.

"How long have I been asleep for?" I asked.

"Just over two weeks," Xavier said as he shuffled closer to me on the chair.

"Wow," I breathed out, my eyes focusing on the wall in front of me. "I want to go home," I wailed.

"I know, angel, me too. I want nothing more than to get you home, but we need to make sure you're okay..." His voice stopped, his eyes moving to Betty, Betty looking back at him.

"What's wrong? Is something wrong?" The panic rose up my throat.

"No, Red. Nothing wrong." He smiled at me, and his damn smile nearly broke my heart. I had so much love for him.

"Then what?" I asked softly.

"Well, we are having a baby." His face lit up; he was practically glowing. His smile was so wide, I don't think I have ever seen him smile so big.

"A baby?" I muttered, my hands pulling out of his as I cradled my tummy.

"Yes, angel, a baby. You're about ten weeks gone." His smile was still plastered on his face.

"Wow," I whispered. I was shocked.

"You're happy though, right?" he asked, his smile fading every second I made him wait.

"I am. I really am. Just a little shocked." I choked, a little laugh leaving before I wiped the stray tears from my eyes.

"I've got one last thing to tell you... Well, ask you..." he muttered.

I turned my face to look at him, my head tipping to the side slightly.

I watched as he pushed off his seat, his eyes going to Betty before they focused on mine. God, I could just lose myself in his beautiful eyes. He dropped to one knee, pulling out a black leathered box.

"Royal, my angel. Marry me, please? For real, not for a debt, not for a game. For real. I can't live without you. If these two weeks have shown me anything, it's that I never want to be without you. You're it for me. Please, say yes."

"Of course, it's always yes. It was always yes," I cried, my hand shaking as he slipped the most stunning oval diamond, sitting on a thin band of diamonds, onto my finger. It was the most perfect engagement ring.

I was so overwhelmed.

It was all coming together.

I was besotted with him. He was my perfectly imperfect fiancé.

I was finally getting my happy ever after.

***

The next few months were a whirlwind. I was discharged from hospital two weeks after I had woken. They needed to run some tests, check the baby daily to make sure everything was going well. And it was.

Once I was home, Xavier waited on me hand and foot, not letting me lift a finger. At first it was lovely, but after a couple of days, I was growing tired of it. We bickered, I was strong willed and so was he.

I smiled at the thought, my eyes darting round the room that I was getting dressed in. We moved a little further out into the country, away from the kingdom and away from Xavier's gothic-style mansion. We found a charming farmhouse, with separate living quarters for Mabel, Christopher and her family. Betty became part of the furniture. After everything that had happened, Xavier and Betty had formed an unlikely bond which made my heart sing. He looked at her like a mother figure, and she was happy to play the part. To both of us.

I felt my lip tremble at the thought of my parents. The pain sliced through me that they wouldn't get to meet their grandbaby, they wouldn't get to watch me marry the love of my life. I closed my eyes for a moment, my hands cradling my tiny bump.

Once I was let out of hospital, the plans for my parents to be laid to rest were made. I stood round the opening, watching their coffins being lowered into the floor, the whole day a blur. All I could focus on was the words, "Ashes to ashes, dust to dust," and the sound of dirt hitting their coffins. I sobbed, I didn't like the fact that I was leaving them there, alone and in the dark and cold. I refused to throw gravel and dirt, I picked my favourite flowers from our garden before we moved and threw three in. One for me, one for Xavier and one for our baby. Xavier had to pull me away, the grief consuming me was too much for me to handle. I had never felt so empty but full in all my life. This baby was a blessing, a blessing from my parents, and that kept me going.

"Royal, darling, are you okay?" I heard Betty's voice pull me from my flashback.

"I am," I said in low voice as I smiled at her, my finger catching the stray tear that tipped over my bottom lid. I didn't want to ruin my make-up.

"It's okay to be sad, it's a special day," I heard her coo as she wrapped her arms around my shoulders.

"I know, it's just so bittersweet, and I don't want to cry on my wedding day," I admitted as I turned to face the mirror, looking at myself.

My hair was pulled into a low bun, flowers threaded through, giving it a slight rustic look.

My eyes were light and bright. Mascara coated over my lashes, making them look even longer than normal. My blue eyes shimmered under the low winter sun.

"Xavier is ready for you," Betty muttered as she looked at me in the mirror, standing by my side.

"And I am so ready for him," I admitted with a small nod.

"Then let's go," she whispered, taking my hand and leading me down to the driveaway where my carriage awaited.

***

The goose-bumps crawled over my skin, the sound of, *Fall on Me – A Great Big World,* echoed around the church. I took a deep breath, my legs slowly moving as I walked down the aisle, my train flowing behind me. Betty had her arm through mine, tears brewing in her eyes.

My gown was a sweetheart neck, covered in beads and diamonds that clung to my thighs, the skirt fanning from my calves. My veil was the same length as my train, it was stunning.

I felt sad, excited and nervous. The feelings were all rolled into one. I was broken that it wasn't my father walking me down the aisle, devastated that it wasn't my mum fixing my dress and make-up. But Betty was both of them and I was so glad I had her by my side.

My eyes focused on him, standing at the end of the small aisle of the rustic church.

It was literally me, Xavier, Betty, Mabel and Christopher. That's all we wanted, all we needed.

Betty kissed me on the cheek as she passed my hand to Xavier's. I handed her my bouquet of roses, all cut from the garden of our home, to Betty.

She stepped to the side, wiping her eyes. I turned my face, looking at her, wiping my own tears from my eyes.

Xavier wrapped his arms around my back, pulling me forward.

"I can't wait to marry you," he whispered, his eyes burning into mine.

"I love you," I whispered back.

We walked out the church hand-in-hand, legally bounded to each other forever.

I finally had my happy ever after.

***

"Keep going, angel." His voice pushed me on, his head pressed next to mine, his hand gripping mine.

"I can't!" I cried out, my skin covered in a sheen of sweat, my head tipping back and resting on the pillow.

"You can, baby, you really can. We are so close to having our baby here," he said quietly, his lips pressing into my temple.

"Royal, one more push. The baby is crowning, chin to chest, darling," the doctor said, her eyes on mine before she focused on our baby.

I had never felt pain like it, but I knew I was close.

Our baby was coming into the world.

I pushed as hard as I could.

"That's it, one last push," the midwife called out.

And I did, I pushed so hard, then suddenly, the room was silent and then all I heard was the piercing scream of a newborn.

I cried, completely overwhelmed when this perfect bundle was placed onto my chest.

"It's a boy," Xavier choked out, a tear rolling down his cheek.

"A boy?" I said surprised as I kissed his head. I was so adamant he was a girl.

"He is so beautiful," I wailed out. "So perfect," I muttered.

"I love you, Red," he whispered as he kissed me softly on my lips, then moved them to his son's head.

"I love you more, beast." I giggled before my eyes fell back to our son.

"Have we got a name?" the midwife asked as she walked over with some ankle tags.

"We haven't chosen, but I have one in mind..." My voice trailed off; my worried eyes moved to Xavier. I took a deep breath; my heart was hammering in my chest.

"Xander Patrick Archibald?" My voice was quiet, but loud enough for him to hear. His face was hard to read for a moment, but then, his beautiful face broke into the most heartbreakingly perfect smile.

"It's perfect," he whispered as he kissed me again.

Epilogue

I watched as Xavier ran around with Xander and Ezekiel, running around on the grass in front of us. My heart burst. I loved him so fiercely and watching him be such an amazing father to our son's was everything.

"No Ez, Xandi's turn." I watched Xander stomp his foot, his head dropping down as he got ready to throw his temper. Xavi had swooped Ezekiel into his arms and was throwing him into the air before catching him.

"Hey, little man, no need to sulk. Daddy has enough time to throw you both in the air," Xavier said softly, his hand running through Xander's red hair as he put Ezekiel onto the floor. I smiled as Zeke ran over to me. "Mama, Mama," he cooed, his hands going to my face as he placed a sloppy kiss on my cheek.

"Oh, baby boy, I love you," I muttered as I swooped him up, kissing him all over. He sat on my lap as we watched Xavi throw Xander into the air, him squealing with delight. Xavier was chuckling loudly.

I leaned back, pulling Zeke with me and cradling him. The sun was sitting low, and I was exhausted. I was heavily pregnant with our third baby and I was wiped.

Xavier looked over, and I waved at him which caused him to pick Xander up and run towards us.

"You okay, angel?" he asked as he sat next to me on the grass, kissing my lips then kissing Zeke's mop of hair.

"I am, but I'm tired. We need to get these two to bed." I let out a little sigh.

"I'll do bedtime, go and have a bath. Daddy needs some time alone with Mummy." His voice was now a low growl, his eyes alight with desire and want.

"Xavi," I said a little shocked, my eyes darting towards the boys.

"Oh stop it, they don't know what I mean." He winked before licking his lips.

"Boys, come on, let's go and have a story and milk before bed."

Xander protested, Zeke jumping up and down at the thought of story time. I stifled a little laugh. Xander was so much like his dad, and I loved it.

"Give Mummy kisses," Xavier said as he helped me up. I bent down, kissing both of them on their lips. "Mummy loves you to the moon and back, my little princes." I smiled as they ran towards our house.

Xavier took my hand in his, holding it tightly as we followed the boys.

After my bath, I flopped onto the bed feeling utterly worn out. I closed my eyes for a moment, feeling the heaviness sweep over me.

"Don't fall asleep on me, angel," I heard his gruff voice say, the bed dipping as he sat next to me.

"I'm not," I muttered, my eyes softly opening as I looked at him. He was so handsome. I would never tire of him.

"I don't know why you want to have sex with me, I am a beached whale." I huffed.

"Royal, baby." He shook his head as his lips hovered over mine. "You are not a beached whale, you are beautiful, alluring and so fucking sexy." He growled before he kissed me, instantly waking me up.

His hand skimmed down the side of my body when I felt something pop, my eyes going wide as I looked between my legs.

"Fuck, Royal. I know you think I'm hot, but this wetness is a little excessive," he teased.

"Piss off, Xavi, my waters have gone." I gasped; I wasn't due for another five weeks.

"Shit!" I heard him call out, running around the room and packing mine and his clothes. The baby bag was already packed and in the baby's room.

"Get the baby bag." I groaned as I stood up, a

346

contraction ripping through me.

I watched as he ran out the room, pacing the floor. I had been getting pains this morning, but I put them down to Braxton hicks as they never developed into anything more. I sighed, my hands on my back as I felt my stomach tighten again. I started to panic, thinking I wasn't going to make it to the hospital.

Betty was in the room in a shot. "Royal, are you okay?" she asked as she ushered me towards the stairs.

"Mmhmm, just not overly prepared." I laughed a little nervously.

"You have done this twice, darling, you will be fine," she reassured me.

"I know," I whispered as I held her hand.

Xavier was by my side in an instant, taking my hand from Betty and giving her such a filthy glare.

"Xavi!" I snapped.

"You're mine," he growled, trying to remind me.

"I am quite aware that I am yours, Xavier, but don't treat Betty like that." I scowled at him.

"Sorry," he muttered to me and Betty. I let out a laugh when Betty rolled her eyes at him. She knew exactly what he was like.

I said bye to Betty, then walked towards the car when another contraction ripped through me. I took a deep breath through my nose, exhaling out my mouth.

"All okay?" I heard the panic in Xavier's voice.

"Mmhmm." I nodded quickly as he helped me into the passenger side before he closed the door behind me.

He was in the driver's seat in a flash, starting the car and driving out of the long winding driveway.

The hospital was half an hour away, in the next town along, and I was now cursing that we had moved so far out.

"I'm worried that the baby will come in the car." I sighed, breathing faster now as I felt the tightening again.

"They won't, I will get you to the hospital." He smiled at me, but his eyes were filled with worry. "I promise."

I reached across the centre of the car, grabbing his hand and squeezing it tightly.

I let out a sigh of relief when I saw the hospital approaching, my heart racing. I was mad doing this again. I fell for Zeke three months after having Xander. I knew we were mad, but our hearts were so full. Zeke had just turned one when I fell with this little miracle. I always knew we both wanted kids, but just not as close together as this.

Xavier pulled outside the hospital doors, just leaving our Discovery parked there. I threw him a glare. "You can't leave it here!" I shouted out as he was round my side of the car, opening the door.

"Watch me," he growled as he helped me out.

I was in my nighty and slippers, and I felt a blush come over me, but I didn't care. I just wanted this baby out.

I walked as quickly as I could to the booking-in desk

"Can I help you?" a young blonde asked over the top of the desk.

"I called from the car; my wife is in early labour." Xavier's voice was full of worry. I gripped his hand, squeezing it gently, letting him know that it'll be fine.

"Oh yes, Mrs Archibald. Can you walk? Or would you like a wheelchair?" she asked as she stepped out from the desk.

"I can walk," I said, but Xavier's voice boomed over mine when he asked for a wheelchair.

I rolled my eyes. "Xavier, I can walk." I sulked.

"Not a chance, get in the chair, Red," he ordered, his eyes going dark.

Before that would scare me, but now, it did something so deep inside of me. It turned me on. I didn't even know how I could be turned on right now, but just being near him turned me on.

I did as he said, sitting in the chair and pouting.

"Don't pout, Red." His lips were by my ear as he rushed to push the wheelchair, not letting the nurse near me.

Typical Xavier.

I was wheeled straight into a private suite on the labour ward, my doctor walking in as I sat on the bed. I cried out as I felt another contraction blow through me.

They were so intense this time round.

"Well, this little one is eager to enter this beautiful world, aren't they?" I heard her chuckle as she stood at the foot of the bed.

"It would seem so," I said through short breaths. Xavier was watching her with beady eyes as she gloved-up, standing next to me and pushing my legs open. I heard Xavier draw in a sharp breath. "I can see you are as protective as ever, Xavier," she said deadpan. I couldn't help the giggle that left my lips.

"Royal, you are eight centimetres dilated, this is going to be quick." She nodded as she discarded her gloves into the bin in the corner of the room. "There is a gown on the chair next to you, slip it on for me, please."

I nodded, standing and slipping my nighty down. I heard Xavier growl as he pulled the curtain round, blocking me from my doctor's eyes.

"Really, Xavier?" I said frustrated, panting.

"Yes," he snapped, his eyes narrowing on mine.

"She has seen my vagina twice, she has seen me birth two children, and now nearly three, and you are worried because she is going to see me naked?" My voice was loud as I groaned at him.

"I don't care, I don't like them looking at you," he snarled.

"Grow the fuck up, Xavier." I moaned out as a contraction sliced through me.

I put the gown on, leaving it undone at the back and climbing back on the bed.

Xavier sulked, pulling the curtain back and revealing himself and me to the doctor and the midwife. I could see the smirk on her face, she knew what Xavier was like.

"I'm going to give you a quick internal, just to make sure baby's position is okay," she said softly as she stepped towards me.

"Is that okay with you, Xavier?" she asked sarcastically.

He didn't reply, just glared at her before he grabbed my hand and held it tightly. He was such an arse, but he was my arse. My loveable, protective arse.

After a few minutes of a silenced room, the doctor came to my side. "Royal, the baby is breeched, they must've turned in the last couple of days. I'm going to have to get you prepped for an emergency section." Her voice was quiet now, timid. I saw the look on Xavier's face, but it instantly changed when he looked down at me. I cried out as the pain shot through me.

"You are not cutting her beautiful skin." He shook his head ferociously side to side.

"This isn't your choice, Xavier, it's mine," the doctor said sternly.

"You know, this doesn't get any easier for me," he growled low, his voice just over a whisper.

"I get you, mate." My eyes rolled, a sigh leaving me.

"It doesn't get any easier for me either," I said through gritted teeth, the sweat beading on my forehead.

I heard the alarm buzz in the room as five midwives ran in, rushing round the bed and prepping me. Xavier stepped back, his face laxed, his eyes filled with worry and panic. He felt helpless, and I knew how hard this was for him. But I needed him to be strong for both of us because I was close to crumbling. I didn't want this, of course I didn't. But I needed what was right for me and the baby, and it was this.

I turned my head to the side, looking at him. My eyes told him everything. In that instant, his beautiful face glowed, his lips parting as he mouthed that he loved me, a small smile creeping on his face.

"Royal, I need you to sign this," the doctor said rushed as she handed me a piece of paper and a pen. My eyes darted over the words, *death, death of your unborn child, cuts, scars, internal damage, the hospital will not be held responsible...*

I was in a daze, the burn in my throat apparent as the tears streamed down my face as I signed the paper, my mind filling with images of my perfect boys.

It needed to be okay. It was going to be okay.

I handed the doctor the paper before I was wheeled out of the room and down to theatre. My heart was thumping against my chest. I was petrified.

Xavier was right by my side, clinging onto my hand.

He was muttering to me, reassuring me that everything was going to be okay.

I was pushed through the theatre doors when I felt Xavier's hand pulled from mine.

"Xavier, you need to stay here while we get her ready." The doctor's voice was assertive.

"Your scrubs and hat are there, wash up and get them on, please. Once done, sit there and we will call you in."

I saw his jaw clench, his eyes dark as I was wheeled away from him.

I was lifted off the bed and on to the operating table. I started to shake, everything trembling.

"It's going to be okay," my doctor reassured me.

"I need him. I need him here." My voice was shaky, I was breathing fast, my chest tight, all the memories flashing back of when I was shot.

I couldn't do this without him.

"Please, I need him here." I started to cry, ignoring the pain searing through me. His voice echoed around the theatre.

"I'm here, baby," he said softly as he stood beside me. "I'm here."

Within minutes I was completely numb, laying on the table wired up as I focused on Xavier. The blue sheet was up, we couldn't see anything. He kept me distracted, pushing my hair from my face and talking to me about how perfect it was going to be. Our three babies all at home, watching them growing up and growing old together.

A single tear left my eye, slipping down my cheek and onto the bed beneath me. His thumb was there, wiping it away. He gripped my hand, bringing it to his mouth as he brushed his lips across the back, planting soft kisses.

"I love you," I whispered when we heard a piercing cry.

Xavier shot up, his eyes tearing up before he looked down at me. "We have a daughter," he choked out before he sat down next to me and cradled my hand again.

"A girl?" I sobbed happy tears as she was placed on my chest. Perfectly pink and plump.

I felt my heart explode; our family was complete.

***

I was back in the room, cuddling our beautiful baby girl, Xavier sitting next to me, his finger firmly in her little clutch. Her tiny fingers were grasping so tightly.

"No one will ever hurt you, my angel," I heard him whisper to her.

My heart fluttered, him sweeping me off of my feet.

I pushed the memories of us out of my mind as soon as they filled it, back when we first met.

"What are we going to call her?" he asked as he looked at me, his eyes all glassy from the tears that he had shed.

"What was your mother's name?" I asked. He had never told me before.

"Amora." His voice was a whisper, his face breaking into the most beautiful smile I had ever seen.

"Amora it is. Amora Mya Archibald." I breathed out as I looked down at her.

"It's beautiful, Red. I am so fucking in love with you," he whispered before leaning over and kissing my lips.

Our moment was short lived when we heard two excited screaming boys running into our room, Betty behind them holding a big pink balloon.

"Mama, Mama," they both shouted as they ran towards the bed.

Xavier reluctantly pulled his finger from Amora's grasp, swooping them both up so they could see me and their new baby sister.

"Baby." Zeke pointed.

"Yeah buddy, it's a baby," Xavier cooed.

"She's pwetty." Xander sighed as he snuggled into his Daddy.

"She is, isn't she? Just like Mummy." He looked from Xander and over to me, his face breaking my heart. I could never do my feelings justice for him.

I was completely and utterly head over heels in love with him.

It was always him, he saved me. I saved him.

I was the cannonball that shot through to his soul,

breaking him from his darkness.

"What you thinking, angel?" he asked as he placed the boys either side of me, being mindful of my stomach.

"Just thinking how lucky I am to have you," I admitted, my eyes getting teary.

"Oh, no, love. I am the lucky one." He shook his hand as he leaned down over me, his lips brushing against mine. "You're always mine, Red. My reason for existence, my reason for breathing. I love you so fucking much, angel."

"I love you," I managed before his lips covered mine.

My perfectly imperfect love.

My happy ever after.

The End

Acknowledgements

Firstly, to my husband Daniel. Without you, none of this would have been possible. You support me in my dream, and push me when I feel like giving up. I couldn't do this without you by my side. I love you.

My amigos, thank you for being my ear when I have my moments of doubt, thank you for being my BETA readers. I am so glad I met you.

Thank you to my BETA readers Natalie and Suny.

Lindsey, thank you for editing my book. I am so grateful to have met you.

Leanne, thank you for not only being an amazing, supportive friend but for also making my books go from boring word documents to an amazing finished product. I am so lucky I got to meet you two years ago.

My bookstagram community, my last thanks goes to you. I will never be able to thank you enough for the amount of love and support you show me. Thank you.

If you would like to follow me on social media to keep up with my upcoming releases and teasers the links are below:

Instagram: http://bit.ly/38NEN4B
Facebook: http://bit.ly/38QuJYI
Reader Group: https://bit.ly/3dKAXfA
Goodreads: http://bit.ly/2HMUXPZ
Amazon: https://amzn.to/2HOJUpf
Bookbub: http://bit.ly/2SSvISD

If you loved my book, please leave a review.

Printed in Great Britain
by Amazon